The Trap

Book 3 of Keeper and His Tiger

A Novel by **Aidan Red**

Copyright

Published by Red's Ink and Quill, Wichita, KS

For information on other works by Aidan Red, Science Fiction and Fiction, published or forthcoming, visit RedsInkandQuill.com or AidanRedBooks.com

eBook ISBNs:

978-1-946039-37-8

1-946039-37-3

Softcover ISBNs:

978-1-946039-36-1

1-946039-36-5

To my family and friends that have supported me and have made the challenge of creating and bringing life to my stories so rewarding.

¤-¤-¤-¤-¤

My many thanks to my editors and cover designer.

Content Editing by Trenda London,
http://ItsYourStoryContentEditing.com

Copy Editing by Amy Jackson,
Copy Editing and Proofreading, http://AmyJacksonEditing.com

Cover by Amy Queau,
Q Design Covers and Premades, www.QCoverDesign.com

Tiger's nerves were on edge, but the plan was simple, though dicey. *Just intercept the hired assassin and stop him,* she reminded herself. *What could go wrong?*

Contents

Contents
(Continued)

Prologue

Saturday, May 21

Billie Mattis woke slowly from a troubling dream of ghostly images, memories flashing through her mind. She opened her eyes, surprised to see she was in a hospital room; then she remembered! The bullet wounds in her back and her chest just above her left breast and lower in her left side, just above her waist, reminded her of her foolishness. The pain persisted, though dulled by the medications.

She remembered Keeper's deeply concerned expression and tears, and how they had shocked her when he and the others had found her, leaning against the truck's open door, bathed in her own blood and that of her attacker, barely able to move. He was crying—she had not expected that—when he sat down beside her and lifted her onto his lap.

She remembered her intense relief as he had held her, and how she had melted into his cradling arms. Then, suddenly it seemed, he was laying her out on a stretcher and the EMTs in green scrubs were taking her away from him. The fear was startlingly intense and real, even as he tried to reassure her they were taking her to the hospital and that she was going to be all right. He had said he would follow right behind them, but the thought of being separated from him again had scared her.

Sighing softly, she glanced around the dim room. It was about dawn, she figured, seeing the early morning sky through the nearly drawn blinds. The whiteboard on the wall below the foot of her bed listed her nurses, their shifts, and her doctor's name. The off-white privacy curtain was pushed back against the wall near the head of her bed and the door to the hallway outside her room was ajar, letting the light cast a tapered line

1

across the floor, widening as it climbed up the wall beside the bathroom door.

She sighed and turned her head, smiling, seeing Keeper, her Billy Carson, the same Billy Carson that had asked her to marry him, and the same Billy that had come to find her, answering her fervent prayers. He was dozing in the chair beside her bed, holding her right hand, their fingers gently intertwined. He had been sitting with her for almost every waking moment she had since she came out of surgery. But now seeing him was different. He was resting peacefully, his head bowed with his strong chin nearly touching his chest. She watched him, remembering how quickly they had become involved once they had met again, she a horse rancher's daughter and he a dishwasher at the Streetcar Diner—a sanitary technician, as he called himself.

Oh god! Was he ever angry with me.

He had reason to be! At least three times now! You keep trying his patience; I'm surprised he puts up with it, much less still wants to marry an inconsiderate, temperamental, spontaneously irrational—

I know, she told herself softly. *I really do have to listen to him more.*

If her mind had arms and a face, she knew it was folding them across its chest and emphatically nodding with a huff.

Billie remembered how she had tried to follow him around after they had briefly met in the diner over a spilled and broken dish of soup, each time getting herself deeper and deeper into the unsavory parts of town, and him finally rescuing her from being dragged off in the homeless village in the northwest part of town.

After that she had pleaded for his help, and he and his friends had taken the time to start teaching her how to defend herself, and he had named her Tiger. She had volunteered with him at the soup kitchen on East Crescent, had backed him up when he unexpectedly faced the drug dealer Pink—the night he had kissed her for the first time—then again when they had faced Pink and Knife the night Knife had tried to fulfill his contract to kill Billy—Keeper, as he was known to the people on the streets.

He had lived homeless for the past seventeen years, trying to find enough evidence to pin the murder of his parents on the man that had killed them.

Shortly after his parents had died, Keeper had almost gotten what he needed. A distraught man tried to settle in an alley in the city center, admitting to setting a car on fire to kill the occupants. The man had named her recent boss, Mike Hammersmith, the senior partner in Boster, Lange and Hammersmith's architectural design firm, as the one that had murdered them and paid the man to help. But before his friends could get the man to tell his story to the police, the man had killed himself, and Keeper had been forced to wait all over again.

Billie had searched for information concerning the car wreck, but could not find anything about a wreck that had killed any Carsons. Instead, she had found information on the wreck that had killed her family's close friends, Bill and Dorothy Hawke, and their son William, her special friend, Willum. She was ten when it had happened and Willum was fourteen.

She had tried to stay mindful of Keeper's concerns for her safety, learning everything he and his friends—all living in the basement of the old, unused Duckard's Department Store building—had taught her. She had gone routinely with him to the soup kitchen and tried to make him proud of her. Until, that is—

Monday, almost two weeks ago?

Yeah. When he told me about Knife having a contract to kill him.

And he wanted you to stay home and stay safe—

I couldn't just let him face Knife alone—

He wasn't alone. He had Lynx, Cat, Hammer, Mace, Stretch—

I know! But I needed to be there too!

She sighed deeply and calmed her rising anxiety.

I needed to be there too. I couldn't let him face Knife without me.

Knife was going to kill you—

I know.

She sighed again, remembering the muzzle of Knife's pistol aimed squarely at her face as she now looked at her hand, her fingers curled up between his. Laying beside him, she was thankful they were both still alive, still together. She relished the comfort his touch gave her.

She smiled. It was just last week he had confirmed their engagement was real, and not the ruse it had started out as when he had drawn the chain around her wrist, a simulated *tat* to keep her safe while they volunteered. And last week he had actually asked her to set a wedding date, asking her to marry him. She had accepted and then explained why when he had asked why she would want to marry a dishwasher. Then a couple of days later, during another of their Saturday afternoons in the Forest, a park between St. Anne and St. Charles Streets, Keeper had told her who he really was, William Carson Hawke the Third.

Talk about being surprised.

I wouldn't call it surprise. You yelled at him and almost ran away.

Yeah. Maybe I did over react a little.

Ya think? You actually punched him in the chest!

Well, what do you expect? Him telling me he's Willum, after I mourned him for all of these years? I couldn't believe he was telling me the truth. And...and...and then he called me Willa-Willa-Wilhelmina? He hadn't done that to me since I was ten. He knows I hated being called that!

Yeah, he does. Willum knows that. You always did say he was more than a dishwasher.

She absently nodded.

4

He certainly is.

And Wednesday, you almost threw it all away...

She looked at their hands again. She did not blame Billy for being angry with her. She had come very close to losing it all, to losing Billy, to losing her own life. Again.

No. If that was what it took to keep him alive, it wouldn't have been thrown away...

But now, she was alive and he had the evidence he needed. Despite the odds, her getting shot—thankfully not fatally—and him finding her before she bled to death, they could prove Mike Hammersmith had killed his parents.

Now, all they needed was for Detective Nolan to find him.

Sixty-Six

Saturday, May 21

"I was just wondering," Joey said as he held the paper in front of him, acting like he was reading it.

Copper sat at the far end of the bench and stretched out as if he were relaxing and enjoying the sunshine on a quiet afternoon in the park near the eastside kitchen.

"Went three nights before Keeper showed up," Copper said.

"But you were told each of those nights to move on and not come back," Joey reiterated. "After what happened to Pink, and he had the Knife to protect him and press his case, I'm surprised you wanted to tick Keeper off."

"He didn't sound ticked off," Copper said, and glanced at Joey.

"I'm told Keeper doesn't lose his temper. He doesn't shout or argue, but he's very keen with a knife, and that companion of his, Tiger, is no one to mess with. She doesn't lose her temper either."

"How d'you know all this?"

"I listen. Pink was told to go elsewhere, just like you. But then he went back again and then again. The last time he went with the Knife and three others. Now he's dead, the Knife got his hand cut off, and him and his three pals are all being cared for by the state and county." Joey sighed. "Copper, you're going to have to get a better game plan. Keeper has control. He has for over fifteen years, I'm told, and I think he might have an in with the cops."

"You think he's one of them?"

Joey shook his head. "Keeper does too many things someone with the police couldn't get away with. Not if they wanted things to stand up in court. Of course, Pink don't need no court."

"So you think going into the city center is not a good idea."

"Let me ask you, how many customers you think you'll get there? Two, three, a dozen?" Joey asked and stared at the paper. "You don't see anyone livin' in the alleys. And how many street fighters do you think Keeper has with him? You're a smart man, Copper. You do the math. If you think you can make a profit after you hire enough people to break Keeper, go for it. But I might think twice, myself. A live dealer working in another part of town might be better than another dead one in the city center."

"Yeah," Copper said, fingering the arm of the bench and then slapping it, "but Mr. H paid me to remove Keeper! It's either Keeper or it's Copper. One or t'other gets removed, and I say it's Keeper. He won't 'spect a dealer comin' after him."

¤-¤-¤-¤-¤

"Just the two of you?" Russell asked as he knocked and led Barbara into Billie's hospital room. The bright north light of the afternoon filled the ecru room with its burgundy accents, dispelling some of the room's inherently anesthetic feeling.

"Hey, guys," Billie greeted. "Yeah, just us. My folks and my sister left for home about three this afternoon, I guess. And a couple of Keeper's friends from the diner just left."

"You look like you're doing really good," Barbara said, following Russell in and sitting down in the chair near Billie. "Hey, Keeper," she said, and nodded to Keeper across the bed.

"Hey, Pidge, Mace," he greeted in return.

"Lynx said you were doing good," Barbara continued, "but we wanted to stop and say we miss you."

"Yeah, and thanks," Billie said. "I think I'm gonna live. They let me sit up this morning and stuck this sling on me, and took the IV out after lunch, and I'm hoping they'll let me out for good behavior before long."

"They might not let you out if you keep trying to use that arm before they say you can," Keeper said, and shook his head slightly. "This whole thing hasn't taught her to listen."

Barbara smiled. "I know it can't be much fun being holed up in here, but you have to remember your body went through a lot."

"I know," Billie admitted softly. "At least they let me walk the hallway up to the nurse's station and back and to the bathroom and back."

"I'm sure they aren't going to let you waste away," Russell said. Then he looked at Keeper. "Keeper, mind showing me where the men's room is?"

-◻-

Billy got up and followed Russell through the door, smiling back at Tiger as he turned and started down the corridor.

"What's up, Mace?"

"That Blake fellow," Russell said. "I didn't want to say anything in front of Tiger, but he's been asking around about you. Ferret and Mouse heard him asking up at the kitchen and someone mentioned the Streetcar and that they thought you worked there."

"That was bound to happen sometime," Billy said as they stopped at the men's room door.

"Don't know if he knows yours or Tiger's street names, but I'd watch that one if I were you."

"I agree," Billy said. "At least he hasn't come here looking for her."

"Don't know that anyone's mentioned she was hurt and is here," Russell said. "Also don't know if he's smart enough to know to obey that court order."

9

"Me either," Billy said. "You need to stop or are you ready to go back to the room?"

"We can go back," Russell said. "I just wanted you to know what's going on."

"Thanks. Let me know if you see anyone around the department store."

"We will."

Sunday, May 22

Billie woke with a start, her whole body twitched. She quickly looked around the room and realized she was still in the hospital, but the flash of fear she felt lingered. Confused, she turned her head and saw Keeper, still holding her hand, leaning over the side of the bed, watching her.

"Are you okay, Tiger?" he asked softly.

She nodded and slowly smiled at him.

"What scared you?" he asked without moving.

"I...don't know," she whispered. "I couldn't see it. I guess I was dreaming."

"You were very restless all night," he said, and sat back down, pulling his chair around to face her. "I'm glad you didn't try to roll over with all of your tossing around."

"I'm sure that would've woken me up," she said, and grimaced at the thought of rolling onto her wounded shoulder and side. "Help me up," she added, and pushed the button to lift the head of the bed. "Nature is calling something fierce." She sat up and swung her legs off the bed as he stopped beside her and helped her slide off onto her feet without jarring her shoulder.

While she was in the bathroom, she took the time to brush her teeth and wash the sleep off her face and out of her eyes and then she stared at herself in the mirror. Certain the woman staring back had been out on a wild tear the night before, she picked up her brush and tried to pull it through her tangled hair. She called Billy to help when she realized she couldn't reach her left side or the back. He came and gently attempted to be of some help.

"You're going to have to teach me how to do this right," he said, and leaned from behind and kissed her cheek. "I only get to run my fingers through your hair when we make love. Even when we were little, you'd never let me play with it."

She leaned against the sink, supporting herself with her right hand, and concentrated on the feel of his fingers slowly straightening her tangled curls and the brush as he gently pulled it through her locks.

"Back then, all the boys I knew just wanted to yank and pull my hair, mostly because it was red and different. But now, I think I was wrong and should've let you," she said. "This feels good and I like how your fingers feel when we make love."

"I wanted to feel your hair so badly back then," he said, and smiled. "I think when you broke your leg and I held you was the only time you let me feel it."

When he had straightened and brushed her curls as best he could, he helped her back to the bed and got her resettled. He threw the light blanket over her legs and kissed her fully before he went back to his chair.

"Tell me something," she asked, and watched him as he sat down and took her hand. She continued when he nodded. "How are you going to keep your identity a secret? Mom and Dad will keep their promise but Sandy's the world's worst at keeping a secret. I'll bet she's already told Gil and who knows how many of her friends." She sighed. "You haven't even told your closest friends. What are Max, Mindy, and all of the others going to think when they find out you've told me and my family who you are and not them? What are they going to think when they find out you have means?

"And then, my God, what if Hammersmith hears someone talking about you suddenly being alive? How am I going to help protect you or the others while I'm laid up at home and not able to fight? Who's going to help you when you've made everyone

11

mad because they've found out you didn't tell them? What am I going to say when—"

"Stop, Tiger," he said in a whisper. "Stop. Please." He looked at their intertwined fingers and sighed. "We'll get them together and I will tell them. But not until you're out of here. They might not like knowing, and you know, they might not like that you know and didn't tell them either."

"I know," she admitted. "But however they react, the truth will come out, and they need to hear it from you. I'm yours, Keeper, no matter how they react, but I'm hoping their loyalty and dedication is as good as I think it is. I'd like to be there when you do tell them."

"You will be, Tiger." He smiled and squeezed her hand, wanting to tease her for doing things without telling him she was going to, but he decided this was too serious for a simple tease. "I won't tell them unless you're with me. It affects you and me, and all of them."

"Who else really knows who you are?"

"Only a handful of people, and they have known since a year after the accident." He looked at her and held up fingers as he continued. "Mary and Sid because they are the only family I have left; Mr. Grier Filton at the First State Bank because he has handled my secreted financial needs; Mr. Walter Gibson because he is my legal counsel and is the counsel for Pastoric; Mr. Jim Donaldson of Kelly and Lloyd Architectural Associates; and Mr. Greg Madison, Operations Manager for Pastoric and its separate holdings."

He released her hand and got up. She watched his sudden quiet, his calm, almost a reluctance to continue as he stopped in front of the window and looked down into the courtyard in the center of the building's square.

"I can't remember if I told you, but in December I decided it was time to force Mike Hammersmith to experience another setback and I set a lot of things in motion. I had the clerk in the Land Appraisal and Tax Auditing Department post a tax delinquency notice 'in error.' He posted the notice from eight in the morning until noon the same day and then he pulled it. Frederick Westman jumped on it at six minutes after ten. I used my sources to find out if Westman wanted it or if he was acting as an agent. As you know, Hammersmith had Westman's people tell Frederick that he wanted him to file an offer to pay. I was very pleased, and I watched patiently to see how it would play out and when Hammersmith would discover the offering was denied, and that he couldn't get his hands on the property, again. In a way, I reset his emotional clock back to the time when my dad bought the properties from Mike's father. I wanted to see what he would do, how he would react. I wanted him to slip up."

Tiger nodded absently, remembering parts of an earlier discussion they had had.

"Then, before he did anything in response, I saw you and everything changed. I realized I'd found you all over again and I suddenly didn't know what to do—your undying enthusiasm an ocean swell that captures and overpowers anything in its path. At first, I didn't know you were seeing all of this through your job in Hammersmith's office and I believe I mentioned that discovering I had missed that detail took me aback. But that first night, coming back from the kitchen, knowing I was dragging you into uncharted waters to face prowlers and who knew what in the dark alleys of the city center, I was afraid I was doing something wrong, possibly raising dislikes or distrust. That's when I realized I was still in love with you, and I didn't want anything to happen to you. Later I realized I have been since I first saw you—"

"That's the night you surprised me and kissed me." She relived the feelings of that moment. "That's when I knew you really cared about me."

"I kept my secret as long as I could, until I was certain you loved me, Billy the dishwasher, and not someone else. And, like we talked, it was partially the money thing." He was quiet for a moment. "But I was surprised by your eagerness to learn, to learn how to fight for strangers, to join in my daily struggles and to excel in honing your abilities and thinking. All of us were surprised by your determination and love.

"After risking your life for me, facing the Knife, I had to tell you who you were in love with. I knew I couldn't keep you out of harm's way any longer and I had to tell you the truth."

He turned and she saw his warm smile.

"I also knew we had Hammersmith. At least we had him for hiring Knife and all that went with it. But I must admit I let myself feel relief and elation when I shouldn't have. I thought I had him off the streets until you went searching for clues in my parents' deaths and I realized he was still on the lam and causing trouble. Second, I began wondering why Mike was so interested in the Duckard buildings, and especially after you told me he wanted to tear the warehouse building down and rebuild it. Stretch, Cat, and I went searching and found that strange locked door in the warehouse basement." He pulled the three keys from his pocket. "And when you're better, we're going to see if one of these work.

"When your folks came, concerned over their little girl being shot and asking why, I almost told them the truth. But I didn't. Hammersmith will certainly find out that I am alive, and I'll just have to deal with it. So many things are starting to happen—so many things I've never faced before. At least with the restoration beginning, the buildings will be safe from being condemned."

"I think," Billie said as he sat down and she reached out for his hand, "I'm beginning to worry about him, more and more. I think he's still very close and I'm also afraid of what he'll do next."

"Yeah," he said, and took her hand. "I'm afraid of that too. I guess, with your folks here, knowing who I am, we need to let them know our fears too."

"And what are you going to do about the others? Are you going to tell those in the village?"

He nodded and smiled. "Of course, I'll talk to them."

Sixty-Seven

Billie was sitting up in bed, dressed in her sweat pants and wearing her sweat top with her right arm through the sleeve and the body simply drawn down over her with the sling and her left arm under it. Keeper sat on the far side of the bed in his usual place, holding her hand as they talked quietly and passed the time, enjoying each other's company. She looked up, hearing Abby coming from the hall a long moment before she came bounding through the doorway.

"Tiiggeerr!" Abby squealed as she entered the room, and Billie quickly put her finger to her lips.

"Not so loud, Rascal," she said, and reached to her with her right hand.

Abby grabbed her hand and stopped quickly, staring. "Whoa! Where's your other hand?"

Billie laughed softly. "Under here," she said, and plucked her top. "It's in a sling and I'm not supposed to move it very much. Keeper thought this would be nicer looking when friends like you come to visit."

"Good." Abby nodded energetically and squeezed her hand. "You look funny with only one arm."

"I feel funny too," Billie admitted, and smiled as Cathy hurried in with Todd close behind her.

"Sorry, Tiger." Cathy caught up with Abby. "She's been excited all day. 'When are we going? When are we going?' I swear I think she was afraid you weren't going to be here."

"Abby," Billy whispered, getting her attention. "Come sit with me and let your mom and Todd have those two chairs."

Abby hurried around the bed and he lifted her onto his lap

so she was straddling his legs and facing Billie.

"I'm so glad that you came," Billie was saying. "I'm dying to hear what all's happening. I feel like I'm in isolation."

"Not a lot happening at the moment," Todd said. "I think Stretch has kept you informed on things around the department store block and Mace the village. We expected to see Copper again, but he didn't come last night and the other one hasn't come snooping yet."

"What other one?" Billie questioned, hearing the subtle tone in Todd's voice.

Uncomfortable, Todd looked at Billy.

"Tiger." Keeper looked at her and she could see he did not want to explain. "Blake's been nosing around, asking people at the kitchen about me."

"And you didn't tell me?" She knew her voice sounded peeved, and she was immediately sorry. "I...I know you don't want me to worry and I know I can't do anything about Blake—"

"Tiger," Cathy said, and patted her leg. "We're watching him. We know what he's doing. Maybe not what he's planning, but right now we know. Ferret and Mouse have been keeping tabs on him."

Billie forced herself to relax, breathe deeper, and smiled at all of them. "I know. Thanks. You've all been so much more support and help than I've ever gotten in all my life, and I'm having trouble accepting it gracefully. I realized a few days ago that before I met Billy again, I never had a real, serious friend. I was very surprised when Lori and Beck went with Keeper and you to find me. It isn't like them to drop everything and come."

"It's okay, Tiger," Cathy said. "When I was laid up expecting the 'rascal' there, I had to force myself to rely on my husband and the others even though I lived with them every day. So I really know."

Billie looked at Todd, suddenly aware of his reserved expression, and then saw Cathy's glance.

"Oh, you don't know," Cathy said, and grabbed Todd's hand. "Tiger, Todd's my partner and we are planning to get married as soon as we feel like we can afford it. My husband, Abby's dad, left when I was eight months along and started having difficulties. Keeper arranged for medical help, a doctor from a free clinic, and he got me through it. Todd was by my side through the rest of the pregnancy and delivery and has been with us ever since."

Billie smiled and shook her head. "Silly of me, I guess, to think everything in the world is simple and nicely laid out for us. I'm glad you were there for her, Todd. For both of them." She glanced at Abby. "I think you two have done a great job raising this one."

"Thanks," Cathy said, and smiled at Abby. "We hope so."

"That brings another thought to mind," Billie said, and glanced at Keeper. He nodded and smiled. "I would like to ask you and Abby for a favor." She smiled at Cathy and waited.

"Sure," Cathy said, and looked at Todd and then at Abby's expectant smile.

"Keeper and I are going to have a wedding ceremony out at my parents' ranch next month," she began, and carefully tried to gauge Cathy's expression. "You all, the whole family, will be there. We'll arrange transportation and everything, so all you'll have to do is come. But..." She hesitated and turned to look at Abby. "I was wondering, Abby. Would you be my flower girl for our ceremony?"

Abby's eyes went wide and her smile blossomed to the edges of her face. "Really?"

"Do you know what a flower girl is?" Cathy asked.

"Something Tiger wants *me* to do! For *her!*" Abby was bouncing on Keeper's knees.

"It's a big responsibility, Abby," Billie continued. "Before the bride—that's me—before I can go up the aisle to be with Keeper and start the ceremony, the flower girl has to spread a carpet of flower petals up the aisle. It's a lot of petals."

"I can do it! I can," she finished in a softer voice when she saw her mom shushing her. "I can."

"Good," Billie said, and leaned back against the pillows. "Afterward, we're going to have a big lunch and a big party and I told my dad he had to pick out the best horses for you and Ernest and Richard and Rusty to ride. Have you ever been horseback riding or fishing?"

Abby was speechless and just shook her head.

"Well, you're going to ride horses and also you're going to fish from"—she caught herself, remembering they did not know she and Billy knew each other as kids—"the pier that I used as a kid, when I was about five."

Damn. Almost blew it that time.

She glanced at Keeper to see if he had noticed.

"Really?" Abby's question was almost a whisper.

"Yes, Abby," Billie said, and caught Abby's hand, "and maybe a lot more."

"I don't know what to say, Tiger," Cathy said, obviously trying to absorb all that Billie was saying.

"Please," Billie said as she turned to Cathy and Todd. "Just say 'yes' and come and be a part of our special day. You're already a special part of our everydays."

"Sure. I'm overwhelmed, but sure. Thanks," Cathy said, and turned to Todd, smiling broadly at his nod. Then she continued, "Abby doesn't have anything nice enough to wear to a wedding, but would you go with me to find something simple that she can wear? Nothing very expensive but nice enough?"

"Yes. Simple will work wonderfully, and as soon as they let me out of here, we'll plan on it. But please, Cathy," Billie said, "don't worry about the cost. The flower girl is part of the bride's attendants. We'll pick out something that looks good and that maybe she can wear for other occasions also."

÷

"Todd," Keeper said as he and Billie walked them to the

elevator. "Can you check with all of the others and see how soon they can all get together for a discussion?"

Billie looked at him and gave him a soft smile.

"I'll ask." Todd cocked his head. "Something up?"

"You might say that." He glanced at Tiger. "With the way things are changing, I have some things that I need to bring out into the open. Hammersmith is still at large and we have his influence adding to the worries around the department store blocks and the village, and I have some personal things to say that affect each and every one of us. Nothing bad, I hope, but there are things that need to be discussed."

"Oookay. I'm not sure I have all of that, but I'll let you know tomorrow when everyone can get together."

"Thanks." He shook his hand again. "I'm expecting these guys to kick Tiger out tomorrow sometime, probably after lunch, so we'll be at her place. I'll let the security fellows know to expect you any time you can come. All three of you."

Then Keeper squatted down and hugged Abby. "Thank you for being our friend. I'll see you soon."

He stood up and Abby just stared at him for a moment, then smiling, she waved and followed her mom into the elevator.

¤-¤-¤-¤-¤

Joey walked slowly down the drive between the two freight distribution buildings, squinting into the afternoon sun, which was still three quarters to an hour from setting as he surveyed the dwindling activity at the numerous freight bays. Silent semi-trailer rigs, dirty and road-stained, filled the ramps and blocked most of the bay doors. Joey checked the numbers beside the doors as he walked.

At the far, east end of the drive, he turned and ascended a short flight of stairs to a standard people-sized door beside a closed loading bay. He knocked, and after a long minute, the door opened and he stepped in.

"Afternoon," Joey greeted as Mike Hammersmith peeked out behind him, then closed the door and locked it. "No one followed me."

Joey followed Mike down the long hallway into a well-lit, nicely furnished living space. "This isn't too bad, Mr. H." He let his gaze look over the room.

"Did you get it?" Mike gestured to a chair as he took one under a floor lamp.

"Sure." Joey unbuttoned his shirt front and pulled out an envelope. "It's all the ATM would give me in one day." He handed the envelope and the plastic card to Mike.

"Which one did you use?"

Joey absently watched him count the contents of the envelope. "Two, actually. One up by the hospital and one down by the First State Bank on south Second. I actually went to the one on Second first."

"Did Herb get the body disposed of?" Mike put the bills into his wallet and handed the envelope back.

"I'm sure he did," Joey said, "but he hasn't contacted me and hasn't come by my place yet."

"Well, it's only been four days. You probably should drive back out to the house and see if he's there."

"I could just call."

"And if he doesn't answer that's all you'll know." Mike squared his shoulders and looked at him. "He could be there and just be out of the house."

"Yeah, I guess leaving a message on the answering machine wouldn't help much either."

Mike stared at him a moment. "Have you talked to anyone about the city center issues?"

"Yeah. You know I talked to one of Pink's rivals, that fella called Copper." Joey settled onto one end of a love seat. "He went three nights and was met and asked to leave each time.

The last time, Keeper met him."

"And?"

"He knows about Knife and Pink and is talking to others. One or two guys are not going to push past Keeper, so he's gathering bodies to go with him the next time."

"I see. Like Pink, he's not confident in his fighting abilities."

"Probably. Especially when he knows he's going to have to face Keeper and his group, and that lady friend of his. But I don't see why they keep pushing. You don't see anyone living on the streets down there. I don't think there are any customers there."

"No one living in the alleys?"

Joey shook his head. "Nada, zilch, no one. The place feels deserted."

"Well, Keeper and his friends are there. I know they are."

"I don't see it, but okay, Mr. H." Joey stood up. "I'll go by your place in the morning. Anything else you need me to do?"

"Yes. Find Herb. I think this fellow Copper might need his help in removing Keeper." Mike gave Joey a devious look and stood up. "If you can't find him, you'll have to fill in for him. One or two shots from inside a crowd and he's out of the way." Mike hesitated and rubbed his chin. "That reminds me—Knife was supposed to do another job for me. I want you to check out Frederick Westman's place. He's become very defiant and rebellious, so I need you to go and see him, to explain a thing or two for me."

"Explain something?"

"Dammit, Joey. I want you to rough him up some and make sure he knows that if he continues, I'll make if tough on him. Just don't send him to the hospital. Yet."

"I don't do that—"

"Then find Herb, or get some help! Just get it done!"

Sixty-Eight

Monday, May 23

"Sorry, Keeper." Detective Nolan looked across the coffee shop table and sipped his coffee. "We have tapped his man Joey's phone, but he's only got two calls since the day after Tiger was shot, both from Hammersmith and both short. Too short to trace. First time he told Joey to find a replacement for Pink and the second for him to meet him, but he didn't say where."

"I suppose Joey lost the tail?"

"More like he was gone before we got a tail on him."

"We know he found Copper for Pink's replacement"—Billy looked up as a young couple entered the Bean and Bag and went to the ordering counter,—"but either Copper doesn't know there's no one there to sell to, or he's being paid to set up a confrontation. You might want to put a couple of undercover types around the eastside kitchen and watch that park just west of it. A lot of deals are made there."

"I have one there but another might not hurt. I spoke with the judge this morning and got a court order to seize all of Hammersmith's accounts and freeze his assets." Nolan smiled and took another sip. "They're being served to his banks now. Maybe that will help flush him out. We have a pretty good case against him."

"For hiring Knife? I sure hope so."

"Yes, but did I mention that I got a very interesting phone call Friday evening, about suppertime?"

Billy focused on Nolan's tone and waited.

"Once again, Tiger was right on the money." Nolan drained

the last of the coffee from his cup. "Westman's ex-wife called and told me a number of very interesting things I needed to know about Hammersmith. Between what Tiger found and what Nancy Westman told me, I think we have a good chance to charge him with your parents' deaths and make it stick."

"Wow. I don't understand. What made her contact someone—you—after all of these years?"

"We need to find Frederick to know that," Nolan explained, "but I'm thinking it has to do with Hammersmith's latest push to get those city center properties. Ms. Westman is adamant that Hammersmith either killed someone or had someone killed so he could buy some city center buildings. She claims Frederick found out about it and Hammersmith blackmailed him, threatened to do harm to him and his family if he ever mentioned the subject. The dates align with your parents' deaths."

"Well, I hope you can find him," Billy admitted unnecessarily. "You said you're seizing Hammersmith's bank accounts and freezing his assets. Have you talked to his partners in his business?"

"No. Not yet," Nolan admitted.

"Probably ought to give them a heads-up." Billy finished his coffee. "Tiger and I know them to be decent men, and I would be very surprised if they have any involvement in Hammersmith's past or present unscrupulous activities. They'll need to make plans for continuing their business."

¤-¤-¤-¤-¤

"Thanks, Walter," Billy said into the phone's handset as he absently swiveled Sid's office chair.

"It'll take about a month to actually get it put together," Walter Gibson replied.

"That'll be perfect." Billy smiled as he leaned back in the chair. "I don't want any names mentioned until then."

"I understand. I'll give you weekly updates."

"Thanks again. I'll look forward to your calls."

Billy hung up and stepped out into the hallway to the diner. He closed the office door, went to his bathroom, and changed into his white pants and shirt for work.

"Sorry I had to go out early again, Sid," Billy mentioned as he started scraping and rinsing plates. "Billie said her doctor is going to release her after lunch, so I'll be gone again this afternoon."

"Not a problem." Sid looked around Niles from the kitchen. "I'm glad they're going to let her go home."

Ned stopped and unloaded his tub of dirty dishes and Angie quickly stuck her head in through the archway.

"He's here," she whispered loudly. "I think it's that Blake fella."

Billy wiped his hands and stepped to the archway.

"Fourth booth from the door." She pointed and Billy nodded.

"Yup. That's him," Billy admitted, and went back to his dishes. "As long as Billie isn't here, I can't stop him from eating here. It's Sid's call who he serves."

"Well I don't have to like him." Angie stomped her foot and turned back to the dining room.

-□-

"What can I get you?" Angie asked with a definite edge to her voice.

"Coffee," Blake said as he looked at the menu. "I understand a Billy Carson works here."

"I'll get your coffee." She ignored his question and turned and walked to the counter. She picked up a cup and a coffee pot. "Julie, tell Billy Blake's asking about him."

Julie nodded and went into the back room as Angie went back to Blake's table.

"Have you decided what you want to eat?" she asked as she set the cup in front of him and started filling it.

"I asked you about a Billy Carson." Blake's voice grew loud, his irritation showing as he slapped the table with the menu. "Does he work here?"

"Oh," Angie said, and turned, still pouring the coffee, to point to the kitchen.

She stopped suddenly at Blake's yell. He jumped back, his front covered in scalding coffee.

"Oh, goodness. I'm sorry." She put her hand over her mouth and continued to empty the pot on him.

"You bitch! You did that on purpose!" he shouted, then pushed past her and hobbled to the front door.

"I said I was sorry." Angie smiled as Blake opened the door and looked at the staring faces of the other customers. Then Angie continued in a pleasant voice, "Oh, and Blake, we don't like people that hurt friends of ours. So I don't think you should come back."

¤-¤-¤-¤-¤

"Looks good, Billie." The nurse looked over the doctor's discharge papers. "You have the breathing monitor?"

"Yes," Billie nodded and looked at her mother for confirmation.

Maggie checked her carrysack and nodded.

"Okay," the nurse continued. "I'll get someone up here with a wheelchair."

"Thanks." Billie looked at Sandy as the nurse left the room. Her heart pounded in happy anticipation. "I wish I had something better than sweats to wear. Have either of you heard from Billy?"

"Why?" Sandy asked with a sly grin. "I'm sure Billy has

26

seen you in worse, maybe even less. But no, we haven't heard anything more."

Maggie smiled and shook her head.

Billie ignored Sandy, sat down on one of the chairs, and slipped her foot into a slipper. "You don't think something's wrong, do you?" She looked at her mom.

"Now, now." Maggie smiled. "Don't let your imagination run away with you. Sid said he'd already left the diner when we called." She looked at her watch. "That was fifteen minutes ago."

Billie slipped her second slipper on, and as she stood up, she heard hurried footsteps coming from the hall. She sighed loudly as he slipped into the room and smiled at her.

She stepped to him and threw her right arm around his neck, pulled him to her, and kissed him.

"What? You were thinking I wasn't coming?" He saw Maggie's and Sandy's nods. He held her gently and did not release her as she rested her cheek against his chest. "Well, I was delayed, but I wouldn't skip out on you for anything."

"What delayed you?" Billie asked, and looked up at him.

He quickly retold how Angie had handled Blake when he had shown up at the diner. "I had to help Ned clean up the spill and try to get the diner back under control. Even Sid pitched in."

"Is Angie in trouble?" Billie's forehead wrinkled with concern.

"No. Cathy stopped by the diner after they left here yesterday and told Angie, Julie, and Sid what they had found out about Blake, and what they knew about how he'd treated you. Julie and Carole said Angie went into a fit, so her clock was wound pretty tight when he showed up for lunch."

Billie fought the urge to ask more questions, and the orderly pushing a wheelchair into the room was her reward.

"Miss Mattis?" he asked, and Billie nodded. She glanced at Keeper, happily thinking she would not be called "Mattis" much longer. "Please sit down in the wheelchair and I'll take you down to admissions."

Billie complied and Keeper walked beside her.

As they turned to the front door, Maggie broke their comfortable silence. "Sandy and I drove ourselves so we'll see you at your apartment. Your dad's bringing his car from the parking garage and will be here in a minute to take you and Billy back to your place."

◻-◻-◻-◻-◻

Billie stopped behind her three-section sofa and looked out through the glass wall of her apartment, feeling like she was almost a stranger as she looked around.

Her dad set her backpack beside the kitchen counter. "Billie, I'm going to head back home." He stepped to her and hugged her gently. "Your mom and Sandy said they would do a little grocery shopping before they get here." He glanced at Billy. "I think you'll be well taken care of in the meantime."

"Thanks, Dad." Billie squeezed him. "I think I've learned my lesson and I won't be running around without Billy anymore."

"Good." Bob turned and shook Billy's hand. "Take care of her."

"My pleasure, Bob. Thanks for everything."

"Okay, I'm gone." Bob kissed Billie's cheek, then turned to the door and left.

Billy slipped his arm gently around her shoulders and led her around the sofa. He sat down with his feet on the coffee table and pulled her to him, inviting her to sit down on his legs with her right side to him. "I've been going out of my mind, waiting to hold you again."

"Me too, Keeper," she admitted as she snuggled down and laid her head on his shoulder.

"Before we have visitors," he said, "I want to ask you to take a short walk with me in the morning. Do you think you'll be up to a walk?"

"Outside? I'd love it, Keeper. I feel like my world has closed in on me, like I can't breathe."

"I know how you feel," he said, and smiled, then continued clinically. "But part of that is that punctured lung. If you push yourself too much, too fast, the doc says you could cause permanent damage."

Billie swatted his chest. "I just want to get better," she admitted, and squeezed him. "I am sorry I went off to search by myself. I didn't think it would matter, but I realize I shouldn't have. If you'd been there, I don't think any of this would've happened."

"Maybe not, but I won't speculate. Nolan said the guy that shot you, Herb, was a mean sort, and I suspect he would have shot at us even if I was there."

"Maybe, but thanks for coming to find me. I don't know what I'd have done if you hadn't."

"I had to find you. I had to."

"I'm sorry, Keeper." Billie sighed. "I know I scared you out of your mind and I really am sorry. But my gut told me I had found what we needed, and when Nolan said it wasn't good enough, I about lost it."

"I know," He smiled. "I saw it in your eyes. The wheels were really spinning. But I thought you'd talk to me about it instead of just charging ahead on your own."

"Yeah, I should have, but you know me..."

"Yeah, I do."

Uncertain of the tone in his voice, Billie looked up at him as he stared out the glass wall.

They sat quietly, Billie safely cradled in his arms without saying anything. A half an hour later, the door chime roused them. She slowly got up and the two of them went to let her mom and Sandy in.

"Hey guys," Sandy greeted as they came in and set plastic grocery bags on the kitchen counter. Maggie started putting items in the refrigerator and Sandy put things in the pantry pull-out. "I bet it feels good to be out of there and back home."

"Very good," Billie answered. "It'll be good to get my nightmares under control."

Sandy stopped and looked at her. "I...yes I guess it will. I'm sorry, Billie. I didn't think..."

"It's okay, Sandy. Billy's been a big help." She forced a smile. "I think he sat with me all night, every night—except for part of one—in that stiff, straight-backed chair. Tonight, I'll make sure he's a lot more comfortable."

"I know he did." Sandy glanced at him and smiled. "Mom and I got a room at the inn just down the street on Main so you two can have your time together. And I didn't want to sleep on the floor."

"So what'd you get to fix for dinner?" Billie peered into a sack, changing the subject.

Sixty-Nine

"Do you realize, Mom," Billie asked as she sipped her glass of tea, "this may be the first time you've actually had dinner in a place of mine?"

"I know it's my first time," Sandy said as she stacked their dishes at the edge of the dining table.

Billy stood and collected the stack and had them in the sink before any of them actually noticed. "Billy, stop that," Billie said when she did. "Come and sit back down. We'll get the dishes in a little bit."

"Almost done," he said, rinsing the last plate and dropping it into a slot in the dishwasher.

"Don't stop him," Maggie said softly. "You'll learn to like that kind of help. Believe me."

Billie chuckled. "Thanks for fixing dinner, you two. It was very nice. And that slaw salad stuff you fixed, Sandy—I want that recipe."

"Did you get it written down?" Sandy asked.

"Yup," he said, and smiled as he wiped the counter around the sink. "All done."

"I thought you might like it, Billie," Sandy said. "Knowing how you like cabbage, ramen noodles, almonds, and the other ingredients. So Billy followed me as I made it and jotted it down while you and Mom talked." Sandy frowned and glanced from one to the other. "Man, this is so weird calling both of you Billy."

"Thanks." Billie smiled, then continued. "If it makes you feel funny, just call us Keeper and Tiger."

Chuckling, Billy was almost back to the table when the

doorbell chimed. He greeted Lori and Becky as he opened the door.

"Are we interrupting? Have you finished dinner?" Becky asked as she stopped beside the table and smiled at Billie.

"Just finished," Billie said. "Becky, Lori, you remember my mom and sister Sandy."

"Of course," Becky said. "We got reacquainted with your mom while you were in surgery. Nice to meet you, Sandy."

Lori turned to Keeper and handed him two white paper sacks. "Here're the prescriptions for Billie. I sure wish my insurance was as good as hers."

"Why's that?" Billie asked, watching him open one sack and start reading the labels on the pill bottles.

"No co-pays, no deductibles," Lori said, and settled onto a stool at the eating counter. "Seems it covers everything."

"Hmm," he said, and held up a pill bottle. "Good timing. You have to take one of these with food, and you just ate, so..." He stepped to the table and opened the bottle for her. "The others are before bed tonight and then once daily after that. That one"—he pointed to the open bottle—"is for pain, twice daily with food."

"Bandages, gauze, lotion, and an antibiotic ointment are in the other bag," Lori said.

"Aah, yes," Keeper said as he checked the bag. "Thank you, Lori."

"Are you now my nurse too, Billy?" Billie asked as she took the pill and washed it down with a sip of her tea.

He bowed slightly. "At your service. Yes, only as much as I have to be to be sure you take everything on time."

"Billie?" Lori asked, a more serious tone in her voice catching Billie's attention. "Can we talk to both of you for a minute?"

"Sure," she said, and shrugged, looking at Keeper as he set the pill bottle on the counter. Then she glanced at her mom and

Sandy. "Excuse us for a minute."

They got up and followed Lori into the living area and sat down on the sofa as Lori and Becky settled into the two chairs.

"What's up?" Billie asked.

"It's Blake again," Becky said softly. "He's been pestering Stacy—badgering her would be a better way to put it. Asking all sorts of questions about you, Billy, who you are and how you two got together, how long have you known each other. You know, all those kinds of questions. He's even been asking her how you know so much about him. The restraining order certainly got his attention. He wasn't expecting that at all."

"He's started pressing Stacy because Beck and I won't talk to him," Lori said.

"Well…" Billy smiled and glanced at Billie. "I think he'll have even more questions after his lunch attempt today."

"Huh? What happened?" Lori asked.

Billie chuckled and told Lori and Becky the story as Keeper had related it to her. They agreed it was fitting, but Lori worried about what Blake might do to try and get back at Angie.

"When Todd stops by tonight," Billy said, "I'll see what we can do to keep an eye on Angie and Julie when they're away from the diner. Blake won't like what happens if he tries something."

"You sound like you're discussing battle tactics or something," Sandy said as she stopped behind the sofa. "Sorry, but we can't help but overhear you guys."

"In a way, we are," Billie said, and glanced up at her sister.

"The street fighting you talked to Detective Nolan about?" Sandy asked.

"We keep the detective informed of the big issues," Billie said.

"And we take care of the smaller issues and tell him about them afterwards. If we have to fight to defend ourselves or the others, then we do," Keeper added. "As far as Blake's sudden confrontation today, I'll get a report tonight on how he fared with the rest of his afternoon."

"This is what I've trained for," Billie said, and held her sister's eyes. "Helping Billy and the others is what I want to do."

"And what about college? Did you spend all that time in college to prepare to do this?" Sandy asked, staring at Billie with one hand on her hip. "What about the dreams and ambitions you had then?"

"I think that my college education might come in very handy in helping Billy." She smiled at Sandy without explaining further and then turned back to the conversation.

¤-¤-¤-¤-¤

"You look very tired," Billy said as he sat down beside Tiger on the sofa in the quiet apartment.

"I am," she admitted softly. "I love my mom and sister very much, but tonight I actually couldn't wait for them to leave. I know I shouldn't feel that way, but..."

"I'll start limiting how long visitors stay." He caught her hand. "And I will start sending you up for naps, whether they are here or not."

She chuckled. "You wouldn't."

"Watch me." He smiled mischievously. "And now, you need to go up and get yourself ready for bed."

"Pull me up," she said, and he stood and helped her up. "Bring the bandages. You'll need to change them for me. But can you help me wash my hair first? It's stiff and full of hospital smells."

Seventy

Tuesday, May 24

"Billy, can you come back up here for a minute?" she asked as she leaned over the rail and looked down into the living room.

"Sure," he said from the kitchen, and hurried up the stairs. "What do you need?"

"Fasten me, please," she said, and turned her back to him, holding her bra in place. "I can't reach back and do it with just one hand."

"Hmm. This is a first, you realize." He chuckled and hooked the strap as she looked over her shoulder at him. "Helping you put one of these on instead of helping you take it off."

She smiled and picked a blouse from her closet. "How about this one?" she asked, holding her choice in front of her.

"That looks very nice," he said as he held the blouse for her and she gently slipped her left arm into the short sleeve, and then her right.

"Help me pull it over."

"How's your arm this morning?" he asked as he pulled her hair out and she tweaked the blouse into place. "Is it still stiff? Can you still bend it?"

She slowly bent her arm at the elbow and grimaced. "The elbow's okay, but the shoulder was better while I was at the hospital."

"You haven't had a pain pill this morning," Billy said. "Have you?"

"No," she said sheepishly. "I don't want to take too many of them."

"The doc said twice a day for at least the first week."

He got a pill from her nightstand and a glass of water from the bathroom.

"Here. The last one will be gone Sunday night, so you don't have to worry about taking too many."

She took the pill and he helped her don the sling. He straightened the straps and pulled them snug. He helped her slip into her slacks, and she was putting her nice boots on when he started brushing her hair. She relaxed and concentrated on his ministrations, surprised again by the delightful sensations of his fingers and the brush in her hair.

You didn't have to getshot to get his help.

Hush! I was stupid. Okay? Are you happy now?

"I don't know how to fix it like you do," Billy whispered in her ear, bringing her back to the moment, "but it isn't tangled now. You'll have to teach me what to do if you want me to do more."

"Sure. Thanks," she said, and caught his cheek with her hand. She turned and kissed him before he could pull away. "Maybe Sandy can help me before we go."

She had no more than finished saying that when the door chimed, and Billy went down to answer it.

"Good morning," she heard Billy say when he opened the door. "Your timing is perfect. Sandy, would you go up and help Billie with her hair. I can't seem to get it right yet."

"Sure," Sandy answered, and Billie listened as she climbed the stairs.

"Hey, sis," Billie said when Sandy reached the top. "He really does a great job helping, but I wanted to do my hair up a little today."

"You're looking good," Sandy said as she sat down on the end of the bench beside her. "Why are you so dolled up?"

"Billy and I are going to take a walk," she said as Sandy began working.

"A walk? Where to?"

"I'm not sure. I wanted to get outside and smell the fresh air, and Billy said he had a couple of errands to run nearby. So I'm going with him."

"Are you sure you're up to it?"

"It's my shoulder that's hurt, not my legs," Billie chuckled. "But I'll go slow, and besides, the doc said I need to walk to get my lung back in shape."

"I know," Sandy said as she finished the small bun, letting a few curls still escape capture.

"Would you get the cap that matches this blouse?" Billie asked, and pointed to the rack on the wall beside her closet. "Yes, that one."

Sandy set the billed, chauffer-styled cap and pinned it in place. "Very stunning. Yes, yes, I think that looks very nice."

Billie smiled in agreement as she stood up and checked her look in the full-length mirror.

"Thanks, Sandy," she said as she picked up her purse and started down the stairs.

"How far are you going?" Maggie was asking when Billie and Sandy reached the living room. "Is it safe?"

"Around six blocks one way. I have to talk to Nolan this morning and then a couple of errands. I'm sure it's safe. Joey won't want to be too close to the police station and I doubt he knows who Billie is or where she lives. And we'll be wearing normal clothes, not dressed like we are when we're out on the streets. We'll be watchful." Billy turned and saw Tiger. "Wow. You sure do look great." Then he turned back to Maggie. "Don't worry. We'll go slow and my errands will give Billie plenty of time to rest. We'll only be gone a couple of hours."

"A couple of hours?" Maggie asked in surprise.

"Yes. And Sid sent some microwavable dishes for lunch and

dinner." Billy smiled. "He didn't want you to feel like you had to cook all the time you're here."

"Oh. Well, thank him for us, please." Maggie slowly nodded. "I'm sorry, Billy. I know you won't let anything happen to her, but I do worry a lot, especially after..."

"I know, Maggie." Billy gently took her hand. "I was worried about how you would feel, knowing your daughter had been shot. Being hurt is one thing, but being shot implies something almost sinister. I'll do all that I can to keep her safe."

-¤-

"So, Sparrow followed him?" Billie asked as they turned the corner and strolled north hand in hand along Main.

"Yes," he reiterated. "Blake limped back to his place, an old motel on Eleventh West and Crescent, north of the Streetcar about halfway to the village. She said he went back out around four and headed east along Crescent."

"Any idea where?"

"Not yet. Hammer said he didn't go by the department store and he's not sure if he stopped anywhere near the kitchen."

"I'll bet he needed to find a drugstore," Billie chuckled, "and some liniment."

"Todd said they'd watch better tonight." He smiled reluctantly. "There is that little strip mall up on David and Main."

"Is something bothering you?" Billie finally asked, feeling a tension in his mood.

"Yeah, but it'll be okay." He walked into the next block before he continued. "Mouse told Sparrow that Hammersmith's man, Joey, bought a gun last night. Nolan said there were two men there when you got shot—a Joey and a Herb. Herb is the one that shot you and that you killed when he tried to pull you out of the truck."

"Wait a minute," Billie said, and stopped suddenly. "I'm betting this feeling I've been having is true. Hammersmith is still right here in town! Directing the traffic first hand. Hammersmith hasn't been calling Joey or Nolan would know about it. I'm betting he's been seeing Joey. We need one of our tails on him."

"I have the same feeling."

"So why'd he get a gun?" Billie asked.

He took her arm and started walking again. "Because Herb isn't here to attempt his next killing."

"Who?"

He smiled and glanced at her. "Up until now, with no construction obvious on the Duckard properties, I'm sure he's seen only one thing standing in his way of getting control of them."

"Keeper..." she whispered, and stared at him as the realization settled in.

First Knife and now...

They walked in silence past the Pages Bookstore, and Billie absently wondered how Stacy's morning was going. Then she saw the large stone buildings of police headquarters and the jail in the next block and looked at him.

"You said we are going to see Detective Nolan?"

"Yes. That's one stop, but I want to ask you a serious question before we go any farther."

"Sure."

"Okay. Explanation first and then a question." He stopped and turned to face her. "I realized when you got hurt, that I've been a target ever since I baited Hammersmith and Westman in December. The faceoff with Pink and then the fight with Pink and Knife, your getting shot—though an accident in the greater sense of things—reminded me that Hammersmith has turned hard, devious, and seems to no longer care about what's right or wrong when it comes to getting what he wants. For some reason he wants those properties very badly, and he's willing to risk everything to get them."

Billie listened quietly and squeezed his hand gently.

"I have to be realistic, Tiger. If my luck runs out and something happens to me, my father's entire estate and everything he worked for, everything I hoped to continue in his name, will be gone. Mike will have won. But to keep that from happening, I want to name you as my beneficiary in all things that matter."

Oh shit! I hadn't thought about that.

"What?" Billie heard herself ask. "I can't be your—"

"Yes you can." He pulled her hand to his chest and she looked up into his smile. "I just have to add you to all of my personal accounts and all of my holdings."

That'll take months. There's not enough time—

She blinked, not certain she was hearing him right. "No, nonono, Keeper. You don't want to do that. You should put all of those in a prenup."

"If I had fallen in love with anyone else, I probably would. But with you, no. I want you to share in everything I do or try to do. I feel you understand what I am and what I want to do. You've even had great ideas that have helped me think of better ways to accomplish some of my goals."

She thought a minute, a flash of panic filled her chest, and she shook her head. "We'll figure out how to keep you safe." She nodded absently to herself. "That will be better. I don't have your talent for seeing what needs to be done, or how to set things up so the right thing happens. I can't do what you do. I can help because I can follow your lead. After you show me what to do is when I can help. Besides, it'll take weeks—months—to make those changes, and then you'll have to do it all over again when we get married."

"True. You're right, unless...there is 'one' way to get around all of that." He glanced up the street. "And it would help me satisfy my second, maybe more important desire. Would you consider eloping? We'd still have our 'real' wedding celebration with everyone next month, but in secret..."

"You want to get legally married right now?"

"Yes. Yesterday wouldn't be soon enough for me, but I know how you and your family feel about weddings, the show and the gathering of family and friends. And I don't want to diminish that in any way." He smiled and could see her thinking. "But I was so afraid I was going to be too late when we went looking for you, and I don't want to wait any longer before I show you how very much you mean to me."

Billie stared at him, suddenly surprised by her conflicting emotions. She was unexpectedly standing on the threshold of her new life, suddenly facing the reality of her own desires and feelings, abruptly faced with her parents' inconsistent mantra, to never let herself get too close to someone—

Stop it! This is Billy, Keeper... Willum! All grown up in the right ways. This is what you've wanted since you were a kid.

Yeah.

Billie grinned and straightened, standing more erect, and gently eased her shoulders back.

You love him and he loves you.

"You know, Keeper, I have kept another secret, almost as large as this one would be." She smiled, pushed herself up, and kissed him. "I do want to marry you, and if this is what you really think we need to do, let's do it."

Seventy-One

"Good morning, Detective," Billy said as he led Tiger down the dim hallway and into Nolan's office.

"Aah, Keeper, and Tiger." Nolan stood up, reaching across his desk and extending his hand. "I see you got my message."

"I did"—Billy helped Tiger with her chair as she sat down—"but I need a favor as well, so we're here for two reasons."

"What can I do for you?" Nolan asked as he leaned forward, forearms on the desk.

"Due to Hammersmith's recent change in tactics," Billy explained softly, "I find we are in need of a justice of the peace for a secret, very private ceremony."

Nolan leaned back and smiled at them. He keyed his intercom and said, "Is Justice Parker available?"

A moment went by and the secretary's voice said, "Yes. He's open for the next hour."

"Please tell him I'm bringing two of my special friends up to see him." Nolan stood and gestured to the door and asked as they stepped into the hall. "What prompted this? Besides the obvious attractions."

"It came to Keeper's mind," Tiger explained, "when Hammersmith's lackey, Joey, bought a gun."

"What?" Nolan was startled. "He did? When? How do you know that?"

Tiger smiled. "He hasn't lost our tail yet. Do you have a picture of him? Everyone knows what he looks like except Keeper and me."

"Sure." Nolan nodded vigorously and went back to his

desk. He rummaged around in a drawer a moment. "Here." He handed the picture to Tiger.

"Tiger thinks Hammersmith is here in town," Billy added as they stepped into the empty elevator. "But Joey hasn't led us to his hiding place yet. This morning, Joey took his car and left. We think he went back out to Hammersmith's place, possibly looking for Herb. He wouldn't know that Herb is dead."

"I have a stakeout up there, so maybe we'll figure out what he's up to," Nolan said as the elevator stopped and the door slid open. "I left you a message because I wanted to tell you the New Jersey Police picked up Frederick Westman last night. He had a ticket for London and connections beyond."

"That's wonderful news," Tiger agreed as they followed Nolan to a single door with a textured glass pane filling the top half.

"Justice Parker," Nolan greeted as they entered the office. "I have brought you customers."

¤-¤-¤-¤-¤

"Did you see Nolan's face when you told the justice your real name?" Billie asked as he toggled her phone off and handed it back to her.

"Yes," he said. "I did apologize for keeping him in the dark all of these years. I hope he understands why I did."

"I'm sure he does, Mr. Hawke." She smiled up at him.

He stopped her on the street corner across from the First State Bank, turned to her, and leaned close. "How does it feel, Mrs. Hawke?" He kissed her and pulled her gently to him before she could answer.

"It feels wonderful, Mr. Hawke," she said as he led her across the street. "I feel happy, comfortable, nervous, and giddy all at the same time."

He squeezed her hand and looked down. "Hmm," he

murmured half aloud as he pulled her hand up to look at her wrist.

She saw his concerned expression and followed his gaze as he looked at his own wrist.

"Our tats are beginning to fade a little. Yours more than mine." He absently nodded at a thought. "Splotchy. Might've been something they used to clean you up at the hospital. Probably the alcohol."

"I guess we'll have to redo them." She smiled.

He looked at her and smiled in return, holding her eyes a long moment as a thought formed in his mind.

"What?"

"I think, since we have made their meaning permanent, we should visit a friend of mine and make these permanent also."

"You mean get real tats?"

"Yup. We'll prep tonight and go see Myra at Gothic Ink in the morning."

"Okay, but you said you have a meeting in the morning."

"I'll come by when I'm finished. Here we are," he said, and turned her to the glass front door.

"The bank?"

"Yes. Grier Filton is expecting us. My third order of business today."

Billy led her in and gestured her to the overstuffed chairs at one end of the lobby, but before they could sit down, Grier stepped out of a glass-fronted office in the queue of offices along the front of the building.

"Billy." Grier extended his hand to him. "And this must be the other Billie." He shook her hand as well. "It's very good to finally meet you."

"And you as well," Billie said, and glanced at Keeper. "He told me who you are, but that's about all."

He gestured to his office and led the way. When they sat

down, Grier closed the door and took his place behind the desk.

"Billy told me what happened. I was very sorry to hear that you were injured, but it looks like you have survived. Will it heal satisfactorily?"

"The doc says I'll have some weakness and a good scar for a while, but yes, thank you. I think it will heal fine, with time."

Grier nodded and smiled as he retrieved a folder from the credenza behind his desk. He opened it and slid an information card to her. "Is this information correct? Name, birth date, birth place, parents' names, and so on?"

Billie looked at Keeper as he slid the marriage certificate to Grier, and then she read the contents of the card.

"Yes, this all looks correct. Even my new name." She looked up and smiled at Keeper. "That was the call you made."

He nodded.

"Will you please add your Social on the line provided?" Grier asked, handed her a pen, and gave Billy the certificate back. "And sign the space at the bottom."

She entered the data and signed the form.

"There will be more papers to sign tomorrow," Grier admitted, and smiled as he slid another card to her. "But this will get things started. Please sign and date this one."

She read the names already on the card, Billy's signature and his Aunt Mary's. She looked at him and signed her new name when he nodded.

"Thank you." Then Grier slipped the card into a long narrow drawer and pushed the drawer closed. "You have your key, Billy?"

Billy held it up.

"This way then."

They followed Grier into a room with a heavy gate where Grier fingered the identification tags and stopped at a large drawer. He inserted the bank's key and stepped back to let Billy insert his.

When the safe deposit box was unlocked, Grier opened the door, slid the drawer out, and handed it to Billy. "All of the private viewing rooms are open," he said, and pointed to the rooms off the hallway they had used when they came in. "Call me when you're finished."

Billy led them to one of the rooms and closed the door. "There are a number of things in here that you need to read and at least know what they are and where they are." He opened the hinged top, picked out a small red envelope, and handed it to her. "This is the second key to this box."

She took it and nodded.

"Tiger"—he took her hand—"as I told you before, you are my life, and now my beneficiary and my heir, at least for the things I have here. Like Grier said, the other changes I am making will come quickly, but later. Put this key where it will be safe, in the safe in your apartment or in your safe deposit box." Then he turned back to the drawer. "There is a list here"—he picked up another small envelope—"of all of the people you will meet that are necessary to see that my dreams—our dreams—of helping the under-privileged can happen."

He took a few minutes and removed each article in the box and explained what it was, why it was in safe keeping, and how it fit into his plans and their future. He answered her questions truthfully and tried to explain in enough detail so that she would understand and remember the importance of each item. When he thought to look at the time, he told her they were going to be a little late and suggested they come back another time to finish going through everything.

"Should we leave our marriage certificate here?" she asked as he started to close the lid on the drawer.

"Yes. Good idea. Right now, Grier and Walter are the only ones that need to know, so I think here would be fine."

He put the certificate in the drawer and closed it. They double-checked that they both had a key and he put the drawer back into the vault. Grier locked the drawer door.

As they walked out onto the street, Billie called her mom and asked if they needed them to pick up anything to go with lunch. When she said no, Billie told her they were just a block away and would be there in a few minutes.

Seventy-Two

Joey stopped his car on the driveway in front of the double-wide garage door, punched the button on the remote, and watched the door slowly rise. When it stopped, he drove his car inside and got out. The garage was empty, but he had not expected Herb's truck to be there, thinking that Herb would have gone home or somewhere else after finishing his sordid deed.

Joey walked out and checked the mailbox and found the normal collection of fliers and solicitations. He took them back to the house, but slowed as he reached the concrete pad in front of the garage. He stared at the wide, brown streak from the stained grass side yard to the larger splotch where he knew they had dropped the body while Herb opened the pickup's tailgate. His mind raced and his stomach spoke to him as he relived those frightened moments, dragging that girl from the back pasture to the drive and then dumping her into the truck bed. He quickly looked around, suddenly feeling very exposed, and hurried into the garage and closed the overhead door.

Joey entered the house and put the mail on the kitchen counter, and then slowly checked each room on the main floor. He knew Herb had turned the lights off before they went to check on the light he saw in the pasture, so the lamp on the desk in the office caught his attention. He rationalized that Herb had come back for something and simply forgotten and left the lamp on when he finally left. He looked at the desktop and then opened each drawer, but having no idea what Mr. Hammersmith kept in them, he could not tell if Herb had taken anything.

Upstairs, the master bedroom looked like it had when they had left it. Then he remembered Herb's comment about a maid coming in and cleaning the house, and he quickly wondered which day of the week she came.

He looked out the bedroom window and could see the shed in the treed area in the northeast corner of the property, and he could easily see the trace through the grass where they had dragged the woman up to the house. His stomach felt ill again and he wished Herb had just shooed the girl away; he wished he had not shot her. He wished they knew where Herb was, only because if they did, Mr. Hammersmith would not have insisted he get a gun.

Joey hurried back downstairs and out into the back pasture. He knew he was better off being outside if his stomach rebelled, and he took comfort in the fact that the land dropped away toward the back and the neighbors, such as they were, could not see him. At the shed, he looked at the stained grass in front of it and quickly forced himself to think of something else. He looked around the east side and saw where the girl had stumbled and slipped through the trees coming to the shed, and when he looked at the west side, he noticed the glass window and shrugged when he peered inside. He reinforced his original speculation that she was just looking for a place to stay the night when he noted the shed was nearly empty.

He hurried back to the house, walked through one more time, and then locked the doors and got into his car. He backed out, closing the garage door with the remote, and started back to the city. His anxiety was high and he did not notice the car on the side of the road just east of the property, one man kneeling beside the front tire with a tire wrench and the second man in the passenger seat taking pictures with a camera and a long telephoto lens.

¤-¤-¤-¤-¤

"Sorry we're late," Billy said when they got back to their apartment. "I got to visiting with an old friend and we just lost track of time."

"Your timing is okay." Sandy moved the heated dishes from the microwave to the table. "We got back just a little bit ago ourselves."

Billie went upstairs to freshen up and Keeper washed his hands in the half bath off the kitchen.

"So what were you two up to?" Billie asked as she started back down the stairs.

"Sandy wanted to go to a fabric store," Maggie said as she put napkins and silverware on the table. "Tea or water?"

"Tea," Billie responded. "Water for you, Billy?"

"Yes" came from the bathroom.

"Why a fabric store?"

"An idea I had." Sandy pulled a number of gaily colored cloth rectangles from a sack she had on the counter. She held one up to Billie's blouse. "It matches pretty well, don't you think Mom?"

"Yes, it does," Maggie agreed, and gestured for everyone to sit. "Right colors and everything."

"What I want to do," Sandy continued as she took a place, "is to make sleeves for your sling to match or coordinate with your blouses. So the sling isn't so noticeable. Do you still have that old sewing machine Mom gave you?"

"Thanks, Sandy." Billie smiled as she scooped a spoonful of casserole onto her plate and took a slice of bread from the stack. "I think it's on the shelf in the top of my closet. Is this Sid's Italian Chicken Casserole?"

"I believe it is." Keeper gestured for Maggie to serve herself next. "And it looks like Sandy found the garlic bread."

Lunch was pleasant with general conversation. Billie admitted she was happy to get out and "breathe" again, and Sandy talked a little about the trip she was planning with Gil.

Good for you, girl. Mom looks okay with it.

Billie was pleased their mom had accepted the fact that Sandy was involved in a maybe-serious relationship of her own.

Keeper cleaned up the dishes and loaded the dishwasher.

"I need to get back to the diner," he stated when the counters were wiped and everything was put away. "Thanks for fixing lunch."

Maggie and Sandy waved it off as nothing and Maggie settled in a chair by the front window. Sandy went up to look for the sewing machine.

"I'm supposed to meet Stretch at the department store after work," he told Billie as he stopped before opening the door. He hugged her gently. "I'll work later than usual to make up for a few of the hours I've taken off, meet with Stretch, and should be back here sometime after dark. Maybe eight thirty or nine. "

"Okay." Billie tightened her arm around his waist. "Thank you, Keeper. For the best day of my life." She pushed herself up and kissed him. "Tell Stretch to tell everyone hi for me."

"I will, Tiger. Now I want you to go and take a nap. At least long enough to keep your strength up."

"Am I going to need it later?" She cocked her head and smiled at him.

"Yes, if it's up to me. How much will be up to you." He kissed her and left.

¤-¤-¤-¤-¤

"When did he show up?" Billy asked as he stood behind the dumpster in the department store alley.

"Ferret said he showed up just before midnight last night," Max explained. "Stayed about an hour and then left. He showed up this afternoon about four. Just sittin' on the sidewalk against the building. "

"Talked to him yet?"

"Yeah," Max answered. "Asked him what he was doin' an' he said sittin'."

52

"When did you talk to him?"

"'Bout five."

"Anyone else been around? Is he alone?"

"Nope. Yup."

Billy nodded and pushed himself away from the wall, walked around the dumpster and slowly up the alley toward Baker. At the mouth, he stopped and casually looked in both directions and across the street. Seeing no one else, he walked to the corner of Baker and First, past the fellow sitting against the building. After a long moment studying the streets in front of him, he turned, walked back, and stopped beside the man. Billy leaned back against the wall and slowly lowered himself into a squat.

"I'm Keeper," Billy greeted. "Who're you?"

"Butch," the man said softly, and Billy listened to the tone and timbre of the man's voice. "You the one that took down Knife?"

"No. Tiger did that. I was busy with Pink, drawing Knife's attention off her."

"Her? Tiger's a 'her' and 'she' took down Knife?"

"Cut his gun hand clean off when he shot Pink. He really made her mad."

Butch shook his head. "Keeper's a funny name. Why?"

"So's Butch," Billy countered, and looked at the man's boots and pants. "No why, just a fact. You from around here?"

"Nah."

"What were you lookin' for last night?"

"Last night?"

"Yeah, when you came an' spent an hour hangin' around. About midnight."

Butch was quiet for a minute. "Any law against bein' here?"

"Depends." Billy glanced up and down the street and then looked at Butch's shirt and hands. "You need to wear older-looking boots and less deodorant."

"What?"

"Nolan sent you." Billy waited a long moment for Butch to realize his disguise had failed.

"How'd you know?" Butch finally asked.

"Just do." Billy smiled and waited as a couple and then a man walked past them heading west. When they were out of earshot, he continued. "Your boots are not worn enough and your hands look too clean for the person you seem to want to look like."

"Yours hands look clean," Butch argued softly.

"True, but I'm not trying to look like I live on the street and haven't had a bath in a couple of weeks."

Butch didn't say anything for a while, and Billy finally said, "I'm going back down the alley to the cross. If you want to talk, go down First to the passage and come in. I'll be waiting where it meets the main alley."

Seventy-Three

Wednesday, May 25

Billy's morning started early, but it was not as usual. He smiled as he thanked Simmy for the *Beacon*, vividly remembering a very well-rested and eager Tiger waiting for him when he got home the night before.

Home. The word hung in his thoughts unlike it had since he had come to the city. He smiled and realized home wasn't a place anymore; home was wherever Tiger was. He yawned and suffered Maxie's scolding when he picked up the flowers for Mary and the diner and looked forward to many more sleepless nights with his Tiger.

With the floors mopped and the tables set, flowers distributed and the crew on hand, Billy finished his cup of coffee and his ritual discussion with Angie, changed into his better clothes, and started back to the department store. At seven, he unlocked the security bars to the front door and greeted the first construction crew and its foreman.

"Buster Crane," the foreman said as he shook Billy's hand.

"Billy Carson." Billy returned the introduction and led Buster and his workers inside. "Where are you going to start?" he asked as Buster walked the ground floor and glanced at his partially unrolled plans.

"The outside boys will get the sidewalk protection started today and the inside boys will start clearing the floors."

"You should put someone on the elevators," Billy suggested casually. "They haven't been operated in years but they haven't deteriorated. They'll make moving stuff between floors a lot easier."

"I agree." Buster looked at Billy. "But this ain't my first renovation, son. I know what I'm doin.'"

"Certainly," Billy replied, unperturbed. "That's why we hired you."

"Who's the GC?"

"Marvin Roberts is the general. He'll be here at seven thirty," Billy said. "And myself."

"And who are you?" Buster asked, turning to face him.

"I represent the owner. I'm normally here every day, early and late." Billy smiled at Buster and waited. "You'll work directly with Marvin most of the time, and he and I will work together. We'll also have someone from the architects here two days every week."

"Let me guess…" Buster studied Billy more closely. "You'll be working closely with the architects too."

"Of course. Ultimately, Buster, I'm the one that gets blamed if it doesn't get done right. And if I get blamed for something, it usually trickles right on down." Billy smiled back at Buster. "So it's best if there isn't anything for me to get blamed for."

Buster slowly smiled and nodded. "Okay, Billy. Show me the top floor and the roof."

¤-¤-¤-¤-¤

Tiger greeted Billy with a hug and a kiss when he entered their apartment. She glanced at his wrist and frowned. "I thought you cleaned that off this morning."

"Couldn't and still go to the diner and my meeting." He stole another kiss before he turned and hurried up the spiral stairs. "I'll only be a minute or two."

"No hurry, I guess," Billie admitted as she sat down on the sofa.

"I talked to Myra and she said she can get these done

anytime we can get there. Are you having lunch with your mom and Sandy?"

"Of course. We were coming to the diner to have lunch with you."

"Thanks. I like that."

The sounds of running water drifted down from the bedroom and she waited, thinking about the many times people had noticed their wrist tats and the many times the tats had caused things to happen. She was deep in her memories when Billy lightly touched her shoulder. She jumped and nearly slid off the sofa.

"Sorry, Tiger." Billy was instantly beside her, holding her, keeping her from falling. "I thought you heard me coming."

She released a deep sigh and smiled. "Just remembering everything these tats have caused."

Billy helped her up and she glanced at their bare, normal looking wrists.

"Like you said once," Billy smiled down at her, "I also feel naked without it."

She looked up and smiled. "Take me Keeper. Let's go see Myra and 'get dressed' again."

¤-¤-¤-¤-¤

"Did you have a good afternoon?" Billy asked as Tiger got out of Maggie's car in the parking lot for the River Crest Apartments. "Thanks for dropping her off."

"You're welcome," Maggie said. "Sandy and I are going to do a little shopping. Billie said she'd call us if you need a ride back."

He nodded and then slipped his arm around Billie, careful of her shoulder, and started them toward the garage behind the apartments as Maggie and Sandy drove off.

"Yes, I had a good afternoon." Tiger squeezed his waist. "It was sooo good to get out and eat lunch at the diner again. After that, we went back and I rested a while." She tickled his side, then turned serious. "Are you ready for this?"

He took a deep breath. "Yes. It's time. I just hope they can accept it. Are you ready for this?"

"As ready as you are."

He chuckled.

As they crossed the driveway to the garage, he absently looked around, expecting Abby to come streaking out of somewhere. Then they were inside and he saw all of their friends sitting cross-legged around three edges of the mat. He led Tiger to the center of their semicircle, crossed his legs, and sat down. She settled beside him and slipped her right arm through his left.

Smiling, he looked at the group from one side to the other.

"Where are the kids?" he asked, and looked at Cathy and then Barbara.

"They're playing with Abby in her room," Cathy explained. "From the sound of your request that we all meet, I figured it was more of an adult gathering."

"It is, but you and I know they'll be down here listening at the door." He smiled and chuckled to himself. "Please bring them out so they don't feel they have to sneak around to know what I've got to tell you. It affects them too."

Sparrow was up and out the door before anyone could start to move, and in only a few minutes she returned with the four streaking in ahead of her.

"Thanks, Sparrow." He nodded to her.

When the kids had settled, he scanned the group once more and felt Tiger gently squeeze his arm.

"I need to tell you a few things about me that you don't know, and the time has come when you should. I'll start back a few years ago when I came to the city—"

"You goin' to tell the folks up in the village too?" Stretch interrupted.

Billy nodded and inhaled with a glance at Tiger's smile. "Yes, but we wanted to talk to you first. We'll go up and include them after we're finished."

"Good," Cathy added. "We'll go with you."

"Thanks. As I was starting to say, Cutter and Owl were my first acquaintances when I stumbled into their alley and collapsed, destroying their shelter." He hesitated, feeling his stomach tighten and suddenly finding it hard to speak as he glanced at Cutter, seeing the shared memories pass behind his eyes. "Sorry. Those were very dark days for me." He cleared his throat and tried to continue. "I met Mace and Pidge there, and Ferret and Mouse were kids like me and we formed a friendship. The rest of you came into our friendship over the next year and a little. I was fourteen and suffering from a car accident that killed my folks. I had a broken arm and a cracked hip and internal injuries from a tree that tried to gore me. Mary at the Streetcar got me medical attention and the surgery needed to fix things up."

"You knew Mary from before the accident?" Barbara asked.

Billy nodded again. "She's my aunt. My only aunt. I'll explain more of that later." Then he glanced at each of them and continued. "Once I was on my feet again, I joined the group and lived in a cardboard dwelling but quickly decided an alley was not the right place to live. I talked to some people my father had known and we moved a block away from the alley and started the village. After almost two years there, I got permission to use the basement of the old Duckard's Department Store, and under a strict set of conditions, part of the village moved inside. Red, Spear, and Ditto joined us a few years later.

"You all know me by what I have done and by what we have done together. But I've not told you everything about me."

He felt Tiger's squeeze again as Abby crawled up onto the mat and sat on his other side. She grabbed his arm and looked up with a smile.

"I was content with my reasons for hiding my past and the

truth until I met this woman, again." He glanced at Tiger and then back at the group. "One of the things I didn't tell you was that I had known her for five years before my accident. She was just a kid back then, much smaller and just as feisty and opinionated."

Abby bounced up and down and squeezed his arm. "I knew she was special. Specially when you asked to bring her to the basement and let us help train her."

"You did, did you?"

"Yup." She nodded emphatically. "I did."

"Well, I guess it should be obvious. She stole my heart before I was fourteen."

"Stole you heart?" Abby asked, and tapped his chest, her head cocked in question.

"Yup. Someday I hope you learn what that means and how wonderful it is." Then he looked back at the group and his expression sobered. "As some of you know, I knew the accident was arranged to murder my parents and me. Obviously I survived, and in order to catch the man responsible, I had to let the world to think I was dead. I might as well have been, since it cut me off from everything I cared about and the life that I knew. Pretending to be dead was the hardest thing I think I've ever had to do." He hesitated again and leaned against Tiger, holding her eyes as he remembered. Then he inhaled, squeezed Abby's knee, and continued. "I must apologize for the fact that when I came here, my first mission wasn't for anyone's safety or protection, as some of you might have thought. I don't mean to say that wasn't important, because it became as much of my purpose in life as my first goal had. But my first goal was to find the man or men responsible for my parents' deaths."

He paused and slowly looked at each of them.

"Didja find him?" Abby asked, and pulled his arm around her shoulders.

He nodded. "A few months after I got here, maybe a little longer, Mace saw a homeless man in one of the alleys a block or so down from the department store, and that man eventually confessed to helping cause an accident up at the Chestnut Creek Bridge on State Highway Forty-seven, setting the car involved on fire and killing the people inside. He named Mike Hammersmith and Frederick Westman as the ones that paid him to do it, and then we think he killed himself."

"He was pretty well tormented by what he'd done," Mace added, his voice deep and soft. "He really knew he'd done something very wrong."

"If any of you have searched the public records like Tiger did," Billy continued, "you'll find a number of similarities with my story and an accident that killed a well-known and well-remembered man in the city's history, W.C. Hawke the Second." He took another deep breath and Tiger squeezed his arm. "You know me as Billy Carson, and that name is true. But my full name is William Carson Hawke the Third."

He watched the group and saw some surprised looks, but mostly nods—certainly not the reactions he expected.

"You're not Keeper?" Abby asked, leaning back to look up at him. Then she glanced at Tiger.

"Yes, Abby. I am Keeper and Billie is Tiger. We just have other names, just like your mom and Todd. Like everyone else does."

"That's good," Abby said with a deep exhale.

"We weren't sure about the name," Sparrow said, breaking the silence with a broad smile on her face, "but Falcon and I did some checking a while back with Ferret's and Mouse's help. We figured there was something going on. You knew too much and you knew how to get us keys to what appeared to be an abandoned building. But it was an abandoned building that was routinely cleaned, windows repaired when someone threw a rock through one, or the roof fixed when a leak appeared."

He nodded, feeling like a great weight had been lifted from his shoulders. He looked at Tiger, smiled, and looked back at Sparrow. "I'm glad you knew. My father's firms kept monies available to maintain the buildings until renovations could be started."

"So you're actually rich?" Ditto asked from where he sat in the back near the door.

"Technically," he answered. "Rich mostly because of my friends, like all of you, and because I found this woman again, but to your point, the truth is that I will inherit my father's estates and businesses."

"So, now that you know who killed your parents, why hang out with us?"

"Because I got to know all of you and because all of you helped me when I needed it the most. We grew into a family, Ditto. I'm no different than you are, and I want to make things better in the future."

"We heard renovations were going to start"—Mindy changed the subject—"and Mace confirmed crews began arriving this morning. Why now? Instead of some time ago or sometime yet?"

He explained his growing impatience and his personal need to see if he could get Hammersmith to do something, anything that might help pin the accident on him. He explained how he had baited him and Westman with the idea that the properties were available for back taxes and how he then snatched the possibility away from them, hoping to irritate one of them enough to make them do something they should not do. He explained the recurring appearance of Pink and then Knife and how he had been able to link those events directly to Hammersmith, and that the police had warrants out for his arrest.

"Hammersmith is trying to get the properties identified as abandoned and to show a rise in unsavory inhabitants so he can get the city to condemn the properties. The city would then sell them at auction and he could buy them. We'll talk more about that later.

"Tiger found clues and started searching. She got shot when she found the tools Hammersmith had used to cause the accident. The police have recordings of the assailants when they dragged Tiger away to dispose of her in Chestnut Creek.

Because of your help in training her, Tiger managed to find the strength to kill Herb when he tried to pull her out of the truck."

The group sat quietly and he waited as they processed everything he had shared. There was more to tell, but he wanted to answer their questions before he kept unveiling truths. Finally, Cathy looked at him.

"Are these almost-rent-free apartments your doing?"

"My father's, actually," he admitted softly. "He set up trust funds when I was very young, before I even knew what he did for a living. He set up a number of funds specifically to provide housing, like these, for those that can qualify."

"Qualify?" Ferret asked. "Like the stipulations you set down when you brought us into the basement? And then here?"

"Yes, Ferret." He nodded. "Those requirements were set down by my father and enforced by his managers. The money was made available to rebuild these apartments when I showed the trust managers that you would be able to qualify when they were available. It really was a godsend that they were finished and I could make them available when I did. I had to set the renovations in motion to make it obvious the city center buildings were not abandoned. But by doing that, I lost our space in the basement."

"What about Hammersmith?" Cathy asked.

"That can go a couple of ways." Billy exhaled slowly. "I'm going to assume that Detective Nolan won't find him before he makes his next move. Hammersmith is out to kill Keeper."

Abby suddenly squeezed Billy's arm, and he patted her knee for reassurance.

"For some reason, he is very intent on getting his hands on the Duckard properties. But when he realizes the renovations have actually begun, he'll also realize that removing Keeper won't let him get the properties condemned. I don't think he has figured out who I am yet, but knowing I am Keeper, he will figure I am part of those getting the renovations started and out of anger, revenge, spite, or whatever the reason, he will take his emotions out on me. But I also think he will try to undermine the renovations. That's where I have to pay particular attention."

"What happens if we can't stop Hammersmith?" Falcon asked.

He took a deep breath again and looked at Tiger. "Then I probably won't be having any more of these meetings. Hopefully, the arrangements I'm making, the things I've started, will ensure the projects' and your safety will continue, no matter what happens to me. I don't want to miss anything, so let's hope I can stop him."

"And this guy Blake?" Todd asked.

"He's a wild card and we don't know what he's going to do. He's been served with a restraining order to stay away from Tiger, but as you well know, we really have no idea what he's thinking," Billy said, and retold his experience with Angie at the diner.

"Mouse saw him talking with Hammersmith's man Joey," Ferret said.

"That's interesting." Billy smiled at Mouse. "Unexpected, but not really surprising."

"We'll keep watching and listening," Pigeon stated emphatically, and the rest nodded vigorously.

"Thanks. Thanks to each and every one of you." Billy felt his throat tighten.

"Besides us," Mindy asked, "are Mary and Sid all the family you have left?"

He nodded. "Just them and Tiger. And that makes me think of a happier subject." He winked at Abby and saw her smile brighten. "Next month Tiger and I are celebrating our wedding at her parents' ranch, and we want all of you to come. Tiger mentioned this to Todd and Cathy while she was in the hospital and I'm sure they mentioned it to you, but we want to be sure you know you're all invited. We wanted to have it on the Solstice, but with so many working, we're thinking the Saturday before. So that will be the eighteenth, three weeks from this Saturday." He turned to Tiger and nodded.

"I've worked out the travel details," Tiger said, "with my mom, and we'll get you all there for the ceremonies and the party and then get you back whenever—later that day or the next if it turns out to be an all-nighter and a sleepover. Sort of depends on how much playing, partying, and dancing we do."

"They got horses," Abby added suddenly to the other kids. "An' Tiger said we get to ride 'em."

Tiger laughed. "That's right, Abby. And fishing and games and lots of space to play in."

¤-¤-¤-¤-¤

The afternoon was stretching into evening when Keeper and Tiger left the village and started back to their apartment. Tiger called her mom when they went to the village, telling her mom they might be a little late for dinner, but glancing at her watch, she knew they were not as late as she first expected.

"So?" Tiger asked, squeezing his waist. "How do you feel now that your secret is out in the open?"

"Apprehensive," he admitted, and studied the sidewalk in front of them. He pulled her tighter against him, yet careful of her injured shoulder.

"Apprehensive? I would've thought that would be gone."

"You're worried too." He knowingly glanced at her. "Ditto said what was on everyone's mind. Will I change now that they know? Will I continue to support and defend them? Didn't you feel the unasked questions?"

"Yeah, I did." Tiger looked around as they walked through the Forest on their way to St. Anne. "I guess you're right. I am still worried. I don't want them seeing us as different, or feeling like all of this was just some lark for us to make ourselves feel good."

"All in all, Tiger, I think we'll just keep doing what we've been doing and let them see we still mean what we say. I'm glad they know. I'm glad I've finally told them, even if there are still fears and concerns to calm."

"You'll calm them, Keeper. You always do."

"We'll calm them, Tiger. Together. No matter how long we have to help, we'll help."

Seventy-Four

"Thanks for fixing something for dinner, Maggie." Billy stacked the dishes and then went up to their bedroom to change. "You didn't need to go to the trouble. I could've eaten at the kitchen." He tossed his shirt in the hamper and turned to the closet for his frumpy pants.

"But we couldn't, Billy," Maggie said. "Unless you took us to help."

"What?" He looked over the rail, but Maggie was in the kitchen and Billie and Sandy were in the dining area. "You sound just like Tiger."

"Well? Why not?" Sandy chimed in, and stepped into the living room to look up. Seeing him shirtless, muscular, trim, and very fit with a nicely narrow waist and broad shoulders gave her pause before she continued. "I've...I've talked to Gil and I'm flying down to meet him on Saturday. So I have three nights that I can help."

"And if everything's okay when Billie gets her stitches out on Friday," Maggie added, and stepped up beside Sandy, "I'll be going back home after Sandy leaves. So I have three nights also."

He stepped back into the bedroom and did not say anything. He was pulling his frumpy pants on when Billie reached the top of the stairs and sat down on the bed beside him.

"You too?" he asked, and nudged her with his shoulder.

"Well, it is a lot safer now that Knife and his cronies are gone," she cooed softly. "And we know Copper and his group are not physically dangerous. At least not around the kitchen."

"So?" He looked at her, keeping his expression solemn.

"I can take them by the recycled clothing store and have

them outfitted in a half an hour." She smiled and waited. "And what will they say if Keeper keeps showing up without Tiger? Someone might think Tiger is available or something."

He sighed and smiled at her, shaking his head slowly. "Do they know they'll have to walk?"

She threw her arm around his neck and kissed him fully. She jumped up and hurried down the stairs. "Get your purses. We have a half an hour to be back and changed."

Billy was laughing as he heard Billie open the door and hurry to the elevator. He listened to her excited voice as the door slowly closed and shut the sounds off. He sighed again and pushed himself up, went down to the kitchen, and finished rinsing the dishes and loading the dishwasher.

-¤-

"Turn in here." Billy pointed to the parking garage on the north side of the bus station.

Maggie followed his directions and found a spot near the entrance. As they stepped out onto the sidewalk, he looked at them and smiled.

"I'm not sure your friends would recognize them either," he admitted. "You did good, Tiger." He straightened her sweater and the scarf she had thrown over her shoulders.

"I'll take the sling off while we're there, Keeper." She slowly straightened her shoulders.

"Don't stretch too fast, Tiger," he warned and dug into his pocket. He handed her knife to her. "I took this from you when I found you last week. It's time I give it back."

"Thanks, love. I wondered where it went," she said, and absently flicked the long blade open.

Maggie and Sandy stared, speechless, watching her examine the blade and wipe it on her sweater sleeve. She absently flipped the knife, catching it by the blade, and then flipped it again, catching it by the hilt, smiling at the familiar heft and balance.

"I cleaned it and sharpened it." He held her eyes and

grinned. "I didn't have a lot to do while I was watching the store."

When she folded the blade and slipped the knife into her pocket, he flicked his open and checked its blade. Then he closed it and dropped it back into his pocket.

"You two take this very seriously, don't you, Billy?" Maggie asked softly.

"Very. Like I explained to Tiger, some of these people can be very rough and disrespectful. Some think a pretty woman is a toy for the moment—any moment they want. We can handle most anything that might happen—even with Tiger's wound, she can defend herself. But I have to warn you two, if anything does happen, a confrontation or anything that you feel might turn into an unsafe situation, you let us know, you stay close to one of us, and never, never act like you're afraid."

Tiger chuckled. "Listen to him. He knows what he's talking about."

"Okay, then." He turned Tiger and started up toward Crescent. "Stay bunched up and talk softly if you feel you need to say anything."

They walked the familiar route along Crescent in near silence and he knew Maggie and Sandy were questioning their quick decision to go with them. When they passed the park, darkened in the early evening light by the abundant trees, he noticed Tiger was looking it over as well. He was pleased that she remembered to keep her eyes roaming and paying attention like he had taught her. But then he smiled; he was pleased with everything about her, except maybe her defiance. But then again, he admitted, he had to love that part of her as well.

They crossed the street and he stopped in front of the nondescript building and made a slow gesture.

"We have arrived. Please follow me."

He led them to the side door and Tiger went in first, saying hello to the kitchen manager.

"Randy, this is my mom and my sister. We're going to put them to work tonight and maybe they'll come back for another couple of nights."

"Good, good. Welcome," Randy happily greeted them.

He decided to put Maggie and Sandy on breads and fruits and Tiger on soups when Billy said he would be their runner, figuring he could better keep an eye out for trouble if he did not have to stay in one place.

Tiger showed Sandy and their mom where to put their backpacks, then she stacked their backpacks on top.

"Here, let me help you get out of that," Billy said, and helped her out of her sling and scarf. "Do you want your scarf or the knitted hat for your hair?"

"Hat, but let a few curls hang free."

He helped her set the hat and pin it in place. He put the sling and scarf in her backpack, then led them to the serving line and introduced them to the other servers as some of the kitchen helpers set up an additional row of tables.

"Looks like we're expecting to be busy tonight," Tiger said to her mom as she positioned them behind their respective trays. "Be pleasant, but don't overdo it and don't overreact if someone sounds terse, grumpy, or a little belligerent. I'll be right here if you need help." Then she turned to the soup pot and picked up a ladle.

They were into the beginning of their second hour when Copper came through the line and, seeing Tiger, stopped in front of her.

"Ooh, Tiger. That's very nice," he said, and leaned forward and made a gesture toward her long curls. "I like your hair. It's very nice indeed."

"So does Keeper," she said, catching his eyes with a firm stare. Then she raised her left wrist and tapped the chain tattoo with a finger. "No one else touches the hair, Copper."

He slowly leaned back and smiled as he took a bowl of soup. "I can see why he feels that way. You have a great night,

Tiger."

She nodded and returned to filling bowls, smiling as she looked at the *real* tattoo wrapping around her wrist, her sense of belonging to Keeper reinforced by knowing he had the matching *real* tattoo on his wrist. She inhaled and noticed Sandy and her mom had seen the exchange and were keenly watching her now. Sandy, with her mouth still agape, quickly turned back to her tray when Billie glanced her way.

"Nicely done," Maggie whispered as Tiger set another soup bowl on the counter.

"Thanks," she said, and then turned toward the kitchen. "Soup!"

-¤-

"Who was that guy anyway?" Sandy asked as they walked south toward the bus station.

"Which guy?" Tiger asked absently, and she dropped Billy's hand and slipped her arm around his waist.

"The one that said something about your hair."

"Oh, that was Copper," she replied. "He's the drug dealer trying to replace Pink and move into our 'hood."

"Drug dealer?" Maggie asked. "You don't seem too upset about his line of work."

"Nolan and the other detectives know who sells drugs and most of the other illegal things being done," she admitted. "We let him handle those issues."

"I'm surprised it didn't take much to change his—that man Copper's—mind about touching your hair," Sandy said.

"That's only because he knows of Tiger," Billy explained.

"Knows *of* her?" Sandy looked at him, questioning.

He explained Tiger's reputation on the streets, with Pink, with Knife, and possibly with Blake. "They know she's not one to mess with. She doesn't get angry. She doesn't start fights, doesn't shout about one if it starts, doesn't scream about it, and she doesn't back down from it. Most of them are sure if they

71

start something and it escalates, she'll finish it for them. I think they're more afraid of her than they are of me."

"I'm just new. They know you've never backed down either. Not in fifteen or so years."

"Maybe so, Tiger," he admitted, and then turned to Maggie when they reached the parking garage. He stopped and turned Billie to look at him and held her close. "I know you won't like me saying this, Tiger, but I need to check with Stretch at the department store and then I'll join you at home. Please go home and get some rest." He leaned to her and kissed her. "Please?"

Tiger sighed and nodded. "No, I don't like it. I want to *rest* with you."

"I know. I just want to get an update from Stretch and I don't want to drag your mom and Sandy through the alleys tonight. I won't be long." He smiled and squeezed her, being careful of her shoulder and side. Then he turned to Maggie. "I think she should get home and get some rest. She's had a big day today. Mind dropping her off?"

"Not at all," Maggie said, and unlocked the car. "Where are you going? It's late."

"Just a quick security check with Stretch, then I'll be home." Then he squeezed Tiger again. "I'll fill you in on anything I hear when I get home."

Seventy-Five

Billy found Stretch in his usual place in the alley between the two Duckard's buildings. The continuation of the pedestrian walk protection as it stretched across the north side of the department store was nearly completed, and the construction gate across the alley's mouth was in place but still swung open. He noticed that Butch was gone from his normal spot on the sidewalk.

"Hey, Keeper," Stretch said in a low voice. "I figured you'd have gone home with Tiger after the kitchen."

"On my way, but I needed to see that everything is okay." He sniffed the air, the faint smell of smoke catching his attention. "Tiger's very tired after her second day and I sent her home with her mom and sister. How's Cat?"

"Okay," Stretch said, and smiled. "Being a bit of a nuisance. A pest mostly."

"A pest?"

"Yeah, in a nice way." Stretch lowered his head, smiled, and continued softly. "Now that we've got a place, she's wanting to start a family. I think seeing you and Tiger together has set her to thinkin.'"

"Sorry," Billy said with a thin smile.

"Don't be. We've wanted to for a long time, but never thought we could," Stretch said, and looked back at Billy's smile. "You know, livin' in the basement and all, little to no privacy."

"Yeah, I can see where that would make a difference."

"You doin' okay? After this afternoon?"

"I think so. Tiger brought up a worry, that you or those in

73

the village might think we're helping just to make us feel or look good."

"The young ones, maybe"—Stretch nodded—"but not those that have known you for a while. What I find hard to believe is that Tiger turned her focus from her previous lifestyle to helping us. That had to be your doing."

"Not as much as you might think. She came and asked me to help her. She told me she was ashamed of how her folks raised her, the biases and the life that naturally followed. She had to find her heart again, but once she did, she wanted to learn and help."

Stretch was about to add a comment when an out-of-breath Abby charged around the corner and unexpectedly collided with Billy's legs. She fell back and landed on the ground.

"Keeper! Come quick!" Abby shouted when she recognized Billy. "They're in trouble! Mom sent me to find you!" Abby rolled over and sprang to her feet, instantly running back the way she came.

"Abby! What's wrong?" Billy shouted in response, running out of the alley after her. Stretch was right beside him.

"The village! Someone's setting it on fire! Hurry!"

¤-¤-¤-¤-¤

Maggie parked the car in a visitor's spot and Billie asked them to come up for a cup of tea.

"I know it's late, but I'm not as tired as Billy thinks I am," she said. "I'm fatigued, but I won't be able to rest until he gets back."

"Sure. We can come up for a little while," Maggie said, and they followed Billie through the lobby door.

The elevator ride was pleasant, with Sandy talking about people they met at the kitchen. Billie let them in, switched on the lights, and went up to her bedroom to freshen up. Maggie and Sandy went into the kitchen and Maggie started a pot of water.

"Thank you for taking us tonight, Billie," Sandy said. "It was a real eye-opener to see my new sister in action. I have to admit, that Copper guy was intimidating."

"Yes," Billie said from the loft. "But he's no fool. He knew I could put him down."

"Wow. And modest too," Sandy said, glancing up to see Billie leaning over the rail and looking down at her.

"No, just a fact." Billie shook her head and stopped to look out at the city, her gaze caught by the orange glow to the northwest, just left of the city center buildings. She leaned forward against the rail and focused, seeing the dark spot of the Forest just to the left of the glow and not quite halfway to it.

Shit! It's the village!

"Oh God! Mom! There's trouble," she said, and dropped back on the edge of her bed, strapped her calf scabbard on, and secured her knife. She got up and looked back up at the window.

"What's trouble, Billie?" her mom asked, and saw her staring at the window.

"We have to go!" Billie shouted, and came down the stairs two at a time.

"Where? What's wrong?" Sandy asked as Billie ran for the door.

"Take me to the village! We have to go! Now!"

Billie darted out of the door and hurried to the elevator, keying Nolan's icon on her phone as she waited for her mother and Sandy to catch up.

¤-¤-¤-¤-¤

Billy had Abby on his back and ran straight up Second West until it dead-ended at Hadley. He turned and ran as fast as he could to Tenth West and the village. He never looked back to see if Stretch was with him or not, he just knew he was. At Tenth he stopped, stunned at the riot he beheld: men crowding from all directions, some with torches and some with clubs and pitchforks, all tearing into the cardboard shanties and tents.

Billy inhaled quickly and turned to Abby. "Where's your mom? And Hammer?"

"In the middle," Abby said, trying to keep herself from crying, seeing the horror in front of her.

"Hang on! We're going to find them," Billy shouted, glancing at Stretch. "Don't let go, Abby! Not for any reason!" He felt her arms tighten, her legs wrapped tight around his waist and her nod as he pulled his knife, flipped the blade open, and charged into the fiery chaos.

-¤-

Billy and Stretch started knocking men down as they came to them from behind, shoving and slamming. His fist around the hilt of his knife silenced many as he came to them, stopping the rampant pillage they were causing. At one point Billy saw a familiar shadow; Blake darted away from the fringes of the rioting crowd. Billy was certain of who he saw, but he could not give chase and help the people in the village. He swung at another intruder as he and Stretch worked their way farther and farther into the fray.

"There!" Abby shouted in his ear, and pointed to Lynx and Hammer defending Helen's hovel.

"I see them, but stay on my back!"

"Okay Keeper. I will," Abby shouted above the din, but Billy knew she wanted to go to her mom.

Billy spun around with Stretch at his side and they began sweeping from one side to the other, pushing the invaders back, away from the center of the village. Billy did not want to think about the many people being affected, he just wanted to stop what was happening.

Abby shrieked and Billy jerked to his left and brought his

long knife up in time to stop a pitchfork. He shoved the man back and pressed the attack until he fell backward.

"Mr. Howl? What are you doing?" Billy asked in a loud voice. "Some of these people work for you!"

The man looked at Billy like he had just awoken from a dream. He rubbed his face and looked around, trying to hide his sudden shame. Then he rolled over, pushed himself up, and ran away from Billy, disappearing back through the chaos of the intruders.

Billy turned as another man charged and Abby screamed again. Stretch caught him with a right hook and dropped him at their feet. Another came at them from the right and Billy was beginning to think they were losing ground as he dropped him with an upper cut to the jaw. Then he looked up and saw the commotion on the path from the south. "Oh shit!"

Seventy-Six

Billie could not believe her eyes as they drove up Tenth West and turned the corner at Hadley. Everything she could see seemed to be on fire!

Oh God! No! No!

"Stop here and let me out!"

Maggie slowed, and Billie threw the door open and was out and running before the car had stopped. Sandy was out right behind her, yelling for Maggie to just leave the car where it was and hurry.

-☐-

It only took a minute, and Maggie was out of the car and following Sandy up the path Billie had taken. It seemed men and women were fighting all around them. Some of the women had clubs, brooms, and a few had knives, fighting back, alongside their men, defending themselves and their makeshift homes. Sandy pointed and Maggie looked up to see Billie as her knee came up, doubling a tall man over; he staggered and fell aside. Her fist, clenched around her knife, slammed into the face of another.

Sandy pulled her mom forward, unsure of why they were following Billie but just as certain she did not want to be very far from her in this chaotic madhouse. She saw her mom stoop down and pick something up; it was Billie's sling, and they both looked up to see Billie's blur as she pushed men aside and dropped others, suddenly stopping near Billy and a similarly dressed tall man.

"What in hell are you doing here?" Billy shouted, his anger and worry overflowing in his confused expression as Tiger quickly turned to assess their surroundings.

"Couldn't let you have all the fun, Keeper," she remarked calmly, ignoring the fact that her offhanded remark flamed his ire. She flipped her knife around to shield the blade and pulled Abby off Billy's back. "Come on, let go, Abby. Get down."

Maggie and Sandy quickly knelt and pulled Abby in between them as Billy swung and stopped another man with a club. Seeing Tiger's mom and sister, Billy just shook his head and forced himself to focus on the fight; his questions would have to wait.

By the time they heard the sirens and saw the first of the police cars, the ten of them from the basement family and a half dozen from the village had nearly stopped the attackers, holding them to the southeastern portion of the block. With their arrival, the police officers made short work of rounding up the last of them. The fires were doused quickly and they realized the damage and affected area was not as bad or as large as they had first feared.

Billy, still fighting internally to keep his emotions in check, was holding Tiger tight, talking with Maggie and Sandy, when a strong hand settled gently on their shoulders. "Thanks for getting here, Keeper. Tiger?" the tired face of Falcon said through a thin smile. He cocked his head at Tiger. "Didn't you just get out of the hospital? Like...two days ago?"

"Yeah," she sighed, sheepishly. "I thought I was going to go home and get a nice quiet night's rest after serving tonight, but..."

"We almost had her there," Sandy said softly, her eyes still very large and round as she put her hand on Billie's back, smiling at her. "But she saw the fire and there was no way of keeping her away."

Tiger looked up at him. "I had to come, Keeper. We each work best when we're together. Please don't be too angry. I just couldn't watch and do nothing."

Slowly Billy smiled, knowing exactly how she felt and why she had come. He didn't have to be happy about it, but he knew. He was no different and would have done the same thing had he been in her place. He nodded. "That we do." He squeezed her again as he turned to look at Falcon and saw Hammer and Lynx walking toward them, Abby between them.

"Hey Keeper," Lynx said. "Tiger?" She shook her head and caught Tiger's hand as she continued speaking with Keeper. "I'm glad Abby was able to find you quickly. I was afraid you might still be over at the kitchen."

Billy nodded and Lynx stared at Tiger.

"I saw that man, Blake," Hammer said, holding Lynx with his arm gently around her shoulder, "sneaking away when the fighting started. He had a few troublemakers from the kitchen with him."

"I saw him too," Billy admitted. "Looks like they enlisted a number of normally nonviolent types as well. I was surprised by some of the people that I saw. They were definitely high on something."

"Yeah, drug induced." Falcon looked up, past Billy. "That detective is here, Keeper." He nodded and Billy turned.

"Nolan," Billy greeted.

"Keeper, Tiger." He nodded and shook Billy's hand. "Thanks for the call, Tiger. What are you doing here?" He nodded to the rest of the group and stopped at the two other faces.

"Sort of in trouble again." She glanced at Billy. "Detective Nolan," Tiger added quickly as a matter of introduction, "you remember my mom from the hospital. And this is my sister Sandy. They brought me when I saw the fire."

Keeper, Falcon, and Hammer quickly gave Nolan the details as best they knew. They walked through the disheveled quarter of the village block, surveying the carnage with flashlights in hand as they talked. Twelve of the attackers were still unconscious and randomly scattered where they had fallen, and those able to stand or walk were escorted to the police vans in preparation for their journey to the station. Nolan counted forty-three, including those still on the ground—all of them seriously marked by their encounter.

When Billy had finished giving Nolan the names of the people he knew, Nolan thanked him and turned back to the policemen and their tasks. Billy looked at Falcon, then bent down and pulled a key from his boot. "On the northwest corner of Eighth West and Iowa, in the garage behind the house, there are a number of refrigerator boxes and some extra blankets. Go and get what they need."

Falcon took the key, picked three other men to help, then he left at a trot, leading them toward Iowa. Pleased he could help a little, Billy watched them for a moment as they disappeared into the darkness. He unexpectedly had an idea.

Thursday, May 26

Billy laid the *Beacon* on the counter with the table flowers. He was very tired as he selected a vase from the dry storage room, filled it half full of water, and set the large bouquet in it for Mary to see when she came down for breakfast. Since he had come from their apartment, he did not need to shower, but dressed in his white shirt and pants and went straight to mopping the floors. He knew that if he stopped, he'd fall asleep leaning on the handle. When he had the floors done, the tables repositioned, and the chairs set out as they should be, he distributed the table vases, napkin boxes, and the shakers.

He did not know whether to be happy or angry at Tiger after her stunt the night before. He greatly appreciated her help, and the more he thought about it, he could not really stay mad at her. She had pulled her incisions in the doing, but at least, he sighed, nothing was torn and the wound had not opened.

It was after two when he got her home and nearly three before he got her bandages changed. By then she was wide awake, and insisted on showing him her appreciation for everything that had happened since their walk Tuesday morning. He had tried to control his warring thoughts and accept her appreciation appropriately. He grinned; it had taken all night, but he had managed.

Sid came into the kitchen as he dumped the mop water and rinsed the bucket.

"Morning, Billy," Sid greeted cheerfully. "Oh, look at those. Tell Maxie she's outdone herself this time. Mom will surely love these."

"Morning, Sid," Billy greeted as he put the mop and bucket away, stifling a huge yawn.

Sid poured two cups of coffee from the urn as he usually did, and set one down for Billy. "You look rough this morning. Everything okay?"

"How's Mary this morning?" Billy asked with a nod as he picked up the cup and sipped the hot brew.

"I guess she's okay," Sid said softly, and glanced to the door to their home. "She said she didn't sleep much last night and I asked if she was troubled or something." He sipped his cup. "She said no. She said she was excited to know you had gotten married and can't wait to come to your celebration." Sid shook his head and smiled. "I think when she saw Billie come in the other day, as happy as she was and so full of life, she decided you two had already tied the knot. She said there's something different about you two, but I couldn't tell what she was talking about."

"Well, Sid," Billy said, and smiled into his cup, "you never know what people see or think as they view their surroundings from the perspective that age has given them."

Billy sat his cup down and turned to the door, knowing Sid had not understood what he meant. It did surprise him that Mary thought they were already married, but then, not really. Like she said, there was a lot that was different; he felt it and he knew Tiger felt it. They were both happily different.

He was halfway to the front doors when Angie rapped on the glass. He glanced back and saw that Sid had disabled the alarm, and then he opened the door to let Angie, Carole, Melony, Julie, Kevin, and Niles in. Angie shook her head when he started to ask about Ned, and he reclosed and locked the door.

Sid reset the alarm as Angie went to the back room to hang up her light jacket and Julie stopped to check the back side of the long serving counter. Billy filled six cups as usual and refilled his own, stirred two packs of sugar and one of creamer into one, and handed it to Angie when she came back to the end of the counter. Julie started the second coffee urn and went to hang her jacket in the back room.

"How was your night?" Billy asked Angie as she took her cup, knowing this was the first time he had started their ritual morning conversation in all of the years Angie had worked there.

Angie blinked and hesitated. "It...was pretty good. Had drinks with a friend of mine after work. She just started working the afternoon shift at Custer's."

"I'm sure that was nice," he said, and thought a moment. "Haven't had any problems from Blake, have you?"

"No," she said. "I went home early, but I'm sure he's following me around."

"I got the same feeling last night," Julie said as she sipped her coffee and leaned on the counter from behind, "around eight thirty. At least I think I saw someone duck out of sight when I looked back once. If it was him, he was quick."

"Probably was Sparrow," Billy said, and smiled at Julie. "I was going to tell you she's watching out for you, Julie. Her husband, Falcon, is watching you, Angie."

"Sparrow and Falcon?" Julie looked at him and smiled curiously. "Really?"

"Since Angie went head to head with Blake," Billy said as he finished his cup, "I wanted someone stronger in appearance to be available if Blake tries anything with you, Angie. Sparrow is quick, agile, and a very capable street fighter, but Blake hasn't learned to overlook size yet. Falcon has the physical presence to get Blake's attention and stop him before he starts anything, before he can hurt anyone. Blake would engage Sparrow before he realized he was in way over his head."

"So they're following us?" Angie asked.

"Yes. To help if Blake tries anything. I thought I just said that."

"Why would they do that?" Julie asked.

Billy got up. "Because I asked them to." He turned and went to the sink, rinsed his cup, and put it into the dishwasher.

Seventy-Seven

Joey closed his apartment door, locked it, and tossed his ball cap on the sofa as he made his way to his refrigerator. He grabbed a beer bottle, twisted off the cap, and threw it in the general direction of the trash can as he returned to the living room. Pushing the pile of newspapers aside—all still folded and wrapped with their rubber bands—to make room for himself, he flopped down on the sofa. The entire trip back from Hammersmith's place on Tuesday, he had wondered about Herb, where he had gone, why he had not contacted him or Hammersmith. No messages, no note at the house, no anything. It bothered him.

But the bloodstains on the driveway bothered him more. He was certain a good rain would wash them away, but when he closed his eyes, he still saw them: dark reddish-brown reminders of what Herb had done to that poor girl. That made him remember her pretty face, her red hair peeking from under the scarf, her disheveled sweater completely saturated with blood, like her chest had exploded.

He took a very long swig of his beer and tried to push the images out of his mind. He had been all right until he had gone back to the house...

Joey glanced at the pile of papers and something caught his attention. He absently picked up the paper from on top of the pile and pulled off the rubber band. As he unfolded the paper, he realized it was last Friday's paper and it was the corner of a color ad on the fly page for a Memorial Day sale that caught his eye. He took another sip of his beer, and without thinking about it, opened the paper to the current events summary section on an inside page.

Keeper and His Tiger: The Trap

As usual for a Friday edition, the section was small and he quickly read down the list of reported burglaries and assaults, but the last one held his attention. A John Doe was found dead in a rural area near the Chestnut Creek early Thursday morning. He looked closer at the few sketchy details, only to find that the location was on a Meadowlark Lane near the river.

Joey shivered, and the images of the woman flooded his memory again and he wondered if her body had been discovered already. He shook his head and reread the very short article; John Doe, not Jane Doe. His stomach felt queasy; he did not remember the names of the roads out by Hammersmith's place, but knew the body was found near it. *Damn,* he worried, *was there someone with the woman? Is the John Doe Herb? Did they follow him and do him in? Damn! What happened?*

He turned the bottle up and drank until it was empty. Then he pushed himself up, went back to the refrigerator and grabbed another bottle, then twisted its cap off as he dropped back into the cushions of the sofa. The cap rattled from somewhere in the kitchen; he did not care if it was close to the trash or not.

Halfway through the beer, he picked up his phone and dialed.

"Mr. H, Joey," he said, and sighed deeply. "The bloody mess Herb left on your driveway when he went to dump the girl is still there."

"He didn't go back and wash off the drive?" Mike asked in disbelief. "Any signs that anyone else had been there?"

"No." Joey took another swig from the bottle. "Everything looked like it did when I left, including the blood."

"And Herb has not shown up at your place?" Mike's tone was anxious and Joey did not know why, but he smiled to himself. Maybe he liked seeing Mike squirm a little himself.

"No. But Friday's *Beacon* had a short article. Someone found a body up near your place. A man's body."

"Whose?" Mike nearly shouted.

"A John Doe. No name and no details. Just a body found." Joey studied his beer bottle as he slowly turned it in his fingers.

"The woman?" Mike's words were tense, and Joey was glad there was a phone between them.

"Nothing about a woman. I haven't looked at any later papers to see if anyone has found a woman's body."

"Find out!" Mike shouted, then paused and Joey listened to his panting breaths.

Joey waited without saying anything, and then in a more normal voice, Mike asked, "Seen Westman yet?"

"No. He wasn't home when I went by."

"Keep trying." Mike's voice had an edge to it again.

"Yeah. I know. Make him hurt."

"Yes. A lot, but no hospitals."

"I know." Joey knew he did not sound convincing. He still was not sure how he was going to do it.

"Did you get a gun?"

"Yeah, I got a gun." Joey took another swig. "I could've shot at him last night, but you didn't tell me you were sending that new guy to tear up the homeless village. I didn't hear about it until this morning. I heard Keeper and his Tiger were there."

"I thought you two were talking to each other." Mike's irritation was noticeable again. "Damn! Go help Copper. See what he's going to do now and when," Mike said. "Then let me know. I can't change your bumbling last night, but you can help him get ready for the next time. I want the one they call Keeper. I want him out of the way. For good!"

"Yeah, I know," Joey said heavily, nodding absently to no one. "You keep saying that, but I don't know why you're so worried 'bout it. Copper can't help you now. There's no one there to sell drugs to. A construction team started work on two of those buildings yesterday."

"Work? What work?"

"They're starting to put up sidewalk covers 'round the front sides and have blocked off the alleys."

"Renovating?"

"Looks like it," Joey said, and emptied the bottle to the sound of Hammersmith's scream.

¤-¤-¤-¤-¤

Maggie and Sandy had let Billie sleep and relax most of the day, worried that she was trying to do too much too soon, especially after demanding they go and help defend the village against the threat of the previous night. Maggie was still having trouble realizing that it was her daughter she had watched wielding a knife and easily defending herself against men twice her size and weight, as if they were nothing at all. She had never seen her youngest daughter so confident and unafraid; it was obvious she had taken Billy's training to heart. Sandy had been quiet most of the day, and Maggie assumed she was wrestling with the same sense of surprise from watching her little sister.

The day passed quietly, and Maggie called Billie late in the afternoon to be sure they were still on for another night at the kitchen. Billie said they were, and Maggie picked them up at six thirty and drove to the bus station parking garage.

"I'm sorry that I drug you two into the fracas last night," Billie admitted as she got out of the car. "I didn't think about you coming into the village, but when you did, I was glad you stayed close."

Maggie laughed a guarded laugh. "I wasn't so sure we should've either, but it seemed the best place to be was close to you and Billy."

"I've never seen anything so intense before," Sandy whispered. "It was like stepping into a war movie or something. But it was real."

Billie hugged Sandy. "I'm sorry you saw all of that. Sometimes it's too real."

Billy slipped his arm around Billie's shoulder and turned them toward Second Street East. "Let's talk while we walk," he said, and let Billie and Sandy walk in front of him and Maggie.

-¤-

After a few blocks, Billie switched places with her mom and she slipped her arm around his waist.

"How's the village today?" she asked.

"Recovering." He smiled. "A few minor wounds. Thankfully, nothing life threatening." He gently squeezed her shoulder. "I'm sorry I got mad at you. I was just surprised and concerned."

"Thanks, and I know you were." She inhaled. "Did Falcon get enough boxes for everyone?"

"Yeah, but I've been thinking." He smiled and glanced down at her.

"About?"

"About making small, one-room portable houses available to those that have jobs." He smiled at her startled expression. "About offering replacements for the cardboard hovels, reducing the unsightly appearance of the village and helping those that are trying to get ahead."

"Well," she thought out loud, "there are some complications associated with that idea, but probably nothing to stop it. What about zoning and use of public property?"

He chuckled. "Pastoric owns that block—it isn't public use."

Billie's eyes went wide. "It's one of the other ten?"

He nodded and chuckled again.

"Does Kelly and Lloyd have designs?"

"I guess we should ask."

-¤-

It was late when Billy led the four of them out of the kitchen and crossed Tenth Street East as they headed back toward the city center. As he stepped up onto the sidewalk, he heard his name called from the shadows. He stopped and turned to face the familiar voice.

"Keeper," the voice said as the tall man stepped forward.

"Hey, Stretch," Tiger said.

"Hi, Tiger," Stretch said, and nodded to the other two women.

"Stretch, this is my mom, Maggie and my sister, Sandy. Sorry they weren't in town the night you and Cat came to visit me in the hospital, and I don't think you got a chance to meet them last night. Mom, Sandy, this is Stretch."

"Nice to meet you," Stretch said, and then turned back to them. "Cat, Pigeon, and Hammer are watching the block from the shadows and your 'buddy' Butch came back to watch. He was there last night about nine, and came back tonight and parked in the same place."

"So Butch is trying to make it obvious that someone's there," Billy said softly. "I don't know if that's good or bad, Stretch, but we'll let him stay and see what happens."

"Okay," Stretch said.

He started to turn, but Billy stopped him.

"Stretch? Who got the free cell phones? I can't remember."

"Cat, Pigeon, and Mouse did." Stretch smiled at him and shook his head. "You should've gotten one too."

"Yeah, I should've." He glanced at Tiger. "I really meant to."

"Feels strange for us to have one. Never used one before."

"Lynx and Sparrow didn't get one?" Tiger asked.

"No, Tiger. Lynx is still too worried," Max explained cryptically. "Sparrow just couldn't get away from work when the others went to get theirs."

"Have Cat call Tiger and give her their numbers," Billy said, and nodded. "Call Tiger if any of you need to tell either of us something when we can't talk face to face." Billy took a pen out of his pants pocket and wrote Billie's number in Max's palm. "And give Tiger's number to everyone in the apartments and to those in the village that help us watch. They can call if they need to. This is water soluble, so don't sweat too much."

"Thanks, Keeper. We'll talk more tomorrow."

¤-¤-¤-¤-¤

Billie folded the sling and laid it on her vanity, then switched off the vanity lights. With the room illuminated by the soft nightstand lamp, she sat down on the edge of the bed between Billy's wide spread legs, her back to him. He helped her slip her blouse up over her head and she let it slide off her arms, tossing it onto the foot of the bed.

"Unhook me," Billie sighed softly, and Billy unfastened the clasp on her bra strap. She tossed it on the bed with her blouse. "How does it look?" she asked as he gently pulled at the tape holding the gauze over the smaller entry wound on her back below her shoulder. "It feels stiff when I move my upper arm tonight."

"Hold on. The scab is caught a little." He tried to keep his mind on his task and his eyes from roaming over her back and down to her hips as he tugged as gently as he could and peeled the gauze away from the stitches. "It actually looks pretty good, but it's been bleeding a little. More of last night's exertion," he said, and dabbed the wound with a moist, sterile cloth. "It's just around a couple of stitches, but there's only a little scabbing. Hand me the ointment."

He cleaned the wound and the surrounding skin with an alcohol-wetted cloth and she held the tube up over her right shoulder.

"I think I'll put less gauze over it tonight," he said as he spread a thin layer of the thick cream over the wound, "so it can air out some."

When he had the new gauze patch in place and was satisfied the tape would hold properly, he pulled the gauze off the entry wound on her side. He spread a little of the ointment on the area. "I don't think we need the bandage on this one anymore.

Turn around."

He pushed himself back to the middle of the bed and turned, stretching his legs out toward the foot. Billie stood up and stepped up on the bed, straddling him. She folded her legs and sat down on his thighs, facing him.

He inhaled the beautiful sight of her, and before he did anything else, he slipped his hand behind her neck and pulled her close, kissing her gently as he cupped her breast with his free hand. Her arm wrapped around his neck in response to his caresses as she eagerly returned his kiss.

Trying to ignore what her closeness did to him, Billy reluctantly released her lips and forced himself to focus on the bandage. He carefully pulled the tape holding the gauze over the shoulder exit wound. As he peeled the gauze back, Billie inhaled sharply at the pull on a thread tail. She tried to watch, having seen the stitched wound when Billy changed the bandages earlier—four incisions that formed a silver-dollar-sized, non-symmetrical cross above her left breast—but the size still surprised her and the stiffness in her shoulder worried her.

"It's only been a week, Tiger. And it looks good," he said as he pulled the gauze free and set it aside. "The inflammation is going away and there's not much oozing—just where three of the stitches pulled last night. You see the doc in the morning and should get them out. That'll make a big difference in how you feel, and you probably won't have to tuck your bra strap under your arm anymore."

"Well, I won't be wearing any strapless dresses for a while," she said, and sighed, still looking down at the wound, trying to smile about it. "I guess I'll have to think about that when I pick out a wedding dress."

"To me, Tiger"—he lifted her chin with a curled finger and held her eyes—"for however long you have your scar, it will always remind me of the incredible courage you have and how much of a sacrifice you were willing to make to help me. If you want to wear sundresses or whatever kind of dress, with or without straps, it's certainly okay with me. And I'll probably argue with anyone that dares to criticize you when you do."

She smiled and he gently smeared the oily ointment on the stitched incisions, working it around the thread tails. "I hope I'm not hurting."

"No, it's okay. The ointment feels very good"—she smiled—"and you're getting pretty good at applying it."

"I would really prefer to practice something else," he said as he taped the new gauze in place and moved his attention down to the exit wound on her side.

"I've been wondering," Billie said, changing the subject. "Do you know if Cathy and her husband ever divorced? I mean officially?"

"No, I don't know. This one looks good too." He collected the old gauzes and leaned over to pile them on the nightstand.

"Cathy said she and Todd wanted to get married, but she said it was a matter of cost." Billie held his eyes and smiled. "I'm curious if it isn't something more fundamental keeping them apart."

"I guess you'll have to ask Cathy for more details. He's never come around since he left her. With us all living together in the basement, I would've known if he had."

"If they were never divorced, would you mind if I see what I can do to fix that?"

Billy smiled at her. "And what if you can fix it?"

"If it can be fixed, and if it can be done in time, would you mind having them get married with us? Since we already are, it would be nice if someone actually was during the ceremony."

"I think it's a very nice gesture, Mrs. Hawke," Billy said, and leaned forward and kissed her neck, then her chin, and then her lips. "If it can be done in time." He lay back, reached to the nightstand, and switched off the lamp. "But I think you'll have to wait until morning to start, Tiger. Right now, you have a very tired and patient husband that needs you to hold him."

"Oh, I think my husband wants more than to be held." Billie smiled and stretched out on top of him.

Keeper and His Tiger: The Trap

Seventy-Eight

Mike Hammersmith slowly crossed St. Charles from Twentieth Street East, watching the crossing streets once he got into the populated part of the eastside of town. Ever since the day the police had come by his office looking for him, getting out was a huge risk; he felt his Towncar was a flag announcing where he was. He knew he had to use a different vehicle, but tonight he was anxious—he could not just sit and wonder if Joey was right. So against his better sense, he had to see for himself what was happening at the Duckard's buildings.

At Seventh Street East, he drove up to Baker and headed west, keeping his vigil for police cruisers and beat patrolmen, but he did not see any. At the bus station he had to wait as an express pulled out ahead of him. Being stopped as the bus moved onto the street pushed his discomfort up a notch, or two notches.

Crossing Main, he could see the sidewalk covers ahead, and just past First West he pulled along the curb and stared. The alley was closed off with a solid, view-blocking construction gate and the assembly of the sidewalk protection was well underway; renovations had certainly begun.

Mike slammed his hand against the steering wheel and let his frustrations shake him.

Damn! Damn!

As quickly as the anger swelled in him, his worry overwhelmed him. Somehow he had to figure out how to get into and out of that building without being seen. He would have to go out to his place in the country and get his key, then maybe—

A flash of light sweeping across the front of the Duckard's

buildings interrupted his thoughts; a patrol car turned the corner behind him, its search light scanning the construction area. Mike inhaled sharply and slowly drove to the next corner, and as casually as one could while driving, he turned north. He watched in his rearview, hoping he looked like someone on the project checking the day's progress, and the patrol car did not follow him.

Friday, May 27

Maggie stopped her car under the spreading limbs of the huge elm beside the River Crest Apartments' wraparound drive. Billie got out and smiled at her through the open window.

"I shouldn't be long," she said, and hurried to Cathy and Todd's apartment.

She knocked and waited. Suddenly the door swung open and Abby's bright face smiled up at her.

"Tiiggeerr! Mama, Tiger's here!" Abby announced, and hugged Billie tight.

"Come in, Tiger," Cathy called from one of the bedrooms in the back of the apartment. "I'm getting dressed for work. Be out in a second."

Abby pulled her into the living room, plopped down on the sofa, and patted the place beside her.

Billie smiled and sat down. "How are you on such a beautiful morning?" she asked.

Abby responded with a litany of things she had already done and the things she was planning to do now that she was out of school for the summer. She was still in full disclosure mode when Cathy came out and shooed her into her bedroom to finish getting herself dressed.

"Good to see you're up and around," Cathy greeted, still brushing her hair. "What's up?"

"Thanks. I'm going to get my stitches out at ten, but I

stopped by to see if I can ask you a personal question?"

"Sure." Cathy sat down where Abby had been.

"First I have to apologize for not blocking out a time to shop for Abby's dress. I don't really know where this week has gone."

"That's okay. You've been a little busy since you got out of the hospital. But we'll have to take time on a weekend or after work. Maybe next week, after the holiday."

"Okay. We'll plan on an evening or two, and then Saturday if we need it."

"Thanks."

"Now, this will sound nosy, but did you and your husband ever file for a divorce?"

Cathy hesitated and held her eyes, but did not say anything.

"I only want to know to see if I can help. I don't mean to be prying, but I can't help you and Todd get married if there are legal matters that need to be fixed."

Cathy slowly let her eyes look away. "No. He just left, and we haven't spoken to each other since. I...I've always been afraid to dig into it much, afraid he might come back and try to take Abby."

"Well, will you let me do the looking? What's his name and your married name?"

"His name is Clark Jefferson," Cathy said, still watching her cautiously. "I...I was a Nikleson and we were married in Cincinnati ten years ago."

Cathy spelled the names as Billie typed the information into her touch-screen phone.

"He was from Detroit and I'm from Garland, just outside of Dallas."

"Let me start with this and do some checking, and I'll let you know what I find out, if anything." She smiled and caught Cathy's hand. "I may need more information along the way. Do you mind if I ask if I do?"

Cathy smiled. "No. That'll be fine, I guess."

"Good." She stood up. "Then I'll get started. If you two really want to get hitched, I'd like very much to help make that happen. And if you decide you don't, I'd still like to help you clear this up. Maybe remove a worry or two."

"Thanks, Tiger. I don't know what to say."

Billie smiled and started to the door. "If I can't find anything out after getting your hopes up, I might not want to hear what you do think of to say. Have a good day at work and I'll let you know when I have something."

"Thanks," Cathy said, and Billie slipped out and hurried back to her mom.

¤-¤-¤-¤-¤

As soon as the college's group photo session was finished, Collin Westman, dressed in her mortarboard and long gown with the college's colored sash draped around her neck and trailing down the front, hurried down off the risers and across the grassy lawn to the spot on the curved sidewalk where she and her mother had agreed to meet.

She only waited a moment before her mom arrived with her own camera in hand.

"I was off to the side," Nancy explained, "trying to get a shot of you in the group, but I think the only good place for a picture was out front. Let me get one of you here under the tree."

Nancy stepped back and took a number of pictures before she stopped, lowered the camera, and smiled at Collin. "You look absolutely wonderful."

"Have you seen Dad?" Collin asked bluntly, fearing that she knew the answer.

"Let's sit a minute, honey." Nancy led her to a bench in the ample shade of the mature trees. As they sat down, Nancy continued. "After your dad was here, I heard from him again and he told me he found out the Chesterfield Police had issued a warrant to arrest Mike Hammersmith for the murder and attempted murder of some street people. Also, he said Hammersmith apparently hired a killer—they called him a 'street assassin'—to kill someone that was keeping him from getting some properties in the city center. Same old story. Your dad said the contract with Hammersmith also targeted him, your dad. He said to tell you he's sorry, but he has to hide until they catch Hammersmith."

"Has he?" Collin asked, her years of mixed ambivalence and anger swept away by her sudden, unfamiliar feeling of concern.

"Yes and no." Nancy looked at her hands, clasped in her lap. "I called the Chesterfield Police and talked to a detective there. I told him the whole story about Hammersmith and how he used your dad and what I know about the accident seventeen years ago. Hammersmith had a family murdered, a couple and their son, so he could take some land in the city center." She looked up at Collin. "I told him where to find your dad and they did. He's on his way back to Chesterfield as an important witness against Hammersmith."

"A witness?" Collin asked, scared to believe her ears. "Not an accomplice? They found him and they aren't arresting him?"

"Yes, honey. The detective said they don't have any evidence that your dad has done anything wrong, other than having worked with an unscrupulous man. They want him to testify against Hammersmith. I might also have to testify."

Collin threw her arms around her mom. "Can it be true, Mom? Can Dad actually stop staying away from us?"

"I think there's a very good chance that we can go home again."

Collin held her mom for a long moment, letting her tears flow and her sobs slowly turn to soft chuckles of anticipation.

"After the ceremony is over," Nancy said, breaking the warm silence that had grown between them, "we need to go and pack."

"Pack?" Collin asked as she pushed herself up and wiped her eyes, knowing she had smeared her makeup and had to look terrible.

"I have airline tickets for tomorrow morning," Nancy announced softly, smiling. "I assumed you didn't have anything important planned, so we're going back to Chesterfield to be with your dad when he gets there."

Seventy-Nine

Billy gestured to the chairs in the hospital waiting room and followed Maggie and Sandy in. Tiger checked in with the receptionist and verified her insurance. When she took a seat beside Billy, she had him hold the clipboard and she started filling out the health questionnaire the receptionist had given her.

"I would think they would have all of this from the hospital records," she said, and nudged him. "Didn't you and Mom give them my medical history?"

"Only some," he admitted. "What I gave them was very minimal when I checked you in, and your mom added some to it when the nurses asked specific questions."

"Maybe they should have all of this in some central files so I wouldn't have to spend so much time trying to remember the details and filling these forms out." She bent to the task of checking boxes.

"So you've only been in a hospital once before and now you'd want them to know and keep records on file so that anyone that had to look you up would know that you are a bit of a show-off and that most of your injuries have come from doing something stup—"

"Okay. Okay," she interrupted, and nudged him again. "I get it. No, I wouldn't. Are you happy now?"

"Yes, Tiger." He smiled. "Any time I'm with you."

She smiled and nudged him again and forced herself to finish the chart. She signed it *Billie Mattis*, dated it, and returned it to the receptionist. Then she sat down, leaned against his arm and curled her fingers in his, completely oblivious to the fact that Maggie and Sandy were even in the room and watching her, much less sitting next to them.

When the nurse opened a door beside the receptionist and called her name, she got up and, without releasing his hand, led him to the door with her. The nurse nodded when she said, "He's coming too," and stepped into the hall beyond the door.

The nurse led them to a small examination room and asked them to sit down and wait, saying the doctor would be along in just a few minutes.

"I hope everything's okay," she said, and turned to hold her arm before they sat down.

"It will be, Tiger," he said, and wrapped his arms gently around her. "At least as good as can be expected for a woman with a couple of bullet holes in her."

"Stop it," she said, and slapped his chest playfully. "You know what I mean."

"Yes, I certainly do," he said, and kissed her. "And you know exactly what I mean."

The door opened and the doctor stepped in, reading something in an open folder, and glanced at them. Billy smiled when he realized the doctor was also Billie's surgeon, the one he had met in the hospital. The surgeon hesitated a moment, smiled at them, and then gestured to the chairs. Billy moved and sat down.

"Miss Mattis—"

"Billie, please," she interrupted, and smiled at him as he gestured to the examination table.

"Billie," he said, and smiled. "Thank you. Please take a seat on the table." He introduced himself as she settled on the cushion, her legs dangling over the end.

He pulled a stool out from under a counter and sat down while he studied her chart. He glanced at Billy and asked, "Good to see you again Mr. Carson. May I ask what your relationship is with Miss, ah, Billie?"

"Billie's fiancé," he said. "Also a Billy."

"We're having our wedding celebration in three weeks," Billie explained.

"I see, and your parents?"

"Oh, my mom and sister are out in the waiting room, and my dad is out at their home," she quickly answered.

"I see." The surgeon looked at her chart again. "Was your broken leg the only other time you've been admitted to a hospital?"

"Yes," she answered, thinking. "I don't think there has ever been another time."

"And when was that?"

"Let's see...I was..." She rubbed her cheek, trying to remember..

"Seven," Billy said. "You were seven and it was early August, on a weekend. Your horse fell against a tree."

"Yes, I was seven," Billie said, and looked at the doctor. "That's right." She smiled at Billy for remembering. "Dad told me later our doctor's office wasn't open because it was a weekend."

The doctor looked at him and then at Billie. "I see. Please take your blouse off and we'll see how well you are doing."

When he turned to the counter and began making notes on her chart, Billy got up and unfastened the straps for the sling and set it aside, and then he helped her pull her blouse over her head and he collected it as she slipped it off her arms. He folded it and set it aside with the sling. She saw the doctor noticed his help when he turned back to her, but he did not say anything.

The doctor put surgical gloves on, leaned close, and began removing the tape from the shoulder exit wound area. A nurse entered the room, quickly closed the door behind her, and began collecting the discarded tape and gauze as the doctor removed them.

"Did Billy do the bandaging?" he asked as he worked.

"Yes," she said, and smiled. "He's gotten good at applying the ointment without bothering the stitches too much."

The doctor smiled but did not say anything, quickly turning to the task of clipping the numerous tight loops of thread. Billie flinched with each snip.

He picked up a pair of tweezers and gently pressed the fingers of his other hand against the incision. "This may sting a little," he said, and quickly jerked the first stitch out.

Billie jumped and inhaled deeply, tears coming instantly to her eyes. The doctor stopped and turned to the nurse. "Get me the topical spray anesthetic." He looked at Billie when the nurse left and asked, "Do you usually have a low tolerance to pain?"

"I...I guess so. Usually I can feel the slightest touch easily. If it's uncomfortable, it usually feels like pain. Billy says sometimes it's like I can feel it before I'm actually touched. Is that normal?"

"No," the doctor admitted. "Not for most people, but redheads seem to have a much higher sensitivity to various stimulations than non-redheads. It's different for different people, but from what I see, I imagine you felt this wound excruciating."

"It was worse than I can explain. Every time I tried to breathe, the pain in my chest and down my left side was paralyzing. Couldn't move my left—"

"That's enough, Billie," the doctor said, and put his hand on her shoulder. "You don't need to relive it. Right now, I need you to relax."

The nurse returned with a small, white aerosol canister and handed it to the doctor. "This will feel very cold, Billie. I'll apply it liberally and let it set for a few minutes."

Billie reached for Billy's hand as he stood up beside the table and held it while the doctor sprayed the area around the stitches. Her eyes followed him as he went around her side and began removing the tape and gauze from the entry wound, spraying the area around it as well. Finished, he checked the wounds on her side before he turned to the counter and made more notations. The nurse left and Billie sat quietly leaning against Billy, holding his hand, comforted again by his presence.

When the nurse stepped back in, the doctor turned to Billie. "Okay. Let's see if we can get this over quickly. Take a deep breath and hold it."

She looked up at Billy's face and focused on his smiling eyes as the doctor started plucking the threads, and before she realized it, the exit wound threads were out and the doctor stood up. Knowing what to expect, she held her breath again as he quickly removed the far fewer number from her back.

She exhaled and Billy dabbed the tears from her eyes as the doctor sat back down on his stool and turned to make more notations, and the nurse began swabbing the skin around the wounds with a sanitized cloth.

"You won't need any more gauze, unless the incisions ooze a little," the doctor said. "Keep the skin clean and apply that ointment for at least the next week. If the skin continues to be sensitive or overly tight, use an over-the-counter skin moisturizer." He rattled off a number of butters and oils that would beneficially help her skin.

"I want to see you again in a month, or as soon as you get back from your honeymoon. I assume you'll be taking one," He smiled. "And here's a prescription for more of those pain pills. Only one a day for the next two weeks. As sensitive as you are to the pain, I want you to be comfortable so you'll use that arm and not coddle it. No strenuous exercise and no lifting anything over ten pounds with that arm, but do use it. Only use the sling if your arm feels tired or if you feel like you need it. I'll see how you're doing in a month or so and see where we go from there."

"It's doing okay then?" she asked in a soft, guarded voice.

"Yes, Billie. It's doing very well," he answered, and smiled gently. "Put your blouse on and see the receptionist. She'll give you a list of restrictions and things you need to do." He smiled at Billy. "And you, sir, make sure she gets that ointment every night before bed for the next week and the butter as often as she'll let you apply it."

Then he shook her hand and followed the nurse out of the

door.

-□-

When the nurse stepped into the waiting room and called Billie's name, Maggie started to collect her purse and get up, but stopped when Billie stood up and led Billy to the door.

"What's she doing?" Sandy asked. "Why didn't she take you?"

Maggie smiled, pondering a possibility that flitted through her mind as she finally recognized the sudden change in her daughter—a change in maturity, purpose, and happiness that she had not had even as recent as her last two visits to the ranch. It was new, and she knew something had changed since she got out of the hospital. Was it because Billy had asked her to set a date, or...? She wondered.

"Sandy, dear," Maggie said, recalling Sandy's question. "First, let me say that I think I did you girls a disservice growing up. I have always been very strict with you, afraid of you falling in with the wrong groups, the wrong men, the kind that only saw your background and not yourselves. I never appreciated that you were capable of understanding and evaluating those issues, but seeing your sister and you now, I realize I was trying to shelter you the wrong way and may have seriously hindered how you see other people. For that I am truly sorry—"

"You haven't done anything—"

Maggie held up her hand and smiled. "Your sister has been her own woman for a number of years. Since she went off to college, she has chosen to take care of herself, seldom asking for our assistance in things, often hating it when I offered it, and now"—she looked at Sandy— "your sister has found herself. She and Billy have found each other and your sister isn't mine anymore. She belongs to him. She's my daughter, but no longer my little girl."

"I don't understand."

"Then, my dear," Maggie said, smiling as she picked up a magazine, "Gil isn't the right one."

Eighty

Maggie and Sandy joined them in their apartment for lunch, and when they were finished, Billy rinsed and placed the dishes in the dishwasher. He washed the pans and put them away, and when he was finished, he said he had to get back and work the afternoon.

"We'll leave for the kitchen about six thirty, serve at seven, and try to get away about nine," he said as Billie stopped him at the door. "I'll see you about six."

She pushed herself up and kissed him, holding him with both arms. "You have a good afternoon," she said as she let herself down.

"You too, Tiger," he said, and gave her another quick peck as he opened the door.

Billie turned back to the kitchen counter and opened her notepad and glanced at her mom. "I have Billy's and my guest list put together."

"Oh good," Maggie said, and came to the counter to look over her shoulder. "How many?"

"With our friends from the apartments, the diner, Lori, Beck, Stacy, and Billy's friends, the Willises and the Florentinis, it's fifty..."

"Fifty sounds like a nice number," Maggie said, and nodded vigorously. "I started on our list, and with your grandparents, and your dad's sisters and their families, my brother and his family, and a few more your dad wants to invite, it should be a nice size wedding. Yes, nice size indeed."

Billie looked at her mom, hearing her enthusiasm. "Simple. Remember? Keep it simple and not over the top. No pretenses.

Not too showy."

"Do you want to go look at invitations this afternoon?"

Billie sighed, knowing her mom was ignoring her. "I know we need to, but right now I just want to crash for a while. I feel like the doctor stuck forty needles in my chest and half that many in my back and they're still there. I hate to think what I'd feel like if I didn't have the pain pills."

"I didn't know you were that sensitive to pain," Maggie said.

"I knew I was but didn't know it was unusual," she said, and turned to face them. "The doctor had to use a topical anesthetic just to pull the stitches. He said a low pain threshold is something a lot of redheads have. I guess we're more sensitive than non-redheads."

"More *of a* pain," Sandy teased.

"You can nap for a while and then we could go before Billy gets back," Maggie offered, and waited for her to decide.

"Okay. Give me two hours."

She hugged her mom and Sandy interrupted.

"Okay, Mom. I think we should go to that mall south of here on the other side of the river and see what they have to look at."

"Finch Meadows. We renovated one of the stores there. That is, Boster, Lange and that other guy's design firm did. You'll like it. It has a lot of shops with new stuff and shops for those still young at heart."

"Are you calling me old?" Sandy snipped.

"You are older than me, o' sister of mine," she retorted.

"Girls! Girls," their mom laughed. "All of a sudden you sound like you did back in high school. Come on, Sandy." She hugged Billie again and kissed her cheek. "You get some rest and we'll be back in time to go to the kitchen."

"Thanks, Mom. And you too, Sandy. It means a lot to have you here."

Billie watched them gather their purses and step out into

the hall. When the door closed and the apartment filled with silence, she inhaled deeply and turned to her notepad.

I thought you were going to take a nap.

Just a few minutes for Cathy.

Only a few.

Yup.

She started with the public records in Cincinnati and checked for ten-year-old marriage records. Then she narrowed the search to people named Jefferson. Finding twelve, she did a quick scan down the list and saw the notation for Clark Jefferson and Catherine Nikleson on July 7.

She took a deep breath, crossed her fingers, and changed her search to divorce records, beginning approximately three years later, about the time Abby was born, but nothing came up. She shifted to the local state public records and searched for divorce records about the same time or later. When nothing surfaced, she searched for death notices in Cincinnati and in the Detroit area, and was not sure if she was relieved or not when she did not find one; the results were the same: nothing.

I could be looking in the wrong part of the country, for all I know.

Perplexed, she thought about their situation for a moment.

Clark really had no reason to file for a divorce. He walked away from his obligations, from Cathy and a daughter that he has never met. If he filed, he could certainly face a judgment for back child support. And whether he could pay or not, it would always be something Cathy could hold over his head. No, I don't think Clark would want to file for a divorce unless he could get child support waived. Billie smiled. *Maybe we have a bargaining chip.*

She picked up her phone and touched Nolan's icon.

"Detective Nolan? Tiger," she said. "Do you have a minute?"

"Sure, Tiger," he answered, his voice sounding happy to hear from her.

"I need to ask you for another favor—for a friend of ours."

¤-¤-¤-¤-¤

During the evening of serving, Tiger did not have any encounters, though about the beginning of their second hour, a very nice-looking and articulate fellow stopped and tried to engage Sandy in a conversation. Maggie smiled and watched with her as Sandy stumbled through the situation and finally left the fellow a little deflated with his lack of success.

When Keeper brought another pot of soup, she asked him who the fellow was, pointing him out at one of the tables. Keeper smiled and told her and then went back to the kitchen and another circuit of roaming through the dining area, stopping to visit with someone and then someone else, or a small group here and there.

During their break, she squeezed in between Sandy and their mom, sitting on a bench by the side door.

"That nice fellow that tried to talk to you, Sandy," she said in hushed tones, "is Chase Kelly. He owns a medical supply company here in the city and volunteers to give the elderly and handicapped folks rides to the kitchen three days a week. On the other two nights, when he can come, he only brings his grandmother so she can visit with two very old and less-fortunate friends of hers."

"He's a volunteer?" Sandy asked, suddenly conflicted, and shook her head. "But he looks like everyone else."

Tiger chuckled. "Sandy, we all do. Look at yourself in the bathroom mirror. Here, the beauty is that you judge people by what they do, how they act, how they speak to one another. Not by their dress."

"He must think I'm such a snob," Sandy said as she bowed her head and held her face in her hands.

Tiger raised an eyebrow and looked at her mom. She smiled.

"Sandy," Tiger continued, "I suggest that you just talk to

him about why you're here, what you're doing, what he's doing, and so on, if he asks again. Be real, and don't think about the physical dress. We are all in disguise so those that come here are not offended by seeing us as giving charity or taking pity on them. They need our help and we're here to try and give it to them. From one friend to another."

Sandy looked at her. "You really have changed, haven't you, sis?"

"I have, and I'm glad I have. I have many new and wonderful friends because I let Keeper show me a different world—his world." She straightened and stood up. "Now, if Chase looks at you or talks to you again, say hello like you mean it, sis." With that, she turned back to the door. "Gotta wash up and get back to my pot."

"Wow," Sandy said, a little louder than a whisper as her sister disappeared through the doorway. "I've never seen her like this. So...so..."

"Comfortable? Self-assured? I think we better get used to it," her mom said, and got up. "But like Tiger said, we need to wash up and get back to our trays."

¤-¤-¤-¤-¤

"So, you didn't see Copper all evening?" Tiger asked as they left the kitchen and started west along Crescent with Maggie and Sandy close behind.

"No," Billy admitted. "It makes me curious. I'm told he's been here every night for the last month. He was here the night Pink died and even the nights following."

"Well, things do come up." She tried to make the situation sound less ominous.

"They do." Billy glanced around as they walked. "The other curious thing is that about a dozen other consistent regulars were also missing tonight."

"Do you think something's up? I mean, he's a dealer and the worst he would do is try to get into the buildings. Right?"

"Unfortunately, yes. Something's up." Billy squeezed Tiger's hand as they crossed Second Street East and turned south toward the bus station. "But I think it's more than just dealing in drugs. Mike lost the last round, and I'm certain he'll be trying to make up for it. I don't think it will be tonight, but if something breaks, Butch will contact Nolan and Stretch or one of the others will contact us."

When they reached the parking garage, Maggie asked, "Will you join us for breakfast in the morning? Sandy's flight is at noon, so we'll try to be at the airport a little before eleven."

Tiger looked at Billy and he nodded. "What time should we meet?"

"How about nine?" Sandy asked. "We can pick you up."

"Where do you want to eat?" she asked.

"The Streetcar, of course," Sandy said.

"Good. Tell you what." Billy glanced at Tiger. "If the weather's good, why don't we just meet you there at nine?"

Tiger smiled. "Yes. I'd like a walk."

"Okay. If the weather's bad," Sandy agreed, "we'll call you and come by. Otherwise, we'll see you there at nine."

Eighty-One

"I confirmed that Cathy and her husband never filed for a divorce, and I did not find a death notice for him, so he's still around somewhere," Billie explained as she washed and got ready for bed. "But I figured her husband hasn't filed for one because he might be afraid he would have to pay child support."

"Well," Billy admitted as he brushed his teeth, "a judge might make that a condition."

She had turned the lights out and was sitting cross-legged on the bed when he came out of the bath and finished undressing. "I was thinking," she continued, "that might be something Cathy could use to persuade Clark to agree to a divorce."

"You mean let him off the hook?"

"Yeah, I guess, if you want to look at it that way." She sighed and looked at him. "But Cathy hasn't pursued contact with him, so I'm thinking she might be agreeable with the idea."

"I know that between the two of them in their present circumstances, she doesn't have to rely on any support from him. Abby's fed, clothed, schooled, and loved."

He picked up the tube of ointment and stepped up onto the bed, sat down behind her, and started applying the gel to the back of her shoulder and side.

"I called Nolan when I couldn't find anything in the public records," she said as he pulled her back against him and wrapped his left arm around her. He tried to stay focused as he felt her breasts rest gently on his forearm, and he began gently rubbing the liniment on the shoulder incisions.

"And why Nolan?"

"Cathy and I have an appointment with Justice Parker Tuesday morning. Monday's a holiday, so I had to settle for Tuesday. Nolan helped set it up for us." She lay her head back against his shoulder and let herself relax as he continued to lightly massage the front of her shoulder in slow, expanding circles. The tingles his fingers created made it difficult for her to concentrate on Cathy's issue. "Nolan thinks the justice might be able to help her file a petition for divorce. If Clark doesn't respond within a set time, he might grant it without his signature. Maybe."

"This is possibly the first time I've heard anyone upbeat about getting a divorce." He chuckled. "I guess we'll see what Tuesday brings." He slowly lay back against the pillows and pulled her with him, inhaling the citrus scent of her hair, feeling her length against him, fully arousing him with her presence.

She rolled over, stretched out, and kissed him.

Saturday, May 28

"Morning, Angie," Billy said as he opened the Streetcar's double front doors to let Billie enter first. "Four for breakfast. Has Billie's mom and sister arrived yet?"

"I haven't seen them," Angie said as she turned to take them to their booth. "You seem very chipper this morning."

"It's a long and sordid tale," Billie said, and then turned serious. "I have to ask if Blake has been a problem since you dealt with him."

"Nooo. Billy's friends have been watching and Blake hasn't made any moves."

"I don't like it, Billy." She looked at him. "It isn't like Blake."

"I know," he agreed. "Angie, could you bring us a coffee and a tea?"

"Coming up." Angie hurried to the counter.

"I feel very odd this morning." Billie leaned close to him and spoke softly. "Like there's something afoot, a sensation in the air that's bothering me."

"I sense something too," he said, and squeezed her hand. "Pidge called just before we left, while you were still in the bath getting ready. Joey's been stirring something up this morning in the park near the kitchen, but Sparrow said they aren't seeing Copper anywhere."

"We'll check with them after we get Sandy to the airport," he said as Angie placed a serving tray on a fold-out stand beside the table. She set Billie's cup, two tea bags, and a large pot of hot water in front of her.

"Your mom and sister drink tea also, right?" Angie asked, and with Billie's nod she set two more cups with two tea bags each on the empty side of the table.

"There they are," Angie noted as she glanced up and saw Maggie and Sandy stop just inside the front door. Angie finished putting Billy's cup and a carafe of coffee on the table as Carole quickly crossed the dining room to greet them. Carole led them to the table and then went back to the counter as they settled onto the bench opposite the two of them.

"How are you this morning?" Billy asked, and took a sip of his coffee.

"Very well," Maggie said happily, "but I think Sandy tossed and turned a lot last night." She winked at Billie.

"Yeah," Sandy admitted. "My mind has been replaying all that's happened in the past week, and I think I'm saturated. And watching you, sis, I'm exhausted." Sandy shook her head. "You're out of the hospital a day and you're immersed in your busy routines again. Hand-to-hand fighting to defend your friends, the kitchen and everything else. You wear me out."

Sandy paused when Angie stopped and asked if they were ready to order. When she had everyone's requests entered in her digital hand unit, she said "thanks" and turned to another table.

"What's the plan for Florida?" Billie asked as her sister sweetened her tea.

"Just planning to hang out on the beaches—quiet time with the pretentious. Gil should get there this morning and I'll get there this evening. I have a two-hour layover in Atlanta plus an hour time change." Then she looked at Billy. "I want to thank you, for taking us to the kitchen and letting us help. I know I learned a lot and I can see why Billie has taken to it. Even with the element of danger that exists, I see why you do it."

"You're very welcome, Sandy," he said. "I like to think the people appreciate having the kitchen and the good that it offers."

"Chase said you're a fixture there," Sandy remarked. "I guess he only knows you as Keeper, but he said you go almost every night, with a few exceptions here and there. He'd seen Billie there and I guess everyone figured out real quick that she was yours."

He nodded at Sandy. "I have to admit I tried to make that very clear. Billie didn't know it at first, but I wanted her to be."

"I told Mom this morning that I'll be back in a week," Sandy continued, and glanced at her sister, "maybe sooner, to help her get the ranch ready for your celebration."

"In a week? Or sooner? I thought you and Gil were planning a two-week getaway." Surprised, Billie waited.

"We were, but I told Gil that getting things ready for you was more important." Sandy sipped her tea and glanced up as Angie brought the first two plates and set them down for her and Maggie.

Maggie looked at her oldest and waited a moment. "Are you going to tell her the rest? Or am I going to have to do it?"

"Oh, Mom."

"Don't 'oh, Mom' me. I'm not the one with the problem." Maggie laughed. She looked at her youngest. "Seems your sister has gotten herself into a pickle. She has a date with Chase, a week from Tuesday after they get finished at the kitchen."

Billie chuckled as Angie returned and served the rest of their order.

"I'm hoping you two can take me to the kitchen," Sandy added, almost as a question. "I'm not sure I'm ready to go alone."

"Before you *ever* think about going alone," Billie said firmly, "you'll have to go through Keeper's self-defense training. And even then you shouldn't ever think about a solo trip."

"Sounds like something to look forward to," she said with a wicked gleam in her eye. "When do classes start?"

Eighty-Two

"Do you think Gil's going to be all right with Sandy's plan?" Billie asked her mom as they left the airport parking lot and started back toward town.

"I don't know," Maggie conceded. "I think the problem will be with what she *doesn't* have planned."

Billy smiled as he caught Tiger's hand. "It's always the unplanned thing that changes your life forever." He looked up and noticed an intersection ahead. "Maggie, could you turn right at the next light?"

"Sure. Where do you want to go?"

"There's another kitchen not too far south of the recycled clothing store. I'd like to talk to their manager for a minute."

"Okay." Maggie turned north at the light and followed his directions.

Tiger absently watched the open terrain around the airport as it quickly filled with industrial businesses and multiple freight yards, blocks and blocks of long distribution buildings, semi-trailer rigs, and forklifts.

"Man," she said absently to no one in particular as she studied the vast, teeming industrial district. "This place is so busy and crowded, a body could simply get lost. Disappear and never be seen again."

"What did you say, Tiger?" He followed her gaze and the scene beyond the window caught his attention. "Get lost? Disappear? That's it!"

"What?" Billie and Maggie asked in unison.

"Tiger, check your phone," he said, and asked Maggie to

slow down a bit. "See if Boster, Lange and Hammersmith or any combination of that name have any businesses out here. They do a lot of shipping to support their projects."

Maggie pulled into a parking area in front of one of the buildings and stopped on the street side of the lot.

"What're you looking for?" she asked as Tiger focused on her phone, tapping icons and waiting for connections.

"Leads to Hammersmith," he said, and held up crossed fingers.

Tiger ran a search, and then another, and after a few minutes she looked up with a wide smile. "Three! Mom, jot these names and addresses down."

Maggie dug in her purse and got the spiral pad out and started writing as Tiger read the information off.

"Here," Tiger said, and showed him the phone's map image. "They're a little spread out, but all three are within a five-block area. Mom, go up to the next main street and turn right."

In the next half an hour, Maggie drove them past the three warehouse addresses and retraced their path back to Twentieth Street East.

"I got good pictures of the fronts of each one," Tiger said as Maggie turned and started driving north again.

"Go up to Richmond and turn back west," Billy said as he looked at the pictures. "The kitchen is on the northeast corner at Seventh Street East." He smiled at Billie. "Can you send these to Nolan?"

"I'll call and see." She nodded and took her phone back. "He's still using a flip-phone and I don't know if he can receive and see pictures." Billie tapped the speed dial icon.

¤-¤-¤-¤-¤

The rental car stopped in the driveway of an austere, ranch-style brick house with a double car garage attached. Nancy

Westman opened the driver's door and got out.

"I'll see if my key works," Nancy said to Collin as she turned to face the house. "I'll be right back."

She followed the sidewalk and stepped up onto the front stoop, pulled a key from her purse, and tried it in the lock. When the key turned and the door opened, she stepped inside.

Standing in the doorway, long-forgotten memories assailed her as she looked at the neat and tidy living room with furnishings she had almost forgotten. She took a deep breath and stepped forward, checking the dining room and the kitchen, and then she went down the hall, past the full bath, and looked into the three bedrooms.

When she stepped back outside, Collin got out.

"We'll stay here, Collin," Nancy said as she opened the trunk to get their luggage.

Still unsure of her mother's decision, Collin collected her roller bag and followed her mother into the house.

"You won't remember any of this," Nancy said as she led the way down the hall, past the first bedroom, obviously used as an office, and turned into the next room on the left. "This was your room."

Collin looked at the single bed, the dresser, the bureau, and the nightstand. "This furniture wasn't mine, was it?"

"No, honey," Nancy said, and opened the drapes on a front window. "Your dad had me take your furniture and this is what he bought after we left. I guess he either thought you'd need something if you ever came to visit or he just couldn't stand to see the room empty."

Collin sat on the edge of the bed and looked at her mother in surprise. "It feels like a great mattress." Then she looked around the room, got up, and checked the dresser drawers. "They're all empty, Mom. He hasn't stored anything in them."

"Just this one," Nancy said as she looked at the wide, top bureau drawer.

"What's in it?"

"Pictures," Nancy said, and smiled. "I remember these." She turned and showed Collin.

"You have some of these at home," Collin said, and began searching through the drawer.

"He's had some reprinted. They're all of you. Even some later ones," Nancy said as she stopped at a beautiful outdoor portrait. "When did he take this one? It had to have been in the last year or two. You're wearing the earrings he got you Christmas before last."

Collin stared at the sharp, clear facial picture of herself. "I don't know. He never came and took one that I know of."

Nancy took another deep breath and stepped back into the hallway and stopped, looking into the master bedroom.

"What is it, Mom?" Collin asked as she stepped up beside her.

"That's the furniture we had when we got married. I thought we sold all of this." She smiled and looked at Collin. "We bought new when he finished his first development job, and that's the set I have at home."

She set her bag in the room and went to the kitchen, checked the cabinets and the refrigerator.

"We'll have to go out and get a few groceries," she said as Collin stopped in the dining room. Nancy tapped a phone number into her touch screen phone. "I figure I better let him know we're here," she said as the connection rang.

"Oh, hello. Detective Nolan, please."

Eighty-Three

Maggie stood beside the car as Billy helped her youngest out and looked up at the department store rising up behind the nearly finished sidewalk protectors.

"So, this is the city center department store you keep referring to," she said as Billie stopped beside her.

"Yes, Mom." She smiled. "This is where Billy and everyone lived for years, secretly hidden away in the basement."

Maggie sighed and looked at her. "You let me know if you need anything." Then she hugged her daughter. "But I know that if you're with Billy, you'll have all you need."

"Thanks, Mom," she said. "And thanks for coming in and helping this week. It means a lot—to both of us. Do you want us to come out and help get things ready?"

"When you can. You have three weeks and the two weekends. And I know you have things here to do and also to do to get ready. So, when you can. Oh, and we need to go dress shopping. When do you want me to come in for that?"

"Oh, wow. That needs to be done this coming week sometime," Billie said, suddenly realizing how little time they had. "I have some ideas of what I want, but haven't seen anything yet."

"Okay. I'll do some calling and then come in on Thursday." She turned to Billy. "And do you realize I haven't gotten a proper hug from you yet?"

"I can fix that, Maggie," he said, and put his arms around her and held her like he should.

"I haven't had a son before, and I think I'm looking forward to it." She smiled brightly as he stood up. "And I think you're going to have to start calling me Mom."

"I'll see what I can do about that too, Mom." He smiled. "You be careful driving home, and listen to the weather forecasts. It's starting to look dark out west."

"I'll be careful."

Billy held her door and she slid in.

"I just called Dad," Billie said, leaning down beside her, "to let him know you're just leaving. Drive careful."

"Thanks, I will," Maggie said, and closed her door. She waved as she pulled away from the curb and turned west on Baker.

"Come on," Billy said, and pulled Tiger into the passage to the alley.

At the metal door they waited a moment, checked their surroundings like he always did, and then he unlocked the door and they slipped in. He stopped and looked down the flight to the basement.

"Everything down there will be redone. The space below the two buildings will be combined into a large, secured parking garage with entries on the east and west sides of the block."

He turned and led her across the main floor to an elevator in the southeast corner, just outside the store rooms. He punched the Up button and Billie smiled.

"It works?"

"We got two of them working and signed off yesterday," he said as the door slid open. He gestured her in and then with a flair, pushed the top button. "Penthouse, please."

She chuckled. "This is great. Does it go down to the basement?"

"Yes. When the renovations are done, this one will connect the basement to the second floor, the tenth floor, and our apartment. The other elevators will connect the basement with all of the floors, but not the penthouse."

"So this will be a private elevator?"

"Yes. For those of us living on the tenth floor and above. Entering from the basement or the second floor will keep it secluded from the lower-floor residents." He smiled.

"You're really going to move everyone back here on the tenth floor?" she asked with a hopeful smile.

"I've talked with the architects and that's the new plan for the building," he explained as the elevator stopped and the door silently opened. He guided her out into the empty tenth floor with only support pillars interrupting the vastness. "I've been thinking about offering them each an apartment for a nominal price, give them fifteen years to pay the mortgage off, and thereby giving them a credit standing. I want to match their payments to give the kids funds for college."

"I can set that up for you." She squeezed his hand as he nodded.

"If some don't want that, we can figure out a reasonable lease arrangement like they have now."

"Do you want me to work on ideas for that too?"

"Yes, Tiger," he said as they started walking to the north end of the building. "When we have the details of what we want worked out, we can take it to Grier and Walter and they can help us make it official." He stopped just beyond the middle of the room and turned around. "Like the architects were saying when we had lunch with them, the area along the east wall will have a dedicated space for the utility connections, gas, electric, water, and sewer. The four stairwells and elevator shafts will remain, and just in front of all of them will be a wide hallway that will run north and south, from one end of the floor to the other. This will be the main access to the apartments and all of the building's equipment for the particular floor."

Then he turned and faced west. "Also like the architects were describing, from this hallway, ten apartments on this floor, twelve on the others, will extend to the west wall, where the existing windows will be replaced with a balcony and a floor-to-ceiling glass wall, much like your apartment, only with a door for balcony access. It's a western exposure, so we'll use an adjustable-tint thermal glass to help control the light and heat that comes through the windows. The ceilings are not tall enough to make them lofts, but the height will help with cooling in the summers and general sound deadening."

He looked back to the elevator they came up. "The last two apartments on the south on this floor will be open, single-apartment-size rooms. They'll be our practice and training room and an indoor space for the kids to play in when the weather is bad or they just don't want to go outside."

Billie was smiling from ear to ear as she listened to his description of the plan. Then he pulled her gently as he started to the north stairwell.

"How large are the apartments? I mean, are they two or three bedrooms, one or two baths, and so on?"

"Initially the plan was for two bedrooms, one and a half baths, but I asked the architects draw up a three-bedroom, two-bath option for the apartments, but then I thought the tenth-floor residents should all be three bedrooms with two and a half baths."

"That would be nice," she concurred. "I can see some of them having at least one more child."

"That's likely. Stretch told me he and Cat are thinking about trying to have one, now that they are out of the basement and have some privacy." He winked at her and then continued. "Each of the apartments will have a nice size kitchen, dining area, and a living room, maybe even an additional family room."

At the stairs, he stopped and looked up at the door at the top of the flight.

"The top of this one and the one halfway to the elevator we used are roof accesses," he said, and started up. "Are you okay with climbing stairs?"

"Yes. I'm doing fine," she said as he took her hand and led the way up to the shadowy door.

"When this is finished," he continued, "the stairs will bring you up into a glass entry area with inner and outer doors like the ones at the Streetcar."

He unlocked the chain and the security bar and pushed the door open. The fresh smells and gentle city noises swirled around them as they stepped out onto the roof. Billie stopped and slowly turned around, taking in the full view.

"I didn't realize this is the tallest building in this block," she said as she finished her turn.

"Yes, it is," he admitted. "And the tallest in the city center is only fourteen stories." He pointed as he guided her to the middle of the north wall, smiling at the view himself. "From the top floor of our apartment, the view ought to be splendid. From here to where they've started the apartment construction, about two thirds of the roof will be the garden patios the architects described, separated by shrubs and hedges and trees—mini gardens within a larger garden. And in the very center, a fenced playground inside tall hedges for the younger kids. "

"The patios and gardens will be available to everyone?"

"Originally yes, but I was wondering what you'd think if we separated a few patios on the north and west sides for the exclusive use of our tenth-floor residents. The others would be available to the rest of the residents through a reservation system."

"I like that," she said as she studied the areas. "Maybe make them a little larger than the others with a serious garden separation from the lower-floor residents."

Billy laughed. "Actually, I'm thinking all of the patios out here near the north end should be larger than the ones farther back. People will prefer to be out here and that will naturally make it quieter back near our apartment. Then above the building's perimeter façade wall, we'll have clear, shatter-proof panels all around up to about head height, to keep everyone from falling over the edges."

"That will be nice," Billie smiled.

He pointed to all of the old air-conditioning units. "Those will be replaced with new, high-efficiency units, relocated and hidden in special sound-deadening enclosures. The owner's residence will have its own heating and air and its own utility runs."

They walked around the rooftop for a while and he answered as many of her questions as he could.

"I'll get a copy of the renovation plans," he said, "so we can review the details together." He took in the view again and studied the darkening western skies. "I'm thinking we might get wet tonight."

Billie checked her phone and the local weather app. "Looks like it," she said, and showed him the moving map. "Doesn't look too strong, but definitely has rain and some storms in it. Ought to get to Mom and Dad's place in a couple of hours."

"Good. Your mom should be home before it gets there, but we may have to call a cab to get home without getting soaked." He led her back to the stairs.

They went in and he locked the access behind them.

"I have a favor to ask you," he said.

"What?"

"Our apartment."

"What about our apartment?"

"Decorating. I think you have to take the lead in decorating it for us. We'll work on it together, but you know I don't know how to make it look nice. I mean, compare my apartment with yours and you can see immediately that it would not be good to let me do the decorating."

She turned and hugged him. "I've no doubts we can make it a home, Keeper. Like I said before, I hope you'll always want your Tiger to help you in whatever you do."

"I do, Tiger. You know I do." He held her face in his hands and kissed her long and tenderly.

Eighty-Four

When they got back to the ground floor, Billy asked Billie if she was hungry, realizing they had not eaten since their mid-morning breakfast at the Streetcar.

"I think I'm starved," Billie said as they stopped inside the heavy metal door to the alley.

"Do you want to eat, just the two of us," he asked, "or would you want to see if your friends would like to join us?"

"Since it will be the two of us later…" she said with a twisted smile and a cock of her head. "Are you sure it's okay with you?"

"Yes, I'm sure. It's been a week and a half since you missed your last girls' night out opportunity."

Billie smiled and touched Lori's icon on her phone.

"What're you guys doing tonight?" Billie asked when Lori answered. "Billy and I are thinking about dinner." She looked at Billy. "Where?"

"How about Danny's Steakhouse on Calvin and Duberry?"

She repeated his suggestion. "Can you give us a ride home after? We're up in the city center and may need a ride if it starts raining." She listened a moment. "Okay, we're leaving now."

He unlocked the door and they slipped into the alley. He locked the door behind them and she stopped, looking at the matching door in the warehouse building's wall.

"Keeper? When did you want to look at that strange door in the warehouse building?"

He chuckled. "Like I said while you were in the hospital, I had planned to a week ago, but you got hurt and changed my plans. With this being a holiday weekend, let's talk to Stretch tomorrow and plan on Tuesday."

"Okay."

With a nod, he took her hand and they went out through the construction gate at Second West and then walked north to Calvin. The sky was darker and the clouds had begun to collect over the city by the time they reached Danny's.

"Hello, Lydia," Billy greeted as they stopped at the hostess' station.

"Hello, Mr. Carson," the smiling young brunette greeted in return. "It's very good to see you again."

"I thought I told you that you could call me Billy," he teased.

"Only in private, Mr. Carson. How may I help you?"

"Put four of us under the name Tiger. We'll wait in the lounge."

"Very good. Four under Tiger..." Lydia looked up with wide eyes and looked at Billie, standing close beside him. "Yes, sir, I'll call as soon as I have a table."

He led Billie into the lounge and stopped at the end of the bar. She took the stool and he stood beside her and watched the front door.

"I haven't been here before." She looked around the room and studied the decor.

"I come off and on," he admitted. "I've known Danny for a week or two."

She knew when he said "a week or two" he was implying a *much* longer time.

"How long, actually?"

"Ten years or so," he answered as the bartender leaned over and asked if they wanted anything and Billy replied "Two iced teas." He smiled at Billie's scowl. "Since it's been a while, I thought we should start slow."

"I know." She forced a smile. "I don't have to like it, but I know." She caught his arm and squeezed. "Thanks for taking care of me, even if I protest a little."

"You're welcome, Tiger." He looked up as the bartender set their glasses of tea on the counter. "Would you start a tab under the name Billy Carson? Some friends are joining us and we're having dinner when they call us." Then he turned back to Billie. "You said Lori and Becky were coming. What's Stacy doing?"

"Lori didn't say. Just that she wasn't going to make it tonight." Billie sipped her tea and added some sweetener.

"There they are." He nodded and stepped closer to the front door to catch their attention.

"Starting to look dark and nasty out there," Becky said as they stopped next to Billie. "How are you doing?"

"Better. Much better," she said, and then made a grimacing face. "Got my stitches yanked out yesterday."

"That bad?" Lori asked, making a face of her own.

"I didn't realize until yesterday that I have a low pain threshold. But it seems us redheads have odd traits sometimes. And yes, it hurt. He even had to deaden the skin around the stitches to do it." She finished with a gesture to her chest and shoulder.

"Can I get you anything to drink?" Billy asked, and motioned to the bartender.

They thought a moment and then Lori and Becky each ordered a cocktail. When Lori saw their teas, she said, "I'm sorry, Billie. You're not having anything to drink?"

"Don't worry about it, Lori," Billy said. "You're fine. Her nurse is making her start slowly. She hasn't eaten since breakfast or had a drink since she went out with you guys."

"Okay," Lori said.

"Thank you, Billy," Becky added, "for inviting us."

-¤-

"Is that Billy Carson?" a pleasant male voice asked as a hand gripped Billy's shoulder. "I don't believe it."

Billy turned, grinned at the face smiling at him, and shook the extended hand. "Hey, Danny."

"Lydia said you were here and then I saw your name on a bar tab. I had to interrupt and see if it was true. Hello, ladies."

"This is Danny Willis, the owner of this fine establishment." Billy's hand swept a wide arc as he gestured to the room, and then he turned to Billie and winked. "And Danny, this is my fiancée, Billie, and her close friends Lori Davis and Becky George."

"Fiancée?" Danny looked at him and then greeted Billie. "My, my. Congratulations. And a Billie as well. I'm very pleased to meet you. And both of you ladies." He turned and playfully punched Billy's shoulder. "I didn't think you kept such nice company, Mr. Carson. Are you celebrating anything else that I might like to know about? Beside an engagement, maybe a birthday or anything?"

"Just our recent engagement, for starters," he admitted, and smiled at Billie. "And Billie had an accident a little over a week ago, so we're celebrating the dedication of her two best friends for helping me take care of her, and we are celebrating the beginning of the renovations on the old Duckard's Department Store buildings."

"*Recently* engaged. Very nice. Very nice," Danny said, and smiled. "And it does sound like there's a lot of other things needing to be celebrated." Then Danny looked around the room and smiled. "I need to take care of something, Billy. I'll get back with you in a little bit. Okay?"

"Sure."

And Danny left , working his way through the crowd.

It only seemed like a minute before they heard Tiger's name over the PA system. Billy helped her up and led the way to the hostess station. Lydia smiled, picked up her stack of menus, and led them through the dining room and into a private room with three tables in it. Two were set together under a single tablecloth along a wall, and the third sat in the center of the room with a wine chiller and four chairs nestled up to it.

"Danny said you would enjoy this room more than the crowded dining room," Lydia said, and placed the menus on the table. "Monica will be your server tonight, Mr. Carson. May I ask if you have a wine choice?"

Billy looked at Billie's pleading expression and mouthed an *okay* "Do you have a shiraz blend that we can lightly chill?"

Lydia nodded and Billy asked Lori and Becky if they would want wine with dinner.

They looked at each other and Lori finally asked, "Would a zinfandel blush be all right?"

"Certainly," he agreed, and looked at Lydia. "Please select a nice label for both."

"Thank you," she said, and left the room.

He seated Billie with the chiller between him and Becky and Lori on Billie's opposite side.

"Mom's coming back in town on Thursday to start the dress shopping," Billie began as she settled, "and we'll get the invitations written this weekend and mailed next week, but I hope you know you're coming to the wedding ceremony?"

"You hadn't said anything, but I was sure hoping you'd invite us," Becky said.

"My life's been a little hectic since Billy asked me to set a date," she explained unnecessarily, and squeezed his hand.

"And," Billy said softly, "there are rings to be found."

A young woman in a pleasantly cut dark burgundy dress and complementing lacy over-blouse came into the room with a tray of water glasses, a pitcher, and two cocktails. She set the tray on a side rack. She turned and hesitated, surprised, a grin slowly filling her face as she looked at the two with the same name. She inhaled visibly and moved to the table, setting the water glasses at each of their places.

"Good evening, Monica," Billy said.

Billie instantly recognized Monica as the dark-haired woman she had seen Billy walking with near the college back in April—the one he said was just an old friend. She glanced at Billy's smile for the woman and her almost-possessive smile for him and wondered how he *really* knew her.

Sure looks like more than just an old friend.

Hush! I don't think Billy would lie about that. But her...I'm not so sure...

"Good evening, Mr. Carson," she greeted, but focused on the redheaded woman beside him as she picked up the cocktails from the side table. Who gets these lovelies?" Monica asked as she returned to stand beside the table.

Lori quickly sorted them out and stared at Billy, her expression questioning the unusual treatment they were getting.

Monica looked back at each of them, regaining her poised manner. "Would you like to hear about the specials?"

They nodded and Monica described how the meats were prepared and cooked, and the sauces used on the vegetables. She described the choices in potatoes, from mashed to twice-baked, as well as the additional choices of sides and how they were prepared and seasoned. When she finished with the specials, she mentioned a number of the entrées on the regular menu and described how they were prepared and any special seasonings used.

"I'll let you think about all of that," Monica said, "and I'll get your wine choices."

"What's going on, Billy?" Lori asked when Monica had left the room. "Why are they acting like this?"

"We're just old friends, Lori." He shrugged and smiled.

"Old friends I know don't treat me this way," Becky said with a giggle as she sipped her drink. Surprised, she looked at the glass. "I think this is better than any I've had here in town."

Lori sipped hers and nodded vigorously. "I have to agree. We'll have to come back here again." Then Lori asked, "What were you two doing in the city center?"

Billie chuckled as she smiled at Billy. "Billy has taken care of that department store property for the owners for years and years, and this last week they have started renovating the two buildings. The plan is to join them into connected apartment buildings. He was showing me around."

"How long will the renovation take?" Becky asked.

"Probably a year, maybe late next spring," Billy said. "If the weather's good this summer and fall, they might bring it in sooner."

"So," Lori started, holding up one finger to hold his attention, "let me get this straight: One, you wash dishes for the Streetcar Diner, and two, you 'house-sat' those old department store buildings for their owner." She put up a second finger. "Three, you've been teaching Billie self-defense and turned her into 'Tiger,' a self-defense legend." She put up another finger. "Four, you volunteer most nights at a soup kitchen." She put up her last finger. "You seem to know most people in town and know what they're doing on a daily basis." And she counted her thumb. "When have you had the time to catch this woman's attention and completely change her life? She turns into an awestruck mess every time she sees you or hears your name?"

Billy chuckled. "I don't know, Lori, but I will say it hasn't been easy. I just had to try. What can I say? She is the love of my life. She has been for many years."

"Hear, hear," Becky said, and raised her glass in a toast. "If there's such a thing as soul mates, I think you two come as close as I've ever seen. I hope you have the greatest of lives together."

Monica coughed softly as she entered the room pushing a small cart with two bottles of wine and a second chiller. She set the second chiller on a pedestal between Lori and Becky and said softly, "The question is, Miss Lori, how she caught him. Mr. Carson has set many women's hearts aflutter and made their knees weak, but he has rarely noticed."

Startled, Lori looked at Monica as she returned to her cart and brought the zinfandel and set it in the chiller, and then brought the shiraz and placed it in the chiller beside Billy.

"Shall I pour, Mr. Carson?" Monica asked, poised,

mannered, and smiling as if she had not said anything. She placed a stemmed wine glass at each of their places.

"I think we'll wait on pouring for Lori and Becky," he said. "Give them time to finish their cocktails."

"Yes, that would be good," Monica agreed, and poured Billie the shiraz. She asked if it was chilled enough and Billie took a sip and smiled.

"That's perfect, Monica. Thanks." She smiled and set her glass down.

"Have you decided what you would like this evening? Miss Billie?" Monica asked when she finished pouring and was ready to take their orders.

"Monica," Billie began, "your chef—does he cook medium rare to a warm red center or does he lean toward a pink center?"

"*She* is quite good. If you like warm red, that's what you'll get," Monica retorted with a bit of pride showing. "If, perchance, you find your steak incorrectly prepared, it will be replaced for you."

"Thanks. I wasn't meaning to sound overly particular," Billie said, and smiled. "I'll do the fillet special you described, medium rare. It sounds wonderful."

"Thank you," Monica said. "I'm certain you will like it. Will the vegetables and potatoes be your sides?"

"Yes, thank you," Billie said, and Monica turned to Lori and went around the table.

"I'll bring the bread as soon as I get your orders turned in," Monica said, and slipped out of the room.

"She seems to know you, Billy." Lori looked at him with a raised eyebrow.

"Yes," he conceded, and chuckled with a glance to Billie. "Monica is Danny's middle daughter. Lydia, the hostess, is his younger daughter, and their older sister Nikki took over cooking after they reorganized three or four years ago—hence the subtle challenge when you asked your question, Billie."

Then he picked up his wine glass, straightened his shoulders, and smiled at Billie. "Disregarding my role as nurse, here's to my Tiger. To us and my hope that she never has second thoughts or cold feet."

The glasses clinked and they each sipped, and Billie smiled at him. "A little late for cold feet, love," she chuckled softly. She straightened and pushed her chair back. "I need to go and freshen up a bit."

"Certainly." He got up quickly and helped her with her chair.

"I won't be long." She collected her purse and left the room.

Keeper and His Tiger: The Trap

Eighty-Five

Billie was almost to the hall for the restrooms when Monica came out of a doorway, obviously from the kitchen area.

"Oh, Monica," she said, and stopped.

"Yes, Miss Billie," Monica said. "Did you get directions?" she asked, gesturing to the hallway.

"Yes, thank you. But I really wanted to say I'm sorry if I said anything you disliked about your sister or her cooking. I didn't realize how your restaurant was organized."

"Thank you," Monica said, and smiled. "Mr. Carson helped our dad see that he needed to reorganize the business, and he got Dad to let me and my sisters help, and today is the result of that."

"It looks like you've done a splendid job of it." Billie smiled back. "I take it you've known Billy for a long time."

"Yes, we have," Monica said, and glanced away as if she had a second thought about what she was about to say. "He's been a special person to us. To my dad during his early years with the restaurant, to our family, and to me, especially. It was a surprise tonight to realize he's getting married." She looked directly at Billie and caught her eyes. "I mean, I think it's really great. I wish the best for the both of you, but like many that have known him over the years, I had that girlish fantasy of wondering what it might be like to marry someone like him. Silly, I know, and I know it's mostly out of gratitude."

"Gratitude?" Billie asked. "The restaurant? His—"

"No," Monica said, her voice suddenly very soft. "About five years ago, I was attending night classes at the college, and one very cold night on my way back to my car, I was attacked, beaten, raped, and left for dead. Dad told me Mr. Carson found me, wrapped me in his coat, and carried me back here."

Oh my!

"He called the police and Dad got me to the hospital. A couple of weeks later, Detective Nolan caught the guys that attacked me. They had gone after another coed at the college and Nolan said he got a timely tip." Monica smiled. "No one ever said who tipped him off, but I've always had my suspicions.

"Anyway, while I was recovering, the restaurant's business was about as low as it could go, and Mr. Carson got us pointed in the right direction. It was my therapy, in a way. I still have nightmares, and sometimes Mr. Carson will have a cup of coffee or something stronger with me to let me talk, vent some, and just help me cope.

"I hope you know how much of a rock he's been for our family, and I hope he will be for you too."

"I hope the best for you as well, Monica," Billie said, and caught her hand and squeezed it. "And if you need Billy's support in the future, please call him. We're planning on living here in the city, and he'll probably continue working at the diner, so please don't be a stranger."

"Thank you, Miss Billie."

-¤-

"That took a little longer than I expected," Becky said as Billie sat back down and Billy helped her with her chair.

"Sometimes it does," Billie said, and smiled at Becky without giving any more explanation.

She looked at Billy and smiled, pleased to know that others saw him as being just as special as she did.

God, I love you, Billy. And what you've grown up to be.

"Did you hear about Blake?" Becky asked as she set her glass down.

"No," Billie said, startled, and cocked her head.

Becky waited to continue as Monica returned and set two wood cutting boards on the table, each with a small loaf of wheat and another of dark rye and a glass tub of seasoned spread.

"Your salads will be out in just a few minutes," Monica announced softly before she turned to leave.

"How are your mom and your sister tonight, Monica?" Billy asked.

"Very well, Mr. Carson. Thank you for asking," she replied, smiled at Billie, and turned and left the room.

"Sorry, what about Blake?" he asked.

Lori started laughing to herself as Becky started. "He spent Thursday night in jail. His second visit, I understand. The night he grabbed you and again Thursday."

"In jail?" Billie asked in surprise, and looked at Billy. "Did you know about that?" He just smiled and she turned back to Lori. "What happened?"

"Poor Blake just doesn't get it, Billie," Becky said, and giggled herself. "Last night, Stacy was telling us she and Tom went to Custer's for dinner and drinks, just the two of them. She said she saw your waitress friend, Angie, from the Streetcar while they were there. Anyway, she said they were enjoying themselves when Blake stumbled in and started talking to Stacy in a loud voice, and of course Stacy didn't want anything to do with him and told him to go away."

Billie shook her head, seeing where this was going.

"Well, Blake—being Blake—doesn't get the message and reaches across in front of Tom, trying to grab her arm," Becky continued. "Tom grabbed Blake's wrist and punched him in the face without getting up. Blake went down right there beside their table. He gets up screaming and the same guy in the T-shirt, the bouncer guy, grabs Blake by the neck and without a word, hauls him into that room behind the bar. Stacy said the cops were there in minutes, flashing lights and everything. They hauled him away and put him in jail."

"You're right, Beck," Billie said, still shaking her head. "He doesn't know when to stop."

"Stacy said she talked to someone that saw Blake this afternoon, and they said he had a shiner to beat all shiners."

Billy led the conversation back to happier subjects. Monica served their dinners and waited on their needs. When the food was eaten and the wine drank, Billy asked her for the check.

"No, sir, Mr. Carson," Monica said with a broad smile. "Daddy said he's so pleased to see you finally happy, and for all you have done for us over the years, he wishes you'll accept tonight as an engagement gift."

"That's very nice, Monica. Thank you and thanks to your dad," Billy said, "but now you leave me in a quandary."

"Thank you, but no, Mr. Carson," Monica said. "You do not need to leave a tip for me. It has been my pleasure to see you again and to finally meet your Tiger. It is a very nice surprise. I think half the town is talking about the two of you." She looked at Billie. "Thank you for coming, Miss Billie. It *really* is a great pleasure to meet and talk with you. And it was nice to meet your friends. Thank you, congratulations again, and I hope you will have a pleasant evening." Monica straightened, turned, and walked out of the room.

-¤-

Billy asked Billie if she was ready, and when she nodded, he rose and helped her with her chair. Lori and Becky led the way into the dining room and stopped to wait when Billy and Billie turned to speak with Monica privately. Lori saw Billy hand something to Monica and heard her squeak as she stifled a surprised response. Then Billie hugged Monica before they turned to catch up.

Eighty-Six

It was raining when they stopped at the front door and Becky went to get her car. When they were away, Lori turned in her seat.

"I want to thank you for the evening"—she looked at Billy—"a very unexpected surprise. But do you mind if I ask a nosy question? I don't mean to be rude, but I am curious."

"What is it, Lori?" he asked.

"I only know of your job at the diner," she began. "And I know you said you took care of the department store and I know of all the other things I counted off tonight."

"Lori, don't." Becky reached over and touched her arm.

"And I have no idea what else you do," she continued, "but you've lived, I'll call it differently, and you don't strike me as one that has a lot of affluence. I'm wondering how you were planning to pay for such a grand evening as this was."

He smiled and winked at Billie. "I'll tell you. I woke up this morning, and when I rolled up my sleeping mat and kicked out the rubbish that had blown into my space beside the dumpster, I discovered a wad of one hundred dollar bills had blown in as well. I said to myself, 'self, you can't let these go to waste,' so I decided to do something nice for Billie tonight."

Lori stared at him and saw Billie chuckling.

"Okay, I guess I deserved that." Lori shook her head and stared at the two of them.

"It's okay." Billie smiled. "It's okay. Stop worrying about it."

"How can I? Either you've really gone off the deep end and

aren't thinking straight or there's something going on that you're hiding."

Billie grinned and glanced at him before continuing. "We can't explain just yet, but there *is* a lot going on. I understand your concern, but just trust me when I tell you it's really okay."

As Lori turned around in her seat, her expression reflected the hurt she felt for being left out of whatever Billie was referring to.

¤-¤-¤-¤-¤

Billie snuggled as close to her husband as she could with her left arm carefully draped across his chest. The long day without her sling and without a nap had tired her more than she realized. She had relaxed in his arms as he tended her healing wounds and massaged a lotion into her aching left bicep, and she felt thoroughly comforted and relaxed after showing him how much his attention and company meant to her. Stretched out along his length, she smiled and melted into his warmth, spent from their spiraling, loving emotions, secure as she inhaled his masculine scent with his left arm possessively curled around her, holding her gently, but tight against his side. His right hand lay open, his palm gently against her cheek and his fingers absently fondling the rogue curls that continued down across her neck and shoulder, and her knee and leg lay high across his thighs. His response to her had been just as passionate and loving, carrying her beyond fulfillment more than once.

The thunder and lightning of the night's storm had slowly died away, leaving the gentle rain behind to cleanse the air and nourish the land. It was fitting, she thought, comparing their emotional surrender in unison with the storms, and now, the comfort of each other's loving embrace remained to carry them into the morning to come with the gentle, soothing sound of the rain. She lay beside him, completely immersed, wondering about the things she did not yet know about this wonderful man she had married. She felt anxious to learn more, teased by each glimpse she got into his past and their time apart.

"Keeper?" she asked, gently breaking the warm silence that had settled between them. "What did you do for Danny and his family for him to want to thank you in such a grand way?"

"Not much," he whispered, and kissed the top of her head. "They did the work."

"Monica said they had to reorganize the restaurant and that you pointed them in the right direction."

"Danny almost lost the business. He didn't have the greatest service or food. You name it and it was pretty much a problem. I stopped by to check on Monica one afternoon and Danny asked me a couple of questions—you know, wondering what I thought about this or that. He was trying to figure out how to turn things around, but had run out of ideas."

His fingers started caressing her ear as he spoke, his palm still gently cupping her cheek, and she listened to his slow, steady heartbeat.

"I told him to have his three daughters look at the business with a fresh set of eyes and to put together a list of things they felt should change. I told him to make a list too, but I pretty well knew what his would look like."

She felt his soft chuckle as his chest shook.

"Three days later," he continued, "I stopped back by and looked at what they had come up with, and the girls had pretty well nailed the issues. I had them draft up a financial and a business plan to fix the problems and the girls went to the library, got examples of the documents, and put them together. I made a few constructive comments and then took Danny and them to visit with Grier and Walter. Together they came up with the necessary loans, the plans for physical changes, and the girls took a keen interest in owning and operating the restaurant. Monica took over the bookkeeping and general management, Nikki took over the kitchen and menu decisions, and Lydia took over managing the waitstaff and the dining room. They've gotten better each day since."

"They seem very proud of the restaurant and your help."

"They've earned what they have and I'm very proud of them too."

She thought a moment. "Monica told me about her attack and your help."

"I'm surprised. She doesn't like to think about it. She still has nightmares over it."

"She told me that too. It's no wonder she looked at you the way she did tonight. At first I was almost uncomfortable with her possessive air. And the monetary gift we gave her tonight?"

"For her son. He'll be four this fall. She wouldn't abort the pregnancy after the rape, told everyone it wasn't the baby's fault he existed, and when he was born, she asked me to be William's godfather."

What? William? Godfather?

She pushed herself up and looked at Billy. "She named her son *William*? After you?"

"Yeah, she did," he replied. "I was surprised and didn't really know how to respond to her doing that."

"That was what, five years ago?"

"Four and a few months."

He didn't know you would come back into his life when that happened.

I know, but...

"And the godfather thing? Does that mean you might have to raise him?"

Billy raised his head and looked at her, holding her eyes as his expression turned serious. "Only if something very horrible happened and he was left without any family to support him. Then yes, I guess that means I would be the one to guide and educate him. Custody isn't necessarily an option, depending on a lot of different things, but I would want to consider it. Actually, that's 'we' now." He waited a few long seconds, watching her. "Does that bother you? The possibility?"

Tell him it does! Tell him your first thought was William's another woman's son, as if he was the result of an affair—

No! It was wrong of me to think that. I said I wouldn't jump to uninformed conclusions again, and I did...Damn, I did.

She sighed and lay her head back on his chest. "Knowing you, it shouldn't surprise me, but it did. Other than your question after practice that one day, about me giving you something like Abby, I haven't really thought about having or raising children." She squeezed him as he waited. "It isn't that I don't want a family with you and children, but things have been so hectic, I really hadn't thought that far. I'm still trying to grow into my life as it is now, with you, trying to find out who I really am."

"Well, when the time is better, I want all of the family we can make, together—kids included, but I'm not pushing. We'll decide, but probably not until our life has settled down and there's some routine order in it. Then we might talk about that in a more serious manner."

He turned his head and she pushed herself to him, kissing him, assuring him she was not completely against the idea either.

Eighty-Seven

Sunday, May 29

Joey had waited in the dark since just after ten, leaning against the trunk of a large conifer, hidden beneath the long boughs and sticker needles. A half block down the street from Frederick Westman's house, he checked his watch, noting it was almost one a.m. He had not seen any lights since about a half an hour after he had arrived on the quiet street and taken his refuge.

He spent his time listening to the city sounds and rehearsing what he would do to Westman; Mr. Hammersmith was not very specific other than to rough him up, but not enough to send him to the hospital. So he pondered his options, disliking all of them, disliking the fact that he was there, waiting in the dark on Hammersmith's orders. Herb was better at this sort of thing, but he had not been able to find Herb.

Finally he sighed and crawled out from under the tree, stood, and stretched his back. He picked up the three-foot piece of pipe he had brought with him and slowly started walking toward Westman's house. Joey had convinced himself, that one good smack over the head, breaking a shoulder or arm while he slept would be enough to get the message delivered. No fighting back, no obvious clues as to how it happened, or who did the smacking.

On the garage side of the house, he followed the wall to the people gate in the wire mesh fence, carefully opened it, and slipped through. Then he closed it quietly and crept into the unlit back yard and stopped at the sliding patio door. Quickly glancing around, he double-checked the slide and confirmed there still was no locking bar. Then, smiling to himself at their trusting nature, he pressed on the frame of the sliding panel and was able to shift it enough to let him release the flimsy latch.

In an instant, he had the panel moved enough to slip through into the small dining room. He slid the panel closed and slowly worked his way to the hallway, thankful the slab-on-grade construction eliminated the worry of a creaking floor.

At the end of the hall he looked into the front bedroom, gently pushing the partially open door. In the dim light from the neighbor's backyard light coming through the end window, he could see a form in the single bed and moved closer. At the side of the bed, he stopped and raised the pipe.

Someone stirred in the room across the hall and Joey froze.

There's only supposed to be one person here.

He stared at the form in front of him and saw her long hair, realizing he was seeing a woman in the bed, not a man, not Frederick! He staggered back a step and the images of the woman—her pretty face, her red hair under a scarf, her chest coated in blood—flooded his mind. His stomach threatened to retch as he hurried to the hall door and glanced into the second bedroom.

Someone was in the double bed there, and in the dim light from the same neighbor's backyard light, he studied the shape the figure made in the sheet and knew it was another woman.

Two women? This is Frederick's house, he argued. *Where's Frederick? I can't smack women. No, not women.*

Joey slowly backed down the hall, carefully crept around the dining room table, and was trembling by the time he slipped out through the sliding door and then crossed the back yard and jumped the mesh fence into the next yard.

¤-¤-¤-¤-¤

Billie rolled over and realized she was alone in bed. She

pushed herself up, stretched, and gently flexed her arm and shoulder and looked out through the large window. It was still overcast and raining as she leaned over the railing to see if she could see Billy; he was not in the living room, but she saw the light was on in the kitchen.

Slowly she crept down the stairs and across the dining area to where he sat on a stool reading the Sunday paper, his back to her. She slipped her right arm around his shoulders and kissed him when he turned to see her.

"Good morning, Tiger," he said as he pushed his stool back from the counter, slipped one arm behind her, and with the other, scooped her up onto his lap, his eyes admiring every gorgeous inch of their journey from the top of her unkempt red hair down to the tips of her painted toes.

She kissed him again. "Good morning, Keeper. Why didn't you wake me when you got up?"

"Obviously, you needed the sleep," he said as she reached for his cup of coffee. "And it looks like you might be hungry."

"I don't know how after that dinner last night," she said, and took a long sip, "but I am. Should I fix something?"

"How about going to the Egg and then over to see Cathy and the group?"

"Sure. I need to tell her about Tuesday."

He pulled her to him and kissed her again, unable to get enough of her. But he relented, stood her up, patted her bare bottom and gently pushed her toward the stairs. He smiled, seeing her smile back at him as he watched her hurry up the spiral stairs. He quickly rinsed his cup and followed her up to shower, happily looking forward to getting ready for their day.

-¤-

They were almost finished with breakfast when her phone chimed.

Billy had taken her to the Everything Egg and she had devoured a three-egg omelet, hash browns, a biscuit with gravy, and a tall glass of juice, while he ate his scrambled eggs, bacon, a slice of sourdough toast, and a small glass of tomato juice. She shared his coffee.

"Hello," she said when her phone chimed a second time, and then she handed it to Billy. "It's Nolan."

"Morning," he greeted.

"Keeper," Nolan's voice said. "I wanted to let you know that Westman got here this morning and we have an official time—eight thirty Tuesday morning—for him to tell us what he knows."

"Tuesday. Your place?"

"Yeah. I'll get everything arranged. His wife and daughter are here from Michigan, but I'll probably have to keep him until after he gives us his testimony. Can you be here before eight thirty? I know Tiger has a meeting with Justice Parker at nine, but the meetings will just have to overlap."

"Sure," he said, and smiled at Billie. "We'll be there. Did you get a look at the pictures Tiger sent you?"

"Yes, and I moved two of my undercover men down there to look around."

"Good. Maybe we'll get lucky."

Monday, May 30

Memorial Day

Billie drove up Fifth Street, past the Forest, and turned onto St. Charles. She stopped along the curb in front of a plywood kiosk full of flowers and flower arrangements with a slender older woman sitting on a stool to one side under the extended awning. The rain had let up some, but it was still a steady drizzle.

"Come on," Billy said as he opened his door.

She got out and hurried around the SUV, stopping beside him as the woman greeted them.

"Well good morning, Master Billy," Maxie said.

"Good morning, Maxie," he replied. "I want you to meet my Billie." He gestured as she extended her hand in greeting.

"I've heard a lot about Maxie and the best flowers in the city."

"Thank you," Maxie replied, and smiled. "I figured I'd see you today, Master Billy, being it's the day it is." She turned and pulled a box from under the kiosk's back counter. "These were cut this morning, so they should last a little longer than normal." She pulled the loose protective plastic cover off and stuffed it under the table.

"Thanks." He picked up the box and handed Maxie a number of folded bills. "There's also a coupon in there so your grandson can go to the arcade next time you're at the mall."

She smiled and asked, "When's the big day?"

"Just under three weeks," Billie said. "How'd you know?"

"Just a good guess," she said. "Both of you wearing the same wrist tats, Master Billy calling you 'my Billie,' and that he's talked to you about us on the streets."

"Guess it isn't too hard to figure," she admitted as he put the box on the back seat.

"You're the one he calls Tiger?" Maxie asked as she stuffed the bills in her pocket.

"Yeah," Billie said, and nodded as she turned back to the SUV.

"Good to finally meet you, Tiger."

"You too, Maxie." She waved to Maxie as they got in.

"Take Ninth Street out ten miles and turn east on County Road Twelve," he said as she pulled away from the curb.

-¤-

She saw the country cemetery on County Road Twelve just as Billy mentioned she should turn in and stop just through the archway. When she did, he got out, opened an umbrella, and held it for her. They took the flowers and walked to a large family plot near the center of the cemetery.

He led her to a pair of ornately carved headstones to one side of the stone-bordered grassy plot. He took the withered and dead flower stems out of a large brass-colored vase on the rightmost headstone and set the fresh bouquet in their place. Then he added water from the two bottles he had brought from the Rover.

"This is five generations of Hawkes," he said, and gestured to the four pairs of ornate white stones in front of the massive single carved marble stone at the back of the plot. "Hiram and his wife Mae are at the back, their son Chester and his wife Claudia, in front on the left. Their son Malcolm and his wife Elizabeth next to them. Their son William Carson the First and his wife Betty—my grandparents—next, and lastly my folks, William Carson the Second and his wife Dorothy here on the right. " He sighed and gestured to the rest of the empty plot. "And plenty of space for William Carson the Third and his wife Billie and their family."

"Where did the name Carson come from?"

"Malcolm's wife, Elizabeth, was a Carson," he said. "So the boys were named after her father who made his name in banking and investments. The Hawke name was in construction and minerals."

"And each generation only had a single son? No other siblings?"

"I was never told why that was, but I did think that was odd," he admitted. "Maybe"—he pulled her close and kissed her—"their women just weren't that good in bed."

Chuckling, she held his waist, his arm still around her shoulders. "Maybe it was their men that weren't that good."

He laughed. "Maybe, Tiger."

"I wish I could remember your folks. I mean, I do remember them coming to the ranch, but I don't remember anything like sitting down and having conversations or things like that."

156

"I would be surprised if you did." He hesitated before he continued. "You were only ten when you last saw them, and we all thought our worlds would last forever."

"Yeah." She sighed softly. "I still can't believe I lost mine and then it found me seventeen years later. That ten-year-old girl lost her guiding star and wandered aimlessly, depressed and dispirited with no hopes of ever getting one again." She looked up at him and smiled. "Thank you for finding me again and still wanting me."

"You are very welcome. But I do have to say I think we've done much better than just finding each other, Mrs. Hawke. Much better." He turned her back toward the SUV. "There's one more place I want you to see."

-¤-

"This is your parents' place," she whispered when he had her turn off the county road and stop at the gated arch. "My dad drove us by here once when I was eight or nine. I don't remember where we were going or why we came by, but I do remember this."

He got out and entered a code into a box set in the curved left wing of the stone arch. He got back in as the gate slowly swung wide.

"I'm surprised it still works," she remarked absently as she drove through and followed the quarter-mile drive to the house.

"The estate keeps the lawns, the gates, and the buildings maintained until I decide what I want to do with it all."

She parked on the circle drive and he led her to the front door, entered another code in a keypad, and opened the door. Inside, he turned off the alarm system and then slipped off his boots. She followed his example.

Billy gave her a guided tour through the sprawling two-story house—from the servants' wing, through the kitchen and entertaining areas, the guest rooms, and then upstairs to his old room and the master suite.

"Just your typical midwestern, four-bedroom mansion," he

jested. From the large family room on the back of the house, he showed her the view down and across a native grass meadow to a small lake beyond. "After the accident, I never could see myself living here again."

"How much land did your family have here?" she asked as she looked across the pastures to the trees in the distance.

"This area was Dad's favorite, or so I was told. It averages five miles by five miles—about sixteen thousand acres."

"His favorite?" She looked at him. "There are others?"

He nodded. "Yeah." And then he continued conducting his tour.

When she had seen the whole house, Billy led them back to the front door. They put their boots on and he reset the alarm. Outside, he relocked the door and paused, pulled her to him, and kissed her. She smiled and they ran through the light rain back to the SUV.

"Do you come out here often?" she asked as she started driving back toward the gate.

Billy shrugged and smiled. "Once, sometimes twice a year, Sid would drive me out here so I could see if everything was all right, but I haven't been for quite a while. Until now, it was just a bad reminder and I had actually thought about tearing it down. But now, Tiger"—he looked at her and his smile widened—"I have someone to share my things with. And I want Mrs. Hawke to have some say in how we deal with them."

Eighty-Eight

Huddled against the rain on a small covered porch near the Twentieth Street East end of a freight distribution building, Mindy handed a printout to Josh and another to Max.

"These are the three places Keeper says are owned by that Hammersmith fella's business," she said. "Keeper thinks that detective friend of his has a guy or two hanging around also. Keep your eyes and ears open and let's see if there's any activity."

Mindy pulled her large garbage bag over her head and stuck her head through a hole she'd made in the bottom and her arms through the slits she had made in the sides. Then with a grocery bag over her head and her "homeless" pants and boots sticking out, she looked appropriate for the part. Max and Josh donned their garbage and grocery bags and they stepped off the porch. "You know where we'll be, Red."

Josh waved. "Yes I do, Cat." He ambled slowly down the side of the building and turned into the next drive.

"Come on, Stretch. Ours are this way," Mindy said, and started down the drive past the first semi-trailer backed up to the building.

They took their time and stopped at each of the many overflowing dumpsters along the drive. The city sanitation crews had not picked up on Friday, leaving a lot of trash and garbage in the dumpsters, and Mindy smiled at their good fortune. It made their presence over the long weekend look more legitimate.

When they reached the place that matched Stretch's picture, he pulled a piece of reasonably dry cardboard from a stack wedged between a dumpster and the building wall and placed it on the ground. He pulled his water bottle—disguised as a wine bottle in a paper bag, partially protected by a small grocery bag—from his coat's pocket and then settled down beside the dumpster. He leaned back against the building below a loading bay door. From where he sat, he had a good view of the subject loading bay across the drive.

Cat slowly continued on, dissembling to look and act older than her age. Her address was at the far end of the next long building. When she reached her spot, she found a place similar to Stretch's, but it did not have the same clear view unless she sat in the rain.

She puzzled the situation and finally decided she could prop one of the dumpster's lids partway open and sit under it to get a better view. Satisfied with her solution, she scrounged a collapsed cardboard box and placed it on top of the rubbish in the not-quite-full dumpster with another box to hold the lid up on a slant. She settled down to wait, protected under the lid and reclined against a soft bag of trash.

Red took longer to reach his spot, nearly to Twenty-Fourth Street East and two blocks south of Cat's position. By the time he settled inside an upturned dumpster beside an overflowing one, it was noticeably darker. He checked his pocket watch and figured the weather was making darkness come early.

-ロ-

Cat heard the man before she saw him, as he came around the corner of the building and walked past her reclining in the dumpster and continued across the drive to the next building. He stopped in front of a parked semi-trailer and glanced up and down the drive. She dared not move and hoped she was reclined enough so he would not see her as a person. She held her breath.

The man—older, with white hair and dressed in normal everyday clothes under an expensive raincoat—finally turned, walked the length of the trailer, climbed a short set of stairs, and went in through a person-sized door beside the overhead freight door.

She checked her watch and made a notation in the spiral

pad she had in her shirt pocket. He looked like their man Hammersmith, and she called Tiger's phone to let Keeper know where he was. She stayed and watched for any other activity until it was full dark and the rain picked up again. She noted the time when the other man came just before the rain changed, and she noted when he left, but she decided to call Tiger after she had made her way out of the industrial park. The wind had changed, and she was getting drenched.

Slowly she made the long walk back past Stretch's spot and was not surprised to see he was not there. She knew he would look very out of place sitting there when the heavier rain started; he would have had to move. She wondered about Red, but quickly stopped her thoughts. She had no way to know his situation and would just have to wait until she saw him back at the apartments.

At Twentieth Street East, she turned north, and she planned to cross to the west side of the city at the next through street west. She was reconciling herself to a very long walk in the dark and in the cold rain to get home when her phone chirped softly. Puzzled, she looked at it and saw the call was from Tiger. She answered it.

"Turn around and get in," Tiger's voice said.

Startled, Cat turned around as the Rover pulled up beside her at the curb. The back door opened and Stretch took her hand and pulled her in.

She started to complain about getting everything wet when she realized they had already covered the seats with a large plastic sheet.

"Thanks." She pulled the door closed.

"We couldn't make you walk back in the dark and in this weather, now could we?" Tiger asked, and smiled from behind the wheel.

"You're driving already?"

Keeper turned around in the passenger seat. "She says she won't use her left arm too much," he said, and shrugged.

161

They laughed and Tiger pulled away from the curb.

¤-¤-¤-¤-¤

It was still raining and getting dark when Joey pounded on the metal door beside the freight door. He waited, knowing it took a little time to get from the living area to the door. When the door opened and Mike recognized him, Joey slipped in.

"Did you bring any money?" Mike asked as he stopped beside the overstuffed chair with a floor lamp beside it.

"No," Joey said, surprised he would ask. "You didn't give me a card or tell me you wanted any."

Mike stared at him but did not explain, and Joey decided to remain standing. He knew something was bothering Hammersmith, and he wanted to be able to move if he got irate and started throwing things.

"Okay, okay. I can fix that," he admitted.

"I came to tell you that I can't find Copper anywhere," Joey said. "No one seems to know where he is."

"Copper's gone?" Mike asked as if he did not hear Joey. Joey nodded and Mike slapped the back of the overstuffed chair. "Took the deposit and ran."

"Maybe," Joey said, trying to stay neutral and not raise his ire.

"You said you got a gun?"

"Yeah. I don't like it, but I got one."

"Still no word from Herb?"

Joey shook his head. "No. Maybe that article in the paper was about him. Maybe there was someone else with that woman and he killed Herb when he went to the river."

"Maybe," Mike considered. "That means someone probably saw you kill her."

"No. Not me! Herb did it! He just calmly murdered

someone, and in his normal, dislikable manner, decided to stuff her body under some rocks in the river. He made me help load her into his pickup." He sobered and looked at Mike. "She was a pretty girl too."

"I see it bothers you."

"Sure as hell it bothers me! And you, expecting me to kill this Keeper for you, also bothers me."

"Better watch what you say, Joey," Mike warned. "The Keeper knows too much! I don't know how, but he does! This is not the time to consider changing your mind."

"Yeah. I may have to get pretty drunk to do it, but I'll do it."

"Good. Did you *explain* things to Westman?"

"No. He wasn't there. Just two women."

"Two women?"

"Yeah. I went to the front bedroom and was about to hit her with a pipe I had, but then I saw she was a woman when she rolled over. I nearly freaked out and went the other bedroom. Someone was there too, and it was obviously a woman too."

"So you just left?"

"Yeah! I don't smack women! I don't shoot women! I don't—"

"Shit! You were supposed to get Westman! Now what do I do?"

"I...I..."

"Get out of here, Joey! Go! Find Westman and find Copper! Fix them both!"

Mike fumed and Joey could tell he was looking for something suitable to throw—something big.

Joey turned and hurried to the front door and splashed out into the rain. He did not look back and did not slow down to close the people-sized door.

Eighty-Nine

Tuesday, May 31

Billy arrived early at the Streetcar, like he did every morning he worked. He mopped the floors and set up the tables and chairs, set out the shakers, napkins, and the table flowers. He had his usual cup of coffee with Sid and then a second cup when he let Angie, Carole, Melony, Julie, Kevin, and Niles in. Sid opened the diner at seven as usual for the early crowd, and at eight Billy left for his appointment with Detective Nolan.

He walked the nine blocks straight east on St. Anne. The clouds from the previous days were nearly gone and the bright morning sun felt warm on his face in the damp, cool morning air. He made good time and knocked on Nolan's open office door at eight twenty.

"Morning, Keeper," Nolan said as he stood up and extended his hand. "Coffee?"

"No thanks." He shook Nolan's hand. "Had a couple already this morning. What's the drill?"

"Is Tiger coming to listen too?" Nolan asked as he led Billy back into the corridor.

He shook his head. "She'll be here in time to meet Lynx and then go to their meeting with Justice Parker."

"Okay. I've got you set up in a listening room," Nolan continued as he opened the door to a small room with a table pushed up against a wall and four chairs set out. A wide-screen monitor hung on the wall above the table. "You'll be able to hear and see what is happening in the actual deposition room through the monitor. You can sit here and watch. Write down any questions that come to mind and we'll see if we can get answers after they've finished. You won't be able to interact during this session."

"Who's the woman with Frederick?"

"That's his wife—ex-wife, technically. His daughter is in another listening room." Nolan looked at him and formed a tight smile. "Since you are a survivor of the accident and the son of the victims, I have to put you in a separate room during this session."

"I understand." He decided on a chair.

"The questioning will start in just a few minutes." The door opened and a young female officer stepped in. "Lieutenant Long will be here with you, and if you need anything, she will get it for you. This should run about an hour, and I'll see you afterwards."

He nodded and greeted the lieutenant as Nolan left the room. The lieutenant took a seat next to the door and he took the one he had chosen earlier.

¤-¤-¤-¤-¤

Billie was waiting in the courthouse lobby when Cathy arrived a few minutes before nine.

"Sorry, I'm running late," Cathy said as she folded her light sweater over her arm. "Abby was full of it this morning, asking all kinds of questions: Why was I leaving earlier than normal? Where was I going? All that sort of curious stuff."

"We still have a couple of minutes." Billie led the way to the elevators.

"Do I look okay?" Cathy asked nervously as the elevator door slid open and they stepped out onto the fourth floor.

"Here. Pop in and take a minute." Billie nodded as she took in her simple-but-nice look in a clean, white print dress and matching white shoes. She gestured to the women's room. "I'll wait."

Cathy made her stop quick, dabbing her face with cold water and running a quick brush through her hair. When she came out, she saw Billie waiting at a door farther down the hallway.

"Good morning," Billie greeted the woman in the outer office. "We have an appointment to see Justice Parker at nine."

The woman studied her monitor screen a moment, then smiled. "I'll tell him you're here." She announced them as his nine o'clock and then looked up and said, "Please go right in."

"Justice Parker, good morning. It's good to see you again," Billie said as she entered the Justice's office. She continued when he returned the greeting. "I'd like to introduce a friend of mine, Cathy Jefferson."

He rose and shook their hands and then settled back into his time-polished leather chair. "And what can I do for you this fine morning?"

"We're here…" She glanced at Cathy when she was reluctant to jump in. "…to talk to you about getting a divorce."

The justice looked at Billie with a start. "But you just got—"

Damn! Damn!

"No. No. It's for Cathy," Billie interrupted, since the innuendo obviously did not go unnoticed by the justice. "Cathy's husband abandoned them—her and her then unborn daughter—over seven years ago. There has not been any contact and no attempted contact since. In order for Cathy and her daughter to move on with their lives, I wanted to talk to you about what she can do to get a legal divorce or separation from her husband. You know, where does she start? What can she expect?"

Justice Parker began by explaining the options available and asked a number of questions to better understand the complete situation. Finally, after nearly an hour of discussion, they focused on three roadblocks; the first they had to overcome was finding where Clark Jefferson was today. The second roadblock was to confirm that he was still alive, and the third was to get him to sign a non-contested request for a divorce.

They thanked the justice for his time and left with the task of getting a current address for one Clark Jefferson, previously of Cincinnati.

"Tiger?" Cathy asked when they stopped on the courthouse steps. "Forgive me for being curious, but did I hear the justice right? Are you and Keeper married?"

Billie sighed and smiled. "I figured you heard that. I won't lie to you—we are." She explained that he was concerned that if something happened to him, many if not all of the things he wanted to do for people would not happen. With the rising uncertainty, the escalating fights, the contract that was put out on him, he wanted her to be able to continue his work if something did happen. "In a private, secret wedding, Judge Parker married us and now he has a legal heir, so to speak— someone to keep his ideas going if he isn't able to. I think it was having the contract on him that made him realize how serious things were getting."

"I'm sorry if I'm adding to your burdens," Cathy said, "but it makes sense."

"Huh? Makes sense?"

"Sure. I saw the change when you got out of the hospital. I just assumed it was something to do with being shot, recovering, being alive, but you both changed. Your focus, the way you work together, changed. It's hard to put into words, but you went from a couple planning a future, with all of the normal overtones of not quite being certain of the outcome, to a couple that has put that uncertainty behind them. You are no longer planning a future, but are focused on making a future. It shows."

"I know I feel differently," Billie said, "but I had no idea it was obvious."

"Why do you and Keeper want to keep it a secret?"

"Hammersmith. Like we talked at the apartments,

Hammersmith doesn't know who Keeper really is...the son of his biggest adversary, the one that survived the accident that killed his folks, and we need to keep it that way as long as possible. Hopefully, Nolan's guys can catch him before he finds out. But now it's obvious he's still trying to remove Keeper from the city center. If he succeeds, Keeper will have lost on both fronts." She sighed. "I really don't know what Hammersmith might do, but Keeper doesn't have much of a chance of dodging this one. We do have an ace that Hammersmith doesn't know about, but it won't help Keeper stay alive."

"What do you have?"

"Frederick Westman is giving his testimony to the court this morning." She thumbed back toward the building. "He knows Hammersmith killed Keeper's parents, and with his testimony and the evidence I found at Hammersmith's place, Nolan says we have a solid case against him. I think we can even show, to a reasonable degree, that he was at the scene when it happened."

"Wow," Cathy said, but quickly sobered her surprise. "But like you said, that doesn't help Keeper in the meantime."

"Even if Nolan finds Hammersmith and takes him in, too many things have been set in motion. At least one person, Joey, is out to kill Keeper. We think Copper is involved in more than just trying to sell his drugs. And now, Keeper has to rely on us to hear what's going to happen, what's being said, and to keep him informed." She smiled a tight smile. "He needs us more now than ever."

¤-¤-¤-¤-¤

Billy stretched his long legs out under the table in front of him and slouched back in the straight-backed metal chair. He watched the large, wide-screen monitor of the interrogation room as two police detectives entered and took seats across from Frederick and his ex-wife.

One detective started the interview with introductory

169

remarks, telling everyone the conversations would be recorded by audio and video means. He asked his initial questions, confirming Frederick's name, address, family details, and his business, and continued by verifying his relationship with Mike Hammersmith and how long that relationship had existed. At the end of the opening session, the first detective handed the second detective a folder, which he opened, and began reading from a page within it. Specifically, he asked what Frederick remembered about Mike's dealings with customers early in their business relationship.

Even though some of the revealed details were new to him, Billy listened with an almost detached air. It wasn't until the second detective asked Frederick about Mike's seemingly obsessive actions regarding the city center blocks where the Duckard's Department Store buildings sat that he began to pay attention.

Frederick explained that Mike had been concerned with getting ownership of those buildings from the first time they had met and all during their working relationship. He further explained how Mike had changed about eighteen years previous, constantly calling W.C. Hawke, the owner, and demanding that he sell the properties, each time adding more and more made-up reasons for why he should.

Billy remembered hearing his dad's side of a few of those calls and suddenly, knowing what happened a year later, his heart pounded as he focused on the details and how his dad had casually explained the calls as just someone that did not want to take no for an answer.

Frederick explained that he was never on any of those calls and that he did try to make Mike see reason. Mike kept making the calls. Then one night, just before the Labor Day weekend, at the end of their workday on Friday, Frederick recounted Mike coming into his office.

"Fred," Mike had said with a sparkle in his voice, rubbing his hands together. "I think I have finally found a way to get those Duckard buildings."

Frederick said he had asked Mike what he was talking

about. He knew W.C. Hawke was not going to sell them to Mike—or anyone, for that matter.

"Don't worry about the details," Mike had told him. "By Monday it will just be a matter of starting the paperwork to change the ownership information."

Billy twisted in his chair, suddenly uneasy as he remembered his side of what had happened that Labor Day: the accident, the fire. He caught himself absently glancing at the door beside Lieutenant Long and wondering if Billie was finished with the judge, wondering if Lieutenant Long would go and find her if he asked her to. He glanced at the time feature on the monitor and knew she would still be in her meeting with the judge.

Billy took a tissue from the box on the table, wiped his eyes and blew his nose, and then turned back to listen to Frederick as he described Mike's actions the following week, when he had found out that W.C. Hawke did not own the properties in his name—rather some company of his owned that central cluster of eight blocks, along with ten others scattered about the city. Frederick said Mike went ballistic, shouting expletives and cursing Hawke for what he had done to him.

Billy felt the odd combination of an upset stomach at hearing the other side of the happenings and the feeble feeling of victory for his dad thwarting Mike in the end. He suddenly did not know if he felt like shouting for his dad's success or crying because the loss of his parents was so futile, pointless. Hammersmith had let his emotions guide him and had not planned his moves to guarantee his success. He was a poor detail person and Billy's parents were lost because of it.

Billy folded his arms across his chest and stared at his feet with blurry, unfocused eyes.

The interview dragged on and Frederick's ex-wife explained how they found out a week later what Mike had done and how Mike blackmailed Frederick so he would not go to the police with what he knew. Mike had made certain the homeless man, a fellow named Johnny Hill from a village down near the river on the east side, thought he and Frederick had planned the accident together. Just another layer added to the lie to keep Frederick from squealing.

When the deposition was over and after a very long few minutes, Billy finally wiped his eyes again and realized the young lieutenant was no longer guarding the door. He shook his head and wiped his eyes as he stood up. Glancing back at the monitor, he saw that the screen was dark, the meeting finished, and he let the details run around in his mind as he stepped out into the corridor and walked to the elevator.

When he had gone into the room to listen, he had thought of a number of questions to ask, but now, walking out into the bright morning, he knew they did not make any difference. Frederick and his ex-wife had given Nolan and the police what they needed if they could just catch Mike.

Billy had no more tears to shed over his loss, and now he just fought to keep his anger under control. He and Billie had found each other again and now he owed her everything and was focused on keeping her as safe and cared for as he could. He would not allow himself to lose control now.

As he stepped out onto the wide stone porch in front of the police station, he thought about Mike's motives; no one knew why Mike wanted the Duckard's buildings so badly.

He smiled to himself and descended the steps to the street. *Maybe, just maybe, we will know more this afternoon.*

¤-¤-¤-¤-¤

"How'd the testimony go?" Billie asked him as Angie set their lunch orders in front of them. "Thanks, Angie."

He nodded and sipped his water. "Like you said it would." He smiled at her and picked up a sandwich half. "He knew what Hammersmith had done and gave detailed descriptions of how he set it up. Very much like you assumed. Hammersmith arranged the assistance of the homeless man but made sure the man thought Westman was part of the setup. I guess he felt that if the man was caught and said anything, Westman would be in as much trouble as he would be."

"Is there something off about Hammersmith?" she asked, and then smiled at her onion burger.

"I'm sure there is."

"I may have messed up again," she confessed, and took a bite.

"How so?"

"This is sooo good," she admitted through a mouthful, and shook her head. "Sorry. Justice Parker made a comment this morning and Cathy heard it. Later, she asked if we were married and I wouldn't lie to her."

He smiled. "That's okay. I think your mom thinks something's going on too."

"Mom? Why do you say that?"

"Just the way she looked at us a few times"—he smiled and nibbled on his fries—"and a few things she said. I think we must be doing something differently."

"Cathy says we are." She chuckled. "And she nailed when."

"Well"—he caught her hand—"I can't hide how I feel about you. I wouldn't know how to try."

She was about to respond when Mouse stopped at the end of the table. "Keeper, Tiger, can I talk to you?"

Billy looked up and quickly slid over to make room for her on the bench.

"What's up, Mouse?" he asked as she sat down. "Can I get you something?"

She shook her head. "Ferret, Sparrow, and I have been listening over on the east side. No one can find Copper, but that man Joey has been asking everyone where he can find you."

"So Copper's split?" he asked absently—a question, but not to either of them. "Or are we just supposed to think he's split?"

"What are you going to do, Keeper?" Mouse asked, and

looked at Tiger.

"I think I'll watch the department store and see if he shows up," he conceded, and looked at Tiger. "Probably ought to give Nolan a heads-up."

Billie nodded and pulled her phone from her back pocket.

"You're going to make it obvious where you are?" Mouse asked.

He nodded. "I'm thinking Hammersmith will have a backup plan—probably his man Joey. He may be a distraction, something to keep us from seeing what's really coming. I think something will break soon, maybe in the next few nights. As hard as Hammersmith is pushing to get me out of the way, there is obviously something urgently pressing on his side."

"We'll have to leave one of us, probably Owl, back at the apartments to take care of the kids," Mouse said, "but the rest of us will be there, on the streets—maybe a few from the village as well. Is Tiger going to back you up?"

"No," he said, looking at Tiger apologetically as she started to answer that she was.

Startled, she stared at him as she pulled the phone away from her ear.

"I want Tiger to find Joey and follow him. To be ready to act if he tries anything." He caught her hand again and squeezed it. "The others will have to watch for Copper. This time, Tiger, I need you to be my eyes on the street. If Copper shows up, I won't have time to look for Joey. And he'll have that gun he bought."

Reluctantly, she nodded and laid her phone on the table. "I left Nolan a voice message."

Ninety

"Did I tell you?" Tiger asked as they walked past the Forest after lunch, heading to the department store. "What I found in a society magazine on Hammersmith about the time he and Hannah got engaged?"

"No," Billy said, and smiled. "What'd you find?"

"Remember I said I thought Hannah had a tattoo barely visible in one of those pictures you showed me?"

"Yeah, I remember."

"In one article in one magazine—her smile was evident in her voice—"there was a picture of the two of them, each with a matching tattoo."

"No!"

"Yup. It was across the back of their left shoulders and around onto their left arms. That part on her arm is what I think I saw in your photo."

"Wow!" Billy said. "So why would he be so adamantly against them now?"

"I'd say something happened between him and Hannah that soured him," she surmised. "A lovers' spat, a quarrel, another man, who knows. I didn't see anything in the articles that mentioned a breakup."

"No, I didn't see anything about a breakup either," he conceded, his voice turning serious and soft. "She just disappeared."

"Oh no! Keeper? You don't think—"

"I don't know, but I think I'm glad we're going to open that room in the warehouse building. I may be wrong, but now it seems odd that she suddenly disappeared without a trace. Nothing ever found, in all of these years."

She was surprised to see Max and Mindy waiting when they reached the department store.

"Aren't you working today?" she asked.

"When Stretch said he was meeting you to open the mysterious room," Cat replied, a serious smile on her face, "I had to be here. I was able to get someone to cover for me and I took the afternoon off."

Billy explained what they were going to do and led them inside. They found Buster Crane on the top floor, reviewing his rolled plans.

"Hey, Buster," Billy greeted. "Are you very busy right now?"

"Hi, Billy," Buster returned the greeting when he looked up. "Not really. What do you need?"

"Two questions," Billy said. "First, do you have enough power cords to reach from the alley door across and down to about the middle of the basement in the warehouse building?"

"I think so," Buster said.

"Second. Can I borrow them and a portable light for a half an hour or so?"

"Sure," Buster said, and turned to the elevator. "I think they're all on either the first or maybe the second floor. What're you looking for?"

"I don't know for sure," Billy said, and followed Buster. "There's an odd locked room in the basement next door, and with some of the strange goings-on around here, I'm going to try to get into it and see what's there."

"I heard there are occasional fights in the alleys," Buster admitted.

"Occasionally, yes," Billy said as they all entered the elevator.

Buster looked at him. "I didn't know this was such a rough neighborhood."

"Maybe it won't be much longer." He smiled as the elevator stopped and the door opened. "I hear the police are trying to locate and arrest the fellow behind the trouble."

"Here they are," Buster said, and picked up a hundred-foot reel. "Two of these ought to get close. Grab that lamp and stand."

-¤-

"There," Buster said as he carried the lamp and stand as close to the bathrooms as he could. "It won't get around the corner, but at least the room isn't completely dark anymore. I can go look for another cord if you want."

"Thanks, but this will probably do," Billy said as he saw Tiger lead Max and Mindy down the stairs to join them.

"We each have a flashlight," Tiger said. "And Stretch has a heavy duty lamp."

"Tiger, this is Buster Crane, the foreman on the construction crew," Billy said. "Buster, this is Tiger, also known as Billie"— Buster nodded and shook her hand. "And this is Max and Mindy. Close friends of ours. They're also known as Stretch and Cat. They were with me when we found the door in question." Billy took Tiger's hand and nodded to Max, Mindy, and Buster. "Let's see if any of the keys work."

-¤-

With the door and the lock illuminated by the flashlights, Billy knelt in front of the door and looked at the shapes of the three keys. After a few minutes, he resorted to trying the first key.

It slipped in but would not turn.

"Here," Max said, and handed him a small container with a short, pointed spout. "Graphite oil. Try just a little."

He nodded, removed the key, and squirted a small amount of the oil into the key slot, wiping the excess away with the rag Max handed him.

He poked the key in and out a few times to spread the oil,

then tried again. "It moved a little this time, but I don't think it's the right one." He wiped the oil off the key and put it in his shirt pocket. He tried a second one. "Moves about the same."

"I think it turned a little farther," Cat said, and Tiger bent close to look.

"I think Cat's right," she encouraged, and he worked it back and forth a few more times.

"Yeah. It turns more each time." He pulled the key out and added a little more oil. Then he tried again and worked the key back and forth. It turned and then got very stiff, turning very slowly. With a little more oil, the key slipped past the stiff spot and turned a full turn. Something clicked and Billy smiled up at Tiger.

"Maybe," he said, then stood up and gently tried the handle. "It turns." He slowly swung the lever down a quarter turn.

He pulled on the handle, hoping the door would swing open, but it stayed.

"Bring the light closer, Tiger." He peered at the plunger in the space between the door and the jamb. "Aaah. The bolt isn't quite clear yet."

He twisted the handle a couple more times and watched as the plunger moved, each time stopping short of clearing the jamb. He added a little more pressure and the plunger moved slightly more, but not enough. Finally, after many attempts, Billy held the handle as far as he could and picked at the plunger with the thin blade of his pocket knife. It finally retracted and cleared the jamb. He pulled and the door shifted.

"Aha!" The panel jumped slightly proud of the jamb.

He stood up and took a breath, then pulled slowly on the handle. The door swung ajar and Max and Buster pulled with their fingers, trying to grip the edge of the door. Suddenly the door swung open with the loud screech of protesting hinges. The lower edge caught a wood scrap and scraped the concrete floor.

Billy quickly held up his hand as Max started to step inside.

"Let it air out a bit," he said, and shone his flashlight into the dark room. "The air might be a bit stale."

Max chuckled. "Just might be."

Max switched his lamp on and flooded the room with light. It was reasonably empty, a few boxes here and there.

Tiger looked at the ceiling. "The light bulbs were removed."

"It's deep," Cat added in surprise. "Twenty feet at least, probably more."

"Yeah," Max agreed. "It doesn't quite go as far as the other building. What's that on the floor, behind the boxes? The one that looks like it has a flashlight on it."

"Wait here," Billy said. He inhaled, held his breath, and stepped into the room.

He took a dozen steps and froze as he shone his flashlight behind the boxes. With leathery skin, a badly decomposed woman with dark hair and wearing a rumpled, dirty white, thigh-length dress lay stretched out on the floor, facedown. He took a step closer, thinking the dress had probably been sullied in her frantic attempts to get someone to let her out.

Leaning closer, he realized she was lying on top of another similarly decomposed body, but this one was wearing equally soiled pants and a shirt, facing up, holding her with his left arm and his other arm reaching down, along her side, his hand tangled in her skirt.

Billy let out his breath and the stale air made him cough and quickly retreat to the open door.

He hesitated a long moment, looking back at the box, then stepped out.

He grabbed the door panel and swung the door nearly closed, dropping a board in the gap to keep it ajar. Inhaling deeply to get cleaner air into his lungs, he turned to look at the faces staring at him in question. He looked soberly at his mate. "Tiger, better go up and call Nolan. Tell him I think we may have found Hannah Quinn."

Ninety-One

Wednesday, June 1

Tiger came down the stairs from their bedroom, dressed in her summer frump, and Billy looked up and smiled at his mate. The light-weight, short-sleeved, short-waisted, slashed-necked jumper atop worn regular-fit pants and scuffed boots took his breath away.

"I don't know if I dare let you out in public," he said, his eyes taking in every curve and nuance of her full, sensual feminine form as he reached out to her.

She took his hand and let him pull her close.

He kissed her and held her tight. "My God, you are absolutely fetching, Tiger. Someone's liable to try to carry you off."

"He better be you," she said, and squeezed his waist, "or he'll get a big surprise. Lynx will be with me, listening. I'll meet her in about a half an hour. Pidge, Mouse, Sparrow, and Cat will be with us on the streets, and you picked four of the guys to be with you in the alleys. Nolan said he'll have three undercover guys there and a number of uniformed policemen patrolling around the area."

"I sure wish I had more time," he said, and she held his eyes, "before we have to go. Seems like the day vanished before I knew it and I didn't get to show you how much you mean to me."

"Don't, Keeper." She squeezed him. "We'll get through this and everything is going to be okay. I know it was a long wait last night and nothing happened, but everyone's ready to wait again. Nolan said he'll pick up Hammersmith once this is over.

I don't know why he's waiting, but he said he wanted to be sure you come out of this in one piece. A lot of us share that understatement."

Billy looked at the clock. "I guess we better get moving."

"You're not dressing in your frump clothes?" she asked, and pushed herself back to look at his pale-colored plaid shirt and lightly worn jeans.

"Not tonight." He smiled. "Do you have your knife?"

"Of course," she said. "Calf scabbard."

He gently turned her toward the door. "It's almost dark. Let's go see who's waiting in the shadows."

¤-¤-¤-¤-¤

Tiger walked with him hand in hand up First Street West into the city center. She left him at Archer and went east a couple of blocks to rendezvous with Lynx, and he went west to the south end of the alley between the two Duckard buildings.

Just below the bus station, she saw Lynx, and trying to act like any normal women that met on the street, they casually walked as if they were catching up on the latest gossip. At Second East, they slipped up to Calvin and started slowly back west, watching the alleys and the cross streets, carefully looking for any signs of someone moving toward the Duckard buildings and Keeper.

"Sorry we're having to do this instead of dress shopping for Abby," Tiger commented absently as she watched people on the sidewalks.

"Not an issue, Tiger. Stay focused. This is more important than a dress."

She mumbled "I know," and saw Lynx look at her. It was obvious that she saw how well Tiger knew how important this was.

At Main, they stopped and watched a shadowy figure, on

the south side of the street ahead of them, turn the corner and slowly wander south. She was certain it was not Joey or Copper, from the man's stature and build, but they watched him until he turned east on Baker.

At the north end of the alley in the block north of the department store, Tiger stopped and looked down its length. She could see the dark alley and the construction gate where Keeper was waiting a block away, but she could not see him. She was waiting to see if anyone crossed the mouth on Baker when Cathy nudged her arm, pointing at Calvin Street.

She turned and saw two figures crossing Calvin, going south on Second West.

"Pidge and Cat," Lynx said softly. "Stretch and Hammer are on First. I saw them behind us when you stopped."

"I think Keeper said," Tiger whispered, "he had Mace, Cutter, Red, and Ditto with him. Is Owl with the children?"

"Yeah," Lynx said with a tinge of sadness in her voice. "She's having a hard time accepting that she isn't as agile as she used to be. At least she does like being with the kids."

"I know." Tiger turned back to the long, dark alley. "And we haven't seen hide nor hair of Joey. Has anyone checked this alley? We've got the streets covered, so I'm thinking we should take a quiet look to see if it's clean."

Lynx gestured for her to take one side and lead the way. She stepped forward and stopped at the corner beside the left wall. Lynx stopped on the opposite side of the alley entrance.

Tiger crouched down and took her knife from her calf scabbard and slowly stood back up, seeing Lynx had her knife ready as well. Tiger nodded and they started forward, each just an arm's length from their wall.

-¤-

"Too damned quiet, Keeper," Russell said as they stopped in the shadows of the alley at Baker, to one side in front of the construction gate partially swung open between the two Duckard buildings.

"Yeah," Keeper agreed, "but we have the A-team on the ground, watching and listening."

"I should've taken Pigeon's cell phone when I came," Russell said, and shook his head. "Wasn't thinkin'. Cat has one and Mouse has hers. If I had've taken one, they could've let us know if they see anything."

"They'll tell Tiger," he said confidently as he scanned the north side of Baker in both directions. "If she knows, that's all I need."

"Haven't seen Butch or any of the others that are supposed to be here," Russell said, following Billy's scan.

"You're not supposed to," he chuckled softly. "If we can see them, so can anyone else."

"True," Cutter said, speaking for the first time in many minutes. "I never realized how many alcoves and storefront recesses there are. Even after watching this area for all these years, waiting last night was like I saw them for the first time."

"Well"—Billy inhaled—"let's see if we're really alone." He sighed, letting his breath out slowly as he looked over his shoulder. "Mouse, Sparrow, and Ferret are in the alleys to the south. Red, you and Ditto stay in the shadows on either side of the mouth here. Cutter, Mace, crouch down at the corners of the building and be ready."

"Ready for what?" Cutter laughed, half to himself. "We can't do much unless one of them runs by, real close. My knife doesn't reach very far."

"I know, Cutter," he said. "Mine either. But tonight, I'm just the bait. Everything's up to Tiger and the rest of the family."

They each took their places and Keeper slowly stepped into the light from the corner streetlamps.

-ࠀ-

The trek down the dark alley was slow, with far more trash, broken crates, and boxes than Tiger was expecting. The alley was not nearly as clean as the one between the Duckard buildings. *But then*—Tiger smiled—*Keeper isn't responsible for keeping this one clean.*

About halfway down, Tiger stopped and dropped suddenly into a crouch as a string of men's silhouettes stepped out of the deeper shadows on the right, stretched across the alley, and blocked their way. She glanced at Lynx and knew she saw them too.

"Damn! A delay we don't need. Watch our backs, Lynx," she whispered needlessly. Lynx had already turned to face them.

"We've got company there too, Tiger," she confirmed, lowering into her crouch, "trying to box us in."

Tiger took a deep breath and eased forward on the balls of her feet. "You fellas need to back away and let us pass," she said in a calm, almost pleasant voice.

"Or what?" one of the silhouettes asked. "We think you're in the wrong alley, Tiger. And when we're done here, we're goin' t' have a bit of fun with you."

That ain't gonna happen.

Don't get cocky.

I know. Just stating a fact.

Tiger felt her anger rising as the middle figure pulled a long knife and the others followed his lead. She focused on him, shook her head, and lunged at his silhouette without uttering a sound.

Nearly within his reach, she sidestepped and dove for the man to her right, catching him off guard. The middle figure tried to turn and block her, but she came up under his extended arm and raked his ribs with the first inch of her blade. He fell too far forward, mouth agape in surprise. The man she targeted staggered when she crashed into him, spinning him to the ground as he tried to slash her. She rolled away from him, spinning back onto her feet. Knife blades clashed in the darkness as she deflected the next, felt her blade slide up the bicep of his knife arm. She smiled at the unmistakable feel of metal grating on bone.

She came up under the next man and pushed him back with

the point of her blade deep in his chest as she spun, kicking the fourth away. Two men dove for her and two men behind her tried to box her in. Her anger flashed and the "Tiger" got loose...

Ninety-Two

Lynx focused on the five men that closed in behind her and Tiger. Out of the corner of her eye, she saw Tiger lunge and she sprang at her five assailants, throwing one man aside with a gash across his chest and sinking her knife into a second's torso as he dove at her. Lynx came up under a third, too close for him to stab her, and rolling to her left, pushing his knife hand wide and raking the side of his ribcage open as she spun to the fourth.

Everything was a blur and suddenly Lynx stopped, crouched as the last two men facing her, backed away, turned, and ran up the alley toward Calvin. With three on the ground around her and no one else challenging her, she spun around looking for Tiger.

Lynx quickly ran to assist, but saw Tiger's silhouette spinning, ducking, and lunging, a dance in the dark with other, larger silhouettes. She tried to keep the images sorted in her mind as Tiger seemed to weave through the narrow flashes of space between the shadows, slashing one with an upward swing of her arm, another swipe across someone else's arm. The chaos of shadows and silhouettes blurred and spun, shrunk and expanded until all of the attackers were moaning heaps on the ground, except the last two. They descended on Tiger oblivious to the losses around them, but in the blink of an eye one folded over on himself, holding his gashed middle, and tumbled sideways. The last suddenly gasped as Tiger raised up abruptly, the silhouette suddenly rigid and still, stretched up on his toes, a prize skewered on the end of her blade. His knife fell in the sudden silence and slowly, knowing he was the last of her assailants, Tiger almost casually pushed him off her knife and watched him crumple to the ground. She stared down at the man at her feet and slowly glanced at the others on the ground around her, inhaling as she turned to look down the alley toward Baker. Into the still darkness Tiger quietly asked, "You okay, Lynx?"

"*Shit!*" Lynx inhaled and looked around them as well. "Yeah. Let's go, Tiger. I'm right behind you."

Tiger walked hurriedly toward Baker, returning to her wary and guarded stance, her arms down beside her, her knife poised, blade forward, ready. She stopped at the south end of the alley, across from where Keeper waited. Lynx stopped beside her, speaking softly into her cell phone.

"Nolan, Lynx. Get someone in the alley between Baker and Calvin, north of Keeper. There's a pile of bodies in need of medical assistance. They're still armed, but less assertive than they were. Tiger's okay. I don't know how many there are for sure. More than a dozen."

Tiger saw Keeper step out of the dark alley as Lynx put her phone in her pocket. She glanced up just as Lynx suddenly pointed past her with her knife. Tiger snapped around and saw Joey as he crossed the sidewalk and slipped off the curb into the street, catching himself before he fell.

-¤-

Joey took another long pull on the bottle he had in the paper sack before he pushed himself up in the deep shadow of the store's front-door alcove. He kept himself leaning back into the dark space and looked again at the alley across the street and a little to his right. He blinked, and the image he saw split and slowly drifted back into a single picture.

He watched as two men stepped out of the alley and stopped on each side, leaned against the buildings, and crouched down, watching. Joey smiled, knowing they wouldn't have a gun. A moment later, he chuckled as Keeper, in a light-colored plaid shirt and faded jeans, stepped out and stood in front of the alley, a bold and daring target.

Too easy, Joey thought, and stepped out onto the sidewalk. He stepped forward and felt the gun in his pants pocket and the bottle in his other hand. He took another step and slipped off the curb, catching himself as he looked down to see what was in his way. He straightened and looked at Keeper, smiled, and shoved his hand into his pants pocket. He wished he had taken another pull on the bottle as he pulled the pistol out. *But I'm here now,* he thought, and blinked, waited a second for his eyes to work together again, then squinting, pointed the pistol and squeezed the trigger.

¤-¤-¤-¤-¤

Mike Hammersmith laid his suitcase in the trunk of the tired and worn-out Civic. He closed the lid, got in, and started driving slowly up Twentieth Street East. He remembered the unpleasant day the city police had come to his office looking for him, the morning after Knife had failed to fill his contract and kill the one they call Keeper.

He had been going to work, a block away, when he had seen the three squad cars stop in front of his building and the uniformed officers rush in. Thankful he was running fifteen minutes or so late that day, he had hurriedly turned around and dropped his Towncar at his city apartment and parked it where it could be seen. Knowing they would soon be watching his apartment, he followed the alley and walked as casually as his racing heart would allow, to his storage garage four blocks away. There he picked up his "beater" car—a dark brown, abused-looking Honda—that he used for his weekend transportation or any other time when he did not need to keep up an "appearance" for clients. It was this "beat-up" car that he drove today as he turned west on St. Charles.

Once he realized the police were onto him, Mike made arrangements to move some of his funds from off-shore foreign accounts into his mother's old bank accounts—the ones in her trust that he conveniently "forgot" to close when she had died. In the past, he had only used her accounts to pay her nursing home bills and medical expenses, and on those few occasions when he needed funds that were harder to trace. But now, with his local personal and business accounts frozen, it was imperative that he have an alternate source of income.

Daylight was about gone when Mike parked in the north end of the alley off Calvin, just east of First Street West. He watched the alley in front of him and behind him for a long moment before he got out, locked the car, and with the appropriate keys in hand, he walked slowly to the alley entrance into the building facing First Street West. Knowing that everyone working in the building quit at four thirty or five, he confidently unlocked the alley door and slipped in. At the south end of the third-floor hallway, Mike jimmied the simple bolt to the last door on his right, ducked inside the dark office, and closed the door softly behind him.

No one was there to listen, but he told himself he should not make unnecessary noise if he did not have to.

Standing in the unlit room, facing the corner where the west and the south windows met, he gently pulled on the cords and opened the curtains a foot, exposing a narrow portion of each window so he could see Baker Street where it passed the two Duckard buildings. The street dimmed in the fading evening light and he waited, watching as patiently as one could when they were expecting, anticipating their greatest desire to come true. He eagerly wrung his hands. Somewhere in that block, the Keeper was about to face his destiny.

Mike did not have to wait long before he saw a couple of shabbily dressed men step out from behind the open construction gate at the alley between the two buildings on the south side of the street. They knelt down at the corners of the buildings and, after a moment, another man, dressed in a normal plaid shirt and jeans, stepped out and stopped on the sidewalk. The man surveyed the street, first to the east, then to the west, and then again to the east. He looked across the street as Mike saw his man Joey step away from a building on the north, cross the sidewalk, and stumble, stepping off the curb into the street.

He really expected Joey to shoot from around the corner of a building or something—anything to be discreet. He certainly did not expect him to step into the street like some old western gunfight. But Mike chuckled, knowing the one they called Keeper would not have a gun.

Then Joey pulled the pistol from his pocket, and as he raised it to point, Mike saw a petite redheaded woman dart out of the shadows and charge Joey. Mike jumped back at the surprise sight, seeing a second figure close behind the redhead.

There were gunshots before Mike could look again, and then the heavy sound of something larger than a pistol. It was close, like it was below him on the sidewalk! Then more gunshots and the ringing sounds of bullets ricocheting off the building; a window cracked in front of him and Mike jumped for the door. Everything was suddenly too close!

Mike hurried up the hall, down the stairs to the back door, and with the barest of glances, checked the alley as he stepped out and ran for his car.

¤-¤-¤-¤-¤

Tiger saw Joey stop and look down, searching around his feet to see what he had stepped on. Then she saw him turn, straighten, and pull the pistol from his pocket.

They were both across the distance to Joey in a mere second. Tiger grabbed his hair and yanked just as she heard the gun's *boom! Boom! Boom! Boom!*

The cacophony echoed through the concrete and glass canyons. Joey stood rigid, arm outstretched his hand frozen holding the pistol aimed high at the building. Tiger held his hair tight in her left hand, his head pulled back and her long knife tight against his throat.

"You twitch or move, Joey, and I swear I'll cut your head off and fill the street with your blood!" Then her eyes flicked aside. "Lynx!" she shouted. "Get the gun. Put it in the plastic bag!"

A second, heavier *boom* punctuated her command and filled the streets. Cathy spun to face the corner at First and Baker.

Several pistol shots echoed in rapid response, the whine of spent bullets filled the air, but Tiger held her breath and did not release her hold or change her stance; she thanked God nothing hit her this time.

Suddenly, it was quiet. And slowly, she could hear the sounds of running feet coming from all directions. Lynx stood up, pulled Joey's arm down, and put the bag over his gun, slowly pulling it from his hand. Tiger slowly realized Keeper and Russell, with two uniformed policemen, were standing around her, Keeper's hand gently resting on her shoulder. She did not relax or lower her knife until the policemen had Joey cuffed.

She stepped back, and as the officers turned Joey to take him away, he froze, stunned. Disbelief washed over his face and his mouth dropped open.

"You? How? You're dead! I saw you! I saw the blood! Everywhere! Herb killed you! Herb put you in the river!"

Tiger leaned back against Billy, his hands gently holding her shoulders, and slowly, she let herself smile. "He tried, Joey, but we traded places. Tiger's alive and Herb's dead."

The officers jerked Joey aside and pulled him away as she turned and jumped up, throwing her arms around Keeper's neck, his arms instantly tightening around her, holding her tight against him.

"I tried, Keeper," she said, "but I was still too slow. Are you all right? Is everyone all right?"

"I'm okay, Tiger. I'm okay," he said, and kissed her before he set her down. "But one of them got Ditto."

"Ditto? Nooo," she whispered, looking up, seeing the pain in his eyes as she absently folded her knife and slipped it into her pocket.

"When he saw Joey pull the gun," he said softly, "Ditto jumped out of the shadows and pushed me down." Then he looked at her, blood splotches all over her slashed-neck sweater and jeans, spatters all over her face and bare shoulder. "Are you all right? You're covered in blood."

"Theirs," she said softly, and took a deep breath. "They tried to stop us and I got mad and...and...the 'Tiger' got loose."

"What's this?" he asked as he held the cut end of her clear bra strap hanging out of her top's slashed neckline and saw the inch-long nick across her shoulder.

She followed his glance and grimaced. "I guess one of them got closer than I thought."

They turned and saw Nolan coming from the corner where the second shot had come from.

"We got Copper. He had a rifle," Nolan said as he stopped, staring at Tiger's blood-covered appearance.

"Did you get the ones in the alley?" Lynx asked, interrupting the question Nolan was obviously going to ask Billie.

"Aaah, yeah," Nolan said, and nodded as he focused on Lynx's question. "Luckily, I had a man close. He counted thirteen bodies in the alley, two dead and the others seriously wounded. He said two men ran out of the alley a few minutes before you called. Were they with the others?"

"Yeah," she said, and smiled. "They had a change of heart when I stopped the other three in the group that tried to box us in. They'll probably tell everyone what happened. Tiger stopped the rest."

"Ten?"

Lynx nodded and Nolan whistled.

"That's why she's got red hair," she continued, "and is covered in blood and I'm not. She takes her fights very close and personal."

"What's her hair got to do with it?"

Tiger looked at her and cocked her head.

"It's a warning flag. Don't mess with her, and for sure don't make her mad. They were trying to keep us from getting here to help Keeper, and Tiger wasn't going to have any of that."

Tiger put a hand on her hip and opened her mouth to throw a retort at Lynx when another shot boomed, muffled by the surroundings of the department store; three more followed in rapid succession.

"Oh shit! Now what, Nolan?" Keeper grabbed Tiger's hand and ran for the department store, past the closed north door and around to the door on the west.

A uniformed officer crouched beside the half open door, then went in. A second officer followed him in and Billy pulled Tiger in behind him.

At the top of the escalator, two men with bright flashlights, holding their badges up, stood beside a body slumped over a cluster of metal cans. One can was open, filling the area with pungent, highly aromatic fumes. The four officers were talking to each other when he and Tiger stepped off the non-operating escalator. Nolan's familiar voice came up behind them demanding to know what was going on. He passed Keeper and stopped beside the slumped man, kicking his fallen gun farther away.

"What's the story?" Nolan asked, and looked at the undercover men that turned to face him.

"We followed this one in," the man he recognized as Butch said. "He was using the fight on the street as a diversion and we found him ready to set this mess on fire. We yelled and he shot Kyle in the arm and then tried for me. I fired twice, Kyle once, and that's where he fell. Anyone know who he is?" Butch rolled him off the cans and onto the floor.

"Damn, Nolan," Keeper said. "He's in violation of his restraining order."

Ninety-Three

It was almost nine thirty that evening when Tiger and Keeper collected Hammer and Lynx in her Rover and followed Detective Nolan out to the freight terminal complex. Tiger only had time to wash her exposed parts—face, neck, shoulder, and arms—before they had to leave to keep up. She turned south off of Richmond and onto Twenty-First Street East, slowing as they passed the block-sized park just north of the complex. She parked where Twenty-First Street joined the ramps around the storage and transfer buildings.

The four of them got out and walked to the second building south, watching the police officers as they lined up between them and the building. Tiger saw the sweeps of the policemen's flashlights in the next alleyway.

"Do you think he's in there?" Lynx asked as the deep sounds of something pounding reached them. "Is that a ram I hear?"

"Yeah. I think Nolan's knocking," Keeper suggested as he scanned the line of officers and the numerous overhead doors mounted in the building wall.

Suddenly the pounding stopped and muffled voices shouted from the other side of the building. Minutes passed before a ground-level overhead door facing them slowly opened. Nolan and two officers stepped out shaking their heads.

-¤-

"Damn!" Tiger whispered loudly as she squeezed Keeper's waist. Then she looked up at him and continued, "Nolan waited too long! I knew he was—"

"Yeah," he said, and squeezed her shoulders, glancing at Lynx and Hammer. "We all felt like he was. At least they have warrants out and the police in the other towns around here can help look for him."

"But Keeper," Tiger said, her eyes full of regret as she looked up at him. "We had him! Days ago! We told Nolan where he—"

"I know, Tiger," he said, interrupting softly. "But now he's still loose. We'll just have to deal with it and stay vigilant. Come on, let's go talk to Nolan." He smiled down at Tiger. "And you, please try to be civil. We don't know the whole story."

Tiger swallowed visibly and slowly nodded.

¤-¤-¤-¤-¤

Billy led a very tired Tiger into their apartment, thumbed the deadbolt behind them, and carried her up to their bedroom. They soaked under the hot shower spray and held each other, letting the heat soften the stark memories, the water slowly eroding the literal and emotional grime, rinsing it away. Their intimate contact reinforced their complete support for each other. She clung to him and he knew he had to be her strength tonight. She had proven herself over and over again, and tonight more than ever.

When they finally dried themselves, donned their light-weight robes, and came down to the living room, Billy turned the sofa toward the city lights. He lay back, propped up against one arm with her stretched out, reclined on top of him, watching the shimmering cityscape through her glass wall. They lost themselves in each other's presence and their distant perspective of the city at night. With his left arm around her waist, he gently massaged the front of her shoulder, working the ointment over her wound.

"I'm glad you didn't pull an incision open," he said, bringing them back to the realities of their day.

"Me too, but I did hurt it some. I can tell I pulled it more than I should've," she said softly, savoring his ministrations. "Not as bad as at the village, but I feel it in my arm, which surprises me."

"Well, you did get pretty physical in the alley. Not to mention nearly jerking Joey over backwards," he said. "I still can't believe you took down ten."

"Like Lynx said, I got mad when they wouldn't move out of the way and when I engaged them, the 'Tiger' really got loose." She sighed. "I didn't have to think—'Tiger' just took over."

"They didn't have a chance," he chuckled softly. "I haven't seen the 'Tiger' when she gets loose, but like I've said before, after seeing you in fight mode, I really don't ever want to be the one 'Tiger' gets mad at." He squeezed her gently and then after a moment he asked, "Have I said thank you or told you how very proud I am of you? You amaze me every day, Tiger."

She was silent for a long moment then asked, "Will I still amaze you when we're not fighting for our turf, or for the safety of the others, or to keep alley squatters out of the 'hood?" Her voice was soft with the color of concern.

"Very much, Tiger," he said. "But I do think we need to find less threatening challenges."

"Is it over, Keeper? The fighting and the dealers?"

"Probably not the dealers," he admitted, "but I think Nolan can handle them. And until he finds Hammersmith, I'm sure things will remain tense. We can't let our guard down."

"I sure wish Nolan had've listened—"

"He told us he just got his search warrant for the freight complex," he reminded her. "If he wants the charges to stick, he has rules he has to follow. But I am surprised his stakeout didn't see Mike leave." He sighed and squeezed her gently. "But you, woman, Keeper's Tiger, are utterly amazing. And I don't use that term lightly. Finding the hidden lights and tools he used after all of these years and figuring out that Westman didn't help him was incredible. Keeper's Tiger is a very intelligent and wonderful woman. And I hope you know I love you very, very much."

Her phone chimed before she could answer, and she glanced

at the screen. Seeing Lori's image, she toggled the speaker on.

"Hey, Lori," she said. "What's up?"

"Did you guys see the news tonight?" Lori asked with an excited edge in her voice. "The shootings down by that department store you and Billy are always talking about? The news said five people are dead! Eleven wounded!"

"Yeah, we heard about it," she admitted in a soft, unemotional voice. "Blake's one of the dead. And also a drug dealer named Copper, and a friend of ours called Ditto. Two other attackers didn't make it. Hammersmith's man Joey was apprehended, and an hour or so later we found out Hammersmith jumped the corral fence—he's disappeared."

"Wow. How'd you know that? The news said they were withholding names. Did you watch a different channel?"

"No, Lori. We didn't." She chuckled.

"Wait. Where were you two when all of this happened?"

"Right in the middle of it." She sighed. "The only good that came out of it is the police have the man that shot Ditto, Keeper didn't get hurt, and the police have new charges against Hammersmith. He is being charged with killing Billy's parents seventeen years ago and for hiring Knife, Pink, Copper, and Joey to kill Keeper."

"You don't sound very happy," Lori admitted. "I think you need a girls' night out. How about tomorrow night?"

"I'm just very tired and we've had a very stressful day...and no," she said, and sat up on Billy's legs, "I don't think I'm up for a girls' night out. But I might be up for a night out with you girls and Billy. I don't think I'm going to be doing any nights out without Billy coming along."

Finally.

Yeah, finally. I get it now.

"I understand, and I'm okay with that," Lori said. "I'll call you tomorrow."

"Okay," Billie said, and toggled the phone off.

He sat up and turned, keeping her on his lap, slipped an arm behind her and the other under her legs, and stood up. "I think it's time, Mrs. Hawke, we find something more enjoyable to think and talk about. Besides, the doctor says your skin needs oiling, and I'm thinking every square inch of it." He kissed her and she flicked the lights off as they passed the switches.

She laid her head against his as he carried her up the stairs.

Ninety-Four

Thursday, June 2

Billie had just made her bed, and had her things hung up and a load of clothes in the washer when her doorbell chimed. She hurried down, opened the door, and hugged her mom enthusiastically.

"Good to see you, Mom. Coffee?" Billie asked, and crossed the dining area to the kitchen. She filled a cup and hesitated, waiting for her mom to say.

"Sure. Why not?" she said, and smiled at her daughter. "You certainly look happy this morning. Something going on?"

Billie slid the cups across the eating counter and then came around and took a stool.

"Yes!" she said, and looked out through the large window. "It's a beautiful day, you're here, I'm feeling wonderful, and Billy is alive and feeling great! And today we're going shopping. Wedding dress shopping!" She picked up her cup and took a sip as her mom settled onto another stool.

"When did you start drinking coffee?"

"It was after I got home from the hospital," she admitted. "We tasted a number of different beans and found a few flavors I like. Hope this one isn't too different for you."

"No, this is fine. Nice. Why the change?"

"Not really a change, Mom. More of an addition," she explained, thinking about it. "I still like tea, but I wanted something else to share with Billy. Everything changed after I met him and he kissed me in the alley the night we met Pink the first time. My tastes changed with the exercise program, the training, and after getting shot, I realized how close I had come to losing him again..."

Maggie watched the seriousness flash across her daughter's face before she quickly returned to her smile.

"Sorry." She grinned. "I guess that's more than you asked for."

"A lot has changed since you got out of the hospital," Maggie admitted, and watched for her response.

"Yes, it has! The only down side is that Hammersmith slipped away before Detective Nolan could nab him. He has been charged for killing Billy's folks on top of all the other charges for trying to have him killed."

"When did he slip away?" Maggie asked, realizing Billie had neatly sidestepped the response she had been expecting. "We heard something about a big ruckus here in town last night. What was all of that about?"

Billie quickly explained the bones of the happening but chose to downplay her and Billy's part in it all. She decided to skip talking about finding Hannah Quinn and the second body in the sealed room. Better, she thought, to look forward, not back. Leave that part to Nolan.

"We have two and a half hours to get started," Billie said, and rinsed the cups, "before we meet Billy for lunch. I have a load in the washer, but I can leave it and dry it later. So are you ready?"

Maggie smiled and picked up her purse.

-¤-

She led her mom in through the Streetcar's front doors and waved to Angie across the dining room, going straight to their booth in the back, beside the archway to the back rooms. She slid onto the bench before Angie could catch up.

"Don't make a fuss, Angie," Billie said as her mom slid onto the bench across from her. "It's just us. You don't have to usher us in every time."

202

"Billie! Yes I do. Especially you and your mom. Sid says so!"

"Well, he should know by now we're family," Billie said as she turned to see if she could see Billy through the archway, missing her mother's sudden smile. "Any good lunch specials?"

Angie said they had two and went through a polished description of each, reminding her of Monica's attention to details when they ate at Danny's Steakhouse Saturday night. She wondered if Billy might have anything to do with her pleasant, poised change and how it lifted the feel of the diner.

"I think I'm going to do the small chicken fry, mashed, gravy on everything. Oh, and fried okra on the side," she said, and glanced at her mom.

"Chicken salad club with the homemade chips," Maggie said, and Angie entered their orders into her digital pad.

"To drink?"

"Water," she said, and Maggie nodded.

"Okay. What are you two up to today? Looks like a nice day out," Angie asked as she put the digital pad in its holster.

"Wedding dress shopping," Maggie announced proudly. "She only has seventeen days left."

"It's coming up fast." Angie smiled. "But trust me, whatever you find, you'll look stunning in it. Ooh, gotta go." Angie turned to check on another table.

"She already does," Billy said as he slid onto the bench beside Billie. He gave her a quick kiss and then said hello to Maggie. "So, how's the hunting going, Mom?"

"Just started." Billie smiled. "We still have a half dozen stores to check out. How's your morning?"

"Quiet. Very nice and quiet," he confirmed as Angie brought their waters and he gave her his order.

"Are we serving tonight?"

"With Mom here and you shopping all day"—he shook his head—"I wasn't planning on it. Probably tomorrow, and then maybe catch up with Lori and Becky afterwards."

She nodded. "Where's dinner then? Do you want me to come home and fix something?"

"Yes, but not tonight." He grinned and held her eyes. "I like your cooking, but you don't need to fix anything after a long day on your feet. How about we take Mom to Nick's? He has a wonderful dinner menu."

She smiled, remembering. "Mom likes Italian."

"What time for a reservation?"

"Oh," Maggie said. "Make it for four of us. I have to pick Sandy up at six thirty."

"Oh! We've been so busy, I forgot she was coming back this weekend. Did everything go okay with Gil?"

"She'll have to explain, but he probably wasn't very happy with her. I think her sister and someone named Chase may have made her realize she wasn't ready to settle just yet." Maggie smiled and sipped her water.

"Seven thirty then?" Billy asked.

"Sure. That will let us get a room and settle in before we meet you."

Billie looked at him and cocked her head. He smiled and looked at Maggie.

"Don't get a room, Mom," he said. "You and Sandy can use my place. I have two beds and the place is clean. It's bachelor plain and very affordable. It's free, and even the neighbors are quiet."

Maggie smiled at them and nodded. "Okay, son."

Ninety-Five

"Good evening, Billy," Miriam greeted as he stopped at the hostess' station. "And you as well, Ms. Billie. We have you down for four."

"Good evening, Miriam," he greeted. "Yes." And he gestured to Maggie. "This is Billie's mother, Maggie, and her sister, Sandy."

"Very nice to meet you," Miriam said. "Would you please follow me?"

He gently pushed Billie forward with his hand against the small of her back as they followed Miriam.

"Father thought you might like the corner booth," Miriam said, and gestured to the large booth with high walls behind the benches. "It will give you a little more privacy than the others. Would you care to hear about the specials?"

"Very much," Billie said as she scooted in first.

Sandy and Maggie took the opposite bench and he sat last as Miriam began describing the specials. When she had finished, she asked what they would like to drink and he looked around the table.

"Is my nurse going to let me have wine tonight?" She looked at him with puppy dog eyes.

He chuckled. "Miriam, does your father still have that special chianti—the one with the smooth finish? And not too terribly dry?"

"Our house reserve. Yes, he certainly does." She smiled as he looked at Sandy and Maggie. When they nodded, Miriam wrote down their choice and left.

"Okay, Sandy," Billie said, and focused on her sister. "What happened with Gil?"

Sandy shrugged. "It's like Mom pointed out—he isn't the right one." She smiled. "When I questioned the change I saw in you after you met Billy again, I guess I was confused and maybe a little jealous. You're alive, sis. And I'm not." She looked away and then quickly at Billy. "And the way you look at my sister and the way you act around her. No man has ever looked or acted that way toward me." She shrugged. "So I decided a change is in order."

"A change?" Billie asked.

"Yup. I put in for a summer internship here at the hospital in pediatrics," Sandy confirmed as Miriam returned with wine glasses and the wine.

"Miriam," Billy asked, "can I trouble you for a stemless glass and a small bowl of ice? Billie likes her reds slightly chilled."

"Of course," she said, and went to the serving station.

He saw Maggie smiling at him and remembered her comment about him knowing her daughter.

When Miriam returned, she asked, "Is this just dinner or are you celebrating something?" She set the glasses out and poured for him to taste.

"I guess you might say we're still celebrating," Billie said, and smiled at him.

"They're having a wedding ceremony two weeks from Saturday," Maggie explained.

Miriam smiled and poured the glasses. "Congratulations to both of you." She briefly laid her hand on Billy's arm, then set the bottle in the chiller and asked if they had decided on their entrée. Billie noticed.

"Internship?" Billie asked when Miriam had gone to turn in their orders. "So you're thinking about staying here in the city?"

"Yes," Sandy said, and raised her glass in a toast. "To my little sister and you, Billy. To finding each other again after all of these years and the very best wishes for your life together. May every day be better than the one before."

They clinked glasses and sipped.

"Thanks, sis," Billie said. "You have what—one more year?"

"And if everything works out and if I like it here, I'm thinking of doing my residency and opening my practice here."

"Really? Oh, that would be wonderful," she said as she reached across the table and caught Sandy's hand.

"When will you know about your internship?" Billy asked.

"Maybe as early as next week. I gave them Mom and Dad's address. Once I know I'm accepted, I'll look for a place."

"Stay in my place until you know and decide what you want to do," Billy suggested, and felt Billie squeeze his arm. "I'm spending all of my time at Billie's and I'm never there anymore."

"Are you sure?" Sandy asked. "That's awfully generous of you. I'll pay the rent."

"Yes, I'm sure, Sandy." He smiled at Billie. "We'll talk about the rent later, but I want your sister to be happy too, and I think she will be very happy to get to know her sister again."

¤-¤-¤-¤-¤

When Maggie and Sandy said their goodnights and retired into Billy's apartment, they turned and started walking back to the Rover in the drive behind the buildings. Billie suddenly stiffened under his arm.

"I think I saw Hammersmith's car a little bit ago," she admitted as she slipped her arm around his waist. "Would you mind if we get Lynx and Hammer to do a little looking around with us before we go back home?"

"No. I don't mind." He studied her eager expression and led her to their door.

"Hey, Keeper, Tiger," Todd greeted when he opened his door.

"Are you and Cathy very busy?" Tiger asked in a rush.

Hammer shook his head and glanced back inside and asked, "Gotta minute?"

"Tiger wants to do a little looking around and was wondering if you'd come with us," Billy explained.

"Sure." He looked at Tiger as Lynx stopped beside him. "Looking for what?"

"Maybe Hammersmith," Tiger admitted. "Maybe not."

They both nodded and stepped out of the apartment. Lynx hurried to Cutter's apartment and brought Owl back to watch Abby. Then she followed them to Tiger's SUV.

As they crossed the Chestnut River going back into town, Tiger started watching each crossing street.

"What're you looking for?" Hammer asked, and started looking at the streets as well.

"I'm not sure," Tiger admitted, and turned south on Seventh West. At Pawnee, she turned and headed back east. "I think I saw Hammersmith's car earlier. Something Keeper said about him not succeeding when he tried to kill him before, and last night he lost again. Nolan has Joey, so it's pretty cut and dried that he hired them."

"I'm not sure I'm following you," Cathy admitted.

"Nolan didn't catch him last night, so I'm thinking he's going to try something else, quickly, while we're all still stirred up."

When Tiger reached the park just west of Hammersmith's design offices, she went around the block, checking the empty parking lot. She looked up at the building. "Aah, someone's in the offices."

"Could be a janitor," Lynx offered.

"Could be. Maybe not," Tiger surmised, and drove back west on Richmond.

At the west side of the park, Tiger spotted the familiar beat-up dark brown Honda in the street side parking spots.

"There's his weekend car," she exclaimed. "I bet he can't use his big car for fear that Nolan or one of the police officers will spot him."

"How do you know it's his weekend car?" Keeper asked as Tiger slowed and stopped beside it.

"That's his license plate—H-D-D-S-G-N-R. He used this car when he came in from his estate on weekends"—she grinned—"when he didn't want customers to know he was in the office."

"Okay, Tiger." Hammer opened his door and helped Lynx out. "What do you want us to do?"

"Let's cut through the park, spread out a little, and wait for him to start back to his car. I'll call Nolan and let him know where he is."

Tiger tapped the speed dial icon on her phone as the four of them started walking across the park. When Nolan answered, she explained where they were and what was happening.

"He's coming. He's also sending some additional officers." She grinned and looked up at Keeper.

"Good intuition, woman." He gently squeezed her shoulders. "I like a woman that can think."

"That's good. You're stuck with this one."

He grinned and they turned back to their pursuit.

After a few minutes of walking, Tiger glanced at the north side of the park and the lone figure walking hurriedly to the west. "There he is!"

Keeper turned and started trotting back the way they came. Tiger whispered loudly at Lynx a few yards away. "He's on the north side of the park. We're going to try to head him off."

Keeper took off in a hard run though the darkness, dodging trees as he closed the distance, keeping Hammersmith in sight. A hundred feet short of the parked Honda, he cut in front of Mike and stepped out of the shadows.

"Stop!" Keeper shouted, and spread his arms as if to embrace Mike, but held his knife tightly in his right hand. "Stop right now!"

Mike slowed, seeing the man suddenly appear and face him. He glanced around and tried to cut to the south, but Hammer stepped in front of him and forced him to stop and turn back the way he came.

"The police have Joey and Copper!" Keeper shouted as Lynx stepped out of the shadows and blocked his retreat to the east. "Give it up!"

Mike turned and took a step to the north, the only direction that seemed available, but Tiger stepped out, mere feet in front of him.

"Hello, Mr. Hammersmith," she said, and flicked the long knife, the blade flashing in the light from the streetlights. "Remember me?"

Mike's expression was hard to read in the dim light, but his surprise showed in his body language. Mike stopped and stepped backwards, and his hand quickly jerked from his pocket.

Keeper saw the flash of silver and recognized the gun. In reflex, he lunged and threw his knife as Mike's arm came up level.

-¤-

Tiger waited, crouched on the balls of her feet, as Mike stopped and stared at her. His surprise hidden in the darkness, she saw him step back and jerk the gun from his pocket.

She lunged, catching Mike's wrist with her left hand as the gun discharged. She felt Mike stiffen and scream a second before her right fist, tightly wrapped around the hilt of her long knife, crashed into his face.

The gun spun away and Mike's knees folded. He fell forward, facedown in the grass, and she stared at Keeper's knife lodged beneath Mike's right shoulder blade.

She looked up as Billy reached her, threw his arms around her, and pulled her tight against him.

"You okay?" he asked in a worried whisper.

"Yeah." She looked down at Mike's unconscious form. "We gotta stop meeting like this, Keeper," she said as Lynx stopped beside them with Hammer close behind.

"Is he dead?" Lynx asked.

-¤-

"No." Keeper sighed as he relaxed his hold on Tiger, bent down, and retrieved his knife. Hammer looked toward the sirens coming from the northeast. "I think you coldcocked him with your right jab. I was just trying to interrupt his aim."

"I guess you called Nolan," Hammer said, and grinned at Tiger's nod.

"I still can't get over how quick you two are." Lynx shook her head as she spoke.

"You want to be here when Nolan gets here or do you want to wait at the car?" Keeper asked, smiling at Lynx and Hammer. "Tiger and I can handle this if you want."

"We'll wait with you. Might help to have witnesses." Lynx squeezed Hammer and cocked her head at them.

"Could be a help at that," he said as the sirens stopped in the street beside the parking spots.

Keeper, with his arm still around Tiger, turned them to face the patrolmen as Nolan's patrol car hurried down Third Street West and slid to a stop behind the Honda. Keeper waved as Nolan got out and hurried across the small clearing toward them.

Ninety-Six

Friday, June 3

"Good morning, Detective," Tiger said as they stepped into Nolan's office.

"Glad you two could come." Detective Nolan got up from his chair. "I reserved a small room so we can talk in private."

Nolan led the way to a small room that Billie presumed was used for a number of different kinds of meetings in the course of a day or week. He gestured to the plain metal straight-backed chairs and took the single placed on the long side of the small table.

Keeper closed the door and sat down beside his mate, across from Detective Nolan.

"Has Hammersmith been charged yet?" Tiger asked before Nolan was completely settled.

"He will be officially charged around ten this morning," Nolan replied, and grinned at her. "Thanks for the call and for stopping him before he got away."

"Any idea on a trial date?" Keeper squeezed Tiger's hand.

"No. Each of the charges will be filed today." Nolan pointed to a finger as he itemized the list. "For being a drug dealer, because he paid the dealers to peddle their wares in the city center and in the village. For entering into a contract to kill you, Keeper, for hiring Knife, and then twice again for hiring Joey and Copper. And lastly, for killing your parents, Mr. Hawke, seventeen years ago." Nolan inhaled and thought a moment. "Yes, I think with what Tiger found and the positive lab results, we can confirm your original testimony, corroborate Mace's earlier testimony, placing him at the scene of the crime."

"So you think you have a good case?" Tiger pressed further.

"Yes, Tiger. I think we have a very good case to put him away for a very long time. One murder and three attempted murders does not make him look very good to a jury. The judge will set an arraignment hearing date in the next few weeks, and then a trial date will be set after the hearing."

"Thanks." Tiger nodded and hugged Keeper's arm. "What about Hannah?"

Nolan flipped through a number of sheets in a folder and then looked up at him.

"Okay. About Hannah. I'm a little confused." He looked at Keeper. "With all of your troubles with drug dealers and street assassins around the village and the department store, what led you to a missing person case like Hannah Quinn?"

He leaned forward and looked at Nolan with a grin. "Hammersmith. He led us to her."

"How on earth—?"

"Because of the arm-wrestling he did with my dad before they were killed," he explained. "As you know, I figured he had something to do with their death. My dad bought the Duckard properties from Warren, Mike's dad, four or five years before they were killed, apparently beating Mike out in the sale. Then Mace saw the man in the alley and I knew. I just couldn't do anything about it."

"Right," Nolan said. "We've been through that part."

Billy explained how he baited Hammersmith and how Hammersmith had Westman respond and offer to pay the back taxes.

"Westman did?"

Then he explained how Hammersmith planned a push to condemn the properties and most likely force them to be sold at auction.

"When Pink showed up, I knew Hammersmith was going

to try to get the properties condemned," he added.

"So what does all of this have to do with—?"

"At first nothing, but I've always wondered what would drive a successful man like Hammersmith to kill someone over a piece of property. I asked Tiger what sort of renovation Hammersmith had in mind, and when she said he wanted to tear the warehouse building down and start over and only renovate the department store building, I began to wonder what was in the warehouse building that wasn't in the other one."

"That's when," Tiger added, "Stretch and Keeper went looking and found the locked room. At first we couldn't figure out what the room was built for, but Cutter remembered Duckard's sold a lot of guns and ammunition and that was where they kept the explosive materials. Cutter said Owl worked there before they closed."

"When we found the room and saw that it was locked," Keeper continued, "I called my contacts and asked if there were any more keys floating around, identified or not. I received three in the mail the following week, but when Tiger got shot, all of my plans were put on hold."

"Things sort of got out of hand over the last couple of weeks," she admitted, "and we remembered Saturday after everything settled down that we needed to check."

"But what about your interest in Hannah?"

"Oh." Tiger pulled a stuffed folder out of her shoulder bag and spread a few images on the table. "That was because we wondered what Hammersmith did before he became a noted architect. As a young man he was quite the ladies' man. We found society rags about him and Hannah and their social life and then their engagement. Then we wondered why he hated tattoos so much—"

"Tiger was fired by Mike for having the mate to this one." Keeper held up his left wrist.

Tiger pushed a picture of Mike and Hannah to Nolan. "You can see what looks like a tattoo on her arm in this one, and..." She slid another across to him. "...in this one. Just after they announced their engagement, they both sported matching tats on their shoulders and upper arm. And that just made us more curious about why he hates tattoos now."

"We brain stormed a few minutes," he said, "and Tiger figured something split them up. I thought of a quarrel but Tiger jumped to another man. Have you figured out who was in the room with her?"

"I see." Nolan nodded. "I'm not sure of your logic process, but we did identify her body by forensics and we found her purse in the room. Driver's license, money, everything seems to be there, locked away when she was. We identified the other body as a male named George White. It appears she was romantically involved with him while she was leading everyone to believe she was happily engaged to Mike. Shortly before she disappeared, George lost his means and all of his properties to his gambling habit. He was homeless at the time they both disappeared."

"So Mike figured out what was happening and caught them," Tiger said softly.

Nolan grimaced. "The evidence looks like he decided to let them have each other, locking them away to let them live their last days and die together. But we can't prove he was the one that locked them away. Unless..." Nolan stopped and pulled an envelope out of his shirt pocket. He opened it and took a small, clear plastic bag out and laid it on the table between them. "Among cash and other things, we found this in a safe hidden in his bedroom, up at his place where Tiger was shot."

They leaned closer and studied the key in the sealed bag.

"That looks like this one." Keeper glanced at Tiger as he pulled the key ring out of his pants pocket. He selected the one he had used to open the steel door and compared the sawtooth pattern and grooves to the one in the bag.

Nolan smiled. "Keeper, if I could get a picture of your key, I think we might have a case to say who locked them away."

"Certainly." He smiled and Nolan called someone on his mobile phone. In minutes, a man with a camera entered the room, and he and Nolan proceeded to take pictures of the two keys.

"Well, that explains why Mike disliked tattoos and homeless people," Keeper said.

"He wanted to get into the building and move the bodies before anyone found out they were there." Tiger grinned at him.

"Looks like it." Nolan handed him his key ring and the man with the camera left the room. "It looks like I can add the murder of Hannah Quinn and George White to the list of charges—now three murders and three attempted murders.

"Now, one more thing. When we went through Mike's personal and work emails, we found a number of interesting emails from a deceased sender claiming Mike had removed enough people, claiming Keeper knows something, and a number of other interesting claims along with telling him he was running out of time. Do you know anything about them, Keeper? And what did you know?"

Tiger cocked her head. "Emails? You never told me about sending him emails."

Keeper smiled and then turned back to Nolan. "The sender is obviously not deceased. You know my full name is William Carson Hawke, W.C. Hawke. Just like my dad and his dad before him. Now Mike, thinking that everyone died in the car wreck, jumped to the conclusion that dad might still be alive or his ghost was somehow—I just pushed his paranoia a bit. Then I set Keeper up as bait, to draw him out."

"But you almost got yourself killed by doing that," Nolan said.

Keeper nodded. "The part I feel the worst about is that Ditto did get killed because I set things up."

"Mace said Ditto pushed you aside," Nolan said, "and got hit instead of you. He saved your life, Keeper."

"I know." He looked at Tiger. "I bet my life on Tiger being able to stop Joey and she did, but I think it was Copper that shot Ditto."

"He did," Nolan agreed. "He saw us coming and got off a rushed shot before we could stop him. Tiger saved you from Joey, and Ditto saved you from Copper. You are a very lucky man, Keeper."

"Yes, Nolan. I am," he said, and smiled softly at Tiger. "Maybe more lucky than I deserve to be, but very lucky indeed."

"Have you made any arrangements for Ditto?" Nolan asked as he closed his folder. "Or is the state going to handle it?"

"Yeah, we did." Keeper smiled. "We bought a plot next to the Hawke's family plot, where my parents and grandparents are buried. We'll have a graveside service when the coroner releases his body."

"The headstone will be ready in two weeks," Tiger added, "and we'll place it after that."

Nolan nodded. "I'm glad Ditto had friends too. He was a good and brave man."

Ninety-Seven

"Ooh, Mama, look..." Abby half sighed as she entered the boutique ahead of Tiger and her mother. "Look at all of the dresses. Are you going to get a new dress?"

Cathy smiled and followed Abby as she gingerly touched the long white and pastel-colored dresses hung on the rack nearest the front door. She looked over her shoulder at her mother as she felt the lacy fabric. She quickly looked around the rack and saw the other racks of similar dresses.

"No dear," Cathy admitted. "Tiger said she saw some that might fit you."

"Me?" Abby turned in surprise and looked at her mother and at Tiger.

"You are going to be my flower girl," Tiger said softly, and grinned. "And your mom and I thought you should have a nice dress for the occasion."

"Wow," she whispered, and turned back to the racks. "They have little ones too?"

"Not little, but they do have your size," Cathy added, and took Abby's hand as Tiger led them to an area off to one side of the store.

Tiger stopped at a rack with nice party dresses and glanced at Abby.

"I think these are close to your size." She winked at Abby. "Now you need to look for something you and your mom like. If you don't see anything, I found a few other stores that might have something."

Tiger stood back and watched as Cathy and Abby searched the two racks, eventually collecting an armful of things for

Abby to try on. Cathy followed her bouncing daughter into the dressing rooms and Tiger found a chair to wait.

The first three did not fit like Cathy wanted and the fourth was a bit too short for Cathy's taste, making Abby look too much like a big toddler. Tiger laughed at their trials and helped Cathy when she needed to look at the racks for other dresses. They were about out of choices until the clerk checked another rack in a different section of the store and came back with two additional dresses—a white and a pale pink one—both similar in style to one that Abby liked, but that did not fit right.

Abby instantly focused on the simpler white dress with an embroidered vest style over-jacket and knee-length skirt. The hem was trimmed with matching white floral embroidery, setting the dress off nicely.

"Ooh, this one, Mama." Abby held the dress in front of her and twirled, watching herself in the mirror.

Tiger glanced at the tag and winked at the clerk. Then she turned to Cathy. "If she leaves the jacket off, she will look wonderful at school functions. I know she's young but if there are any other special occasions, like *another wedding*, she will be the star of the show, except for the bride."

"I forgot about that." Cathy smiled at Tiger. "We haven't found him yet, but we're still hoping."

"Us too," Tiger said, and caught her hand. "Go try this one on, Abby."

Reluctantly, pulled by her excited daughter, Cathy followed Abby into the dressing room. A few minutes later, Abby danced out wearing the dress and jacket. She stopped and stared at herself in the tall mirror.

"Mama? Is that me?" She looked at her mother and smiled when Cathy nodded. "I look... pretty."

Tiger chuckled and knelt down beside her. "You look beautiful."

And Abby beamed.

Cathy watched, tears running down her face as Abby

studied the dress and turned, almost missing it when Tiger gestured for the clerk to come closer.

"Is your seamstress available?" Tiger asked. "I want her to make any necessary alterations. This is so perfect, we want it to look absolutely stunning."

"Yes, ma'am," the clerk said, and hurried into the back of the store.

A moment passed and a woman near Tiger's age greeted them and asked Abby if she could look at her dress. Abby stood very still and listened to the woman as she pinned a tuck here and there and marked places where the dress pulled a little.

"It will take very little alteration," the seamstress said to Abby, turning her around in front of the mirror. "You are a very pretty young lady. Is this for a special occasion?"

Abby looked at Tiger. "I'm going to be her flower girl at her wedding!"

"Wow," the seamstress said softly. "That's quite an honor."

Abby nodded and then looked over her shoulder at her mother. "Am I going to wear this when you and Daddy get married?"

Cathy, caught by surprise, glanced at the seamstress and then stared at Abby for a moment before she put her words together. She was glad the seamstress did not seem to have an opinion about her marital status, one way or another. "Yes, yes you are."

"When will that be, Mama?"

"As soon as we can arrange it, dear."

"Okay." Abby turned her attention back to her image in the mirror.

-¤-

Abby was dancing between them as they walked along St. Anne and Cathy confided to Tiger. "I don't know what I'm going to do if we can't find him and get him to agree to the divorce," Cathy admitted. A dark cloud had slowly formed over her, dampening the earlier joy of the shopping spree. "Thank you for the dress. It's so much more than I expected. You really shouldn't have spent so much on it."

"It's okay," Tiger soothed. "It wasn't that expensive, and besides, when he does agree, we won't have to shop for her again. She'll be set and ready."

"Thanks again. I can't believe how happy she is over it. She's never had a new, really new dress before. And now she has a really beautiful one. I just hope she doesn't start a growing spurt before she gets to enjoy it some."

Tiger chuckled and Abby looked up at them when Tiger continued. "You are very welcome. And don't let yourselves get too depressed over the divorce issues. We'll keep looking, and the clerk in Judge Parker's office is looking also. That might help."

"I sure hope so."

"Don't worry Mama. It'll work out. Keeper always said things would, and now Tiger's telling us too. It'll be wonderful. And soon, I bet."

Cathy smiled at her daughter. "I hope so, dear."

"Wait and see. You said we had to wait to get a home and we did and now we have one. And even if you and Daddy can't get married, he's still my daddy and you're still my mama. And I'll still get to wear my new dress." Abby smiled at her mother and then glanced around in surprise. "Where are we going?"

"Lunch with Keeper," Tiger said.

Abby beamed, smiling from ear to ear. "At the restaurant?"

¤-¤-¤-¤-¤

"You guys found a dress in one day?" Sandy asked as she waited in her sister's living room.

"Yeah, and it needs very little alteration," Billie said as she put her good clothes in her backpack. "You have a change of clothes?"

"Sure. Mom said she'd be back in on Tuesday to take you for a final fitting."

"I think Mom and I went to every store in the city that carried wedding dresses." Billie checked her look in her mirror. "And we found a dress for Abby. What do you think, Keeper?"

"Hmm, I don't know." He smiled at her. "Are you trying to liven up the ol' kitchen?"

"Just a little." She kissed him. "I think a little color should be okay."

He grinned at her and eyed the bright pastel jumper, faded jeans, and her lightly scuffed low-topped boots.

"Come on." She kissed him again and grabbed her backpack. "I've seen that look a hundred times, and you'll just have to wait until we get home."

At the bottom of the stairs, he collected his backpack and followed them out.

-□-

The walk up First and across Crescent was pleasant, and for some reason Tiger felt the air was less tense. She asked Billy if he thought there were more people out than usual, and he said he had to agree that it looked like it. She was feeling almost relaxed by the time the three of them crossed Tenth Street East and reached the kitchen.

They went in and stashed their backpacks as usual, freshened up, and then went to greet Randy and get their duty assignments. Tiger reintroduced Sandy, and the manager was pleased when Sandy said she was trying to get a job in the city and maybe she could help more often. Keeper chose the walk-around duty again, clearing tables and getting anything extra people needed while they ate; Tiger got soups, and Sandy got the breads and fruits.

When Tiger led them out of the kitchen to the serving line, she stopped at the pot and Sandy stood beside her at the trays. She grabbed her ladle and started to fill a bowl, but someone called her name and she looked up to see the entire room standing and facing the counter. Someone said "Tiger" again and then repeated it as they began to clap.

Sandy stepped back and just stared at her sister. After a moment, she glanced at Billy standing at the end of the serving counter with his towel and a wide smile.

Totally unprepared and not knowing what to do, Tiger smiled with a little shrug and started filling bowls. Billy walked around the end of the counter and stopped behind her, slipped his arms around her waist, and hugged her from behind. When the people cheered, she turned around and buried her face against his chest. "What's going on, Keeper?"

The people quieted and she looked back as an older man, walking with short, uncertain but purposeful steps, slowly approached the counter and smiled.

"From all of us to you," the man said, and extended his hand to shake hers.

Billy gently turned her around and pushed her to the counter, and she shook the man's hand in response.

"We don't have much, but we want to thank you for being our friend and for helping Keeper keep things safe for those of us that can't. Everyone knows Keeper, and now they know his Tiger too. You have made this a very happy and pleasant day. Thank you, Tiger. I don't think anyone will mess with Keeper or his Tiger. Bless you, Tiger. Bless you both."

Slowly the man turned and carefully walked back to his table. He turned again, smiled at her, and then sat down.

"I...don't know what to say," Billie said to the room, and inhaled deeply, "except you're very welcome for what little I've done. I'm very glad I could help, and I'm very happy to call you my friends. Thank you."

Someone started the clapping again, and Tiger smiled and wrapped her right arm around Billy's waist. She took his left hand with hers and held them up in front of them to show off the real wrist tats side by side.

"So, that's your sister?" Chase said as he stepped up beside Sandy at the counter. "I know you pointed her out before you left last week, but it really didn't click."

"Hi, Chase," she said, and served the woman that was next in line. "Nice to see you again. Yeah, that's my little sister. She and Keeper are getting married in a couple of weeks, but I certainly didn't know she was a celebrity."

"Well, from the talk I hear"—Chase nodded at them—"she's someone they can trust, and not one to mess with. I hear she caught one of the gunmen Wednesday night. Held him with a long knife until the cops could collect him."

"Really? Well, she is pretty good with that knife. I actually saw her put down six or seven when the village was attacked. Keeper and his friends did a good job teaching her how to defend herself and protect others."

"I understand he's the second man with a gun she's stopped and held for the police. Does this kind of tenacity run in the family?"

"It might. If I get my summer internship here, Tiger says I'll start training in my spare time and then we'll find out."

"Internship?" He looked at her, grinning. "You're looking to intern here? And you're going to train?"

"Hey, Tiger?" Sandy nudged her sister. "Okay to invite another tonight?"

Tiger looked at Sandy and smiled at Chase. "Sure. If he can come, I'll have Lori set up an extra chair."

Sandy looked back at Chase. "We're going out with some of Tiger's friends after. You're welcome to come and I can explain a few things."

"Sure. I'll have to take my rides back, but I can meet you."

"Tiger? Where are we going?"

"Custer's at nine."

Ninety-Eight

Saturday, June 18

Bob, the ranch foreman Jake, and two ranch hands were outside waiting in their Sunday finest when the chartered tour bus arrived and stopped in front of the stable. Bob personally greeted each person as they got off, and one of the hands distributed ceremony announcements and small net bags of quinoa for after the service. Jake and the other ranch hand directed the guests to the path markings for the short walk to the smaller, southern lake.

Maggie looked out the kitchen window and smiled at the procession. She had told Bob earlier how thankful she was the weather was doing its best to make it a great day for Billie, and with the light, scattered clouds and the abundant trees, she knew the sun would not be too hot.

"Billie," she called louder than necessary as she walked through the family room and headed for the bedrooms. "The bus has arrived and your friends are going down to the lake. How are you coming?"

Maggie stopped in the doorway when she reached Billie's old bedroom and smiled at the woman she saw in the stunning, fitted white dress.

"Do you think he'll like it, Mom?" Billie asked as she turned and looked at herself in the full-length mirror.

"Such a silly question," she said as Sandy straightened the short train. "He's been smitten with you most of his life—even when you were young and covered in mud from wrestling in the yard and now, even when you're in your kitchen clothes."

"I'd say what you wear doesn't really matter," Sandy said,

227

and stood up, "but sis, I have to say you are very beautiful. Beaming, in fact."

"Thanks, Sandy," Billie said, and gently pressed the front of the dress with her open hands. "I want to look good for him."

"I think, Sandy," Maggie said, "we're as ready as we can be. Let your father know she's ready whenever they are."

-¤-

On the small stage Bob and the ranch hands had prepared beside the small lake, Billy stood, waiting with Sid as his best man and Stretch as a second groomsman and friend. Lori waited as Billie's bridesmaid beside the open spot for Sandy as her second bridesmaid. He looked up and smiled as Sandy hurried up the aisle and took her place beside Lori.

He looked over the seated guests, hoping the Hawke-vs.-Carson name disclosure in the announcements did not surprise anyone. He and Billie had worried about making the announcement, but in the end he had taken it upon himself to try to meet with and tell everyone ahead of time.

On his side of the aisle, he smiled at his aunt Mary in the first seat of the first row, chatting with those around her. He smiled at the rest of his side of the aisle—their friends from the apartments and others he knew from the city. He was pleased the Willis family had made it, and he was especially happy that Monica had brought little William. Nick Florentini—with his wife and Miriam and his other two daughters—sat near the Streetcar staff and he chuckled to himself, noting it was the first time he remembered seeing Ned on time. Grier Filton and Walter Gibson had settled in the back row with their wives and older children, and all in all Billy was pleased his friends had taken the time to come and share the day with him and Billie.

Most of the people on Billie's side of the aisle he did not know beforehand, but he was happy with how many of her relatives had come. Maggie sat in the first seat on Billie's side of the aisle, with a space for Bob between her and Bob's parents, Billie's paternal grandparents, and his sisters' families. Maggie's parents and brother sat just past them, and Becky and Stacy with Tom beside her, sat just behind Maggie in the second row. Of the others, he only recognized those few he had met or re-met in the past two weeks when they had come out to the ranch to help get things ready for their *big day* .

In that couple of weeks, he and Billie had revisited many of the old haunts they had experienced as kids: the woods where she had broken her leg and cried in his arms until her sister could get help, the lakes where they had fished and paddled around in canoes, the many places she had wrestled and "fought" with him, and the flagstone patio where they had spent quiet nights in front of the fire pit with their folks. He had to laugh. As special as they were, the quiet nights and the fire pit with Billie beside him meant a lot more to him now than it had when they were kids.

Abby, in her very pretty white embroidered dress and vest jacket, stopped at the foot of the aisle with her large basket of flower petals and Billy smiled as she slowly walked to the front, tediously spreading the petals to evenly color the path for Billie. When she was nearly to the front, someone started the processional music and Bob led Billie to the foot of the aisle.

Billy forgot about everything else after that, unable to take his eyes off her as she came toward him in her shimmering, cleanly styled, fitted dress with a modest neckline and short sleeves, accented by her beautiful, curly red hair and a stylish, white, billed cap holding her veil.

The ceremony and the repeating of their vows went more quickly than he remembered it had the first time, though he had to admit later, this time he spent most of the ceremony lost in her beautiful green eyes and speaking from his heart. They exchanged rings and the minister recited the blessing and pronouncement.

He was not surprised that when the minister said he could kiss the bride, she jumped up and threw her arms around his neck, his arms instantly wrapping around her, holding her tight. She held him in her kiss until he finally had to breathe, and they laughed at each other as he slowly lowered her to the stage and then they turned to face family and guests. Behind them, he heard the minister present "Mr. and Mrs. Hawke."

-¤-

They posed for the many traditional wedding pictures along with a few impromptu—some with him holding her, cradled in his arms, her unexpected, polished, white low-top boots peeking out from under the hem of her long dress. They kissed in as many of the pictures as they could, finally forcing the photographer to tell them to stop when he was ready to shoot.

They cut the cake and toasted the guests and each other and did all of the traditional necessities until they reached the time for lunch, after which the party and fun could begin. While the guests began eating, they returned to the house and changed into nice-but-more-casual clothes: new jeans, boots, and matching western-yoked white shirts with their names, "Mrs. Billie Carson Hawke" and "Mr. Billy Carson Hawke," embroidered over the left breast pockets.

"Well, Mrs. Hawke," he asked as he stopped her at the kitchen door. "Have I told you how incredibly beautiful you are?"

"Not in the last few minutes."

"Well, you most certainly are the most beautiful thing I've ever seen, and I have a wedding present for you, Mrs. Hawke." He took an envelope out of his back pocket and unfolded it. "With Mike Hammersmith no longer able to run a renovation design firm, Carl and Robert had to figure out how to keep their business going."

"And how did they decide to do that?" she asked slowly, cocking her head and watching him.

"It seems the best way was to get a new partner and to replace the old business name with a new one." He handed her the envelope.

She opened the flap and took the enclosed letter out and began reading. Her eyes grew wide and she looked up at him. "It says their new business is Boster, Lange and Hawke. Are you—"

"No, you are." He smiled. "If you want it. Walter and Grier have worked on the arrangements for a month, and if you want it, either as an active or as a silent partner, you're a full, equal partner in your new business. Three-way ownership, no juniors and no seniors."

"I...don't know what to say." She smiled, stared at him, and then looked back at the letter.

He smiled back at her. "They also have a new contract to handle the interior decorations and appointments, working with Kelly and Lloyd Architects out of Chicago, for the new Hawke's Residence Plaza in Chesterfield's city center—pending, of course, on the decision of the newest partner to take on the job."

She jumped up and wrapped her arms around his neck. He squeezed her in response.

"Carl and Robert don't know 'who' this Mrs. Hawke is, but they understand the details and that she will have exclusive design control over the owner's residence on the eleventh and twelfth floors and final approval authority for the apartment designs on the tenth floor."

She lowered herself to the floor and then hugged him again. "I know this is just your way to make me go back to work and stop loafing around."

"Maybe, but I understand partners do get to pick and choose what they want to do and how many hours they want to spend doing it. And for the other projects we've talked about, like the small houses for the village residents to replace the cardboard hovels, I know of a very good construction firm in the city that doesn't have any local projects on their plate."

"Hmm. And who might that be, I wonder? The owner wouldn't perchance be remarrying his ex-wife, would he?" she asked.

"I think that's the one." He bent and cupped her face between his palms and gently kissed her again. "And with Carl and Robert's old business closed, they have forgiven the Duckard Project's default payment."

"That's wonderful."

"Only if you want to try, Tiger. It's yours if you want it."

"Might be fun." She folded the envelope and slipped it into her back jeans pocket. "I'll think about it." Then she grabbed his hand, squeezed it, and pulled the back door open. "Come on, you handsome rascal. Let's go eat, party, and play."

-◻-

They were almost to the array of picnic tables and eating guests when Abby saw them, jumped off her bench, and ran headlong into Billie.

"Tiiggeerr!" she squealed.

When Billie knelt down and hugged her, Abby looked up at the two of them, deep concerns in her eyes. "Are you still Tiger and Keeper?"

"Yes, we most certainly are," she said, and squeezed her. "Billy will always be Keeper and I'll always be his Tiger."

"Good," she said emphatically, and smiled. "That's good."

"You need to go and finish eating," Billy added, and hugged her as well. "Then you need to change into play clothes so you can go riding and any of the other things we have to do."

"Okay, Keeper," she said, and ran back to the bench and her mom.

Billy spotted Sid carrying two plates of food through the seated guests, and he took Billie's hand and followed. They stopped and greeted Mary as Sid settled into a chair beside her.

"Aunt Mary," Billy said, "I know you've seen Billie in the diner, but I don't think you've actually met."

"Not officially, Billy," Mary said, and extended her hand to Billie. "I am so happy for you, for the both of you, especially for finding each other again."

"Thank you. It's wonderful to meet you, Mary," Billie said. "I'm also sorry we've been so preoccupied that we haven't taken the time before now."

"With all that you have faced since you two found each other again," Mary said, shaking her head slowly, "and with me only coming to the diner at off-peak times, I knew we'd have to wait to meet." She smiled at them and then caught Billie's hand. "Your mother and father would be very proud of you and of your choices, Billy."

"Thanks, Aunt Mary," he said. "I know Dad understood."

"Now," Mary said, straightening her shoulders and smiling at both of them, "you need to get something to eat and go visit with your guests. We can visit later, at the diner."

Billie leaned over and gave Mary a hug, thanking her again, and then she let Billy lead her away. When they reached the serving line and she had picked up her plate, Angie stopped beside them.

"I thought you were Carson all these years," Angie said.

"I still am. Carson's my middle name, Angie. Remember?" Billy explained again.

"Oh yeah," she said. "And Billie said she was family now. Does that mean you're related to Sid?"

"Sid's my cousin on my mother's side and Mary's my aunt—my mother's sister." He smiled.

"Wow," Angie said, finally putting it together.

"Have you eaten?" he asked, gesturing for her to go ahead of them.

"Oh, sorry," Angie said. "Yes. You should go ahead. I didn't mean to be keeping you."

"No problem, Angie," Billie said, and looked down the table. "Please have more if you like. Are you going to go riding later?"

"Really? I thought that was just for the little kids."

"For the bigger kids too," he said as he gestured for Billie to start ahead of him.

As they settled and started eating, Cathy and Todd stopped and sat down across from them. She was smiling brightly, almost giddy as she slid a thin stack of stapled papers to Billie to look at.

"He agreed. He signed it!" Cathy said happily, barely able to sit still. "And Justice Parker got it stamped."

"Really?" Billie asked in surprise. "You found him and he agreed? It's done?"

"Clark said he didn't know an address where I could be found," Cathy explained. "He wants to remarry too, so he was willing to sign, and not requesting child support cinched the deal."

"I'm so happy for you," Billie said, and caught her hand.

"So what about you two?" Billy asked.

"Early next month," Cathy said, and glanced at Todd. "Judge Parker filed our application on the fifteenth, Wednesday."

"The second or the ninth," Todd added.

Then Cathy looked at Billie with a sheepish smile. "Tiger, will you go dress shopping with me? Nothing fancy like yours, but you do have a nice sense of style and fit."

Billie smiled. "Of course I will. Just say when."

"Thanks, Tiger," she said, then picked up her decree and looked at Billy. "Keeper? Were you serious with what you said to us about the department store?"

"I was," he admitted. "It's completely up to each of you, but Billie and I have set the entire tenth floor aside to be apartments for the rest of our extended 'family,' if any of them, including you three, are interested in living there with us."

Cathy smiled. "That building and neighborhood are more like home than anywhere I've lived since I was a child," Cathy admitted. "And to not live in the basement and to be able to go and come like we belong there, without worry, would be wonderful. You said we could either lease or purchase the apartments?"

"Yes we did," Billie said, and squeezed Keeper's arm. "Either way, the monthly costs will be similar to the rent you pay at the River Crest. To help you decide, we can get together whenever you want and we'll give you all of the details for all of the options."

Cathy shook her head and glanced at Todd and then turned to Billy. "Why are you doing this? It's so...so...generous."

"I want to share my good fortune." He covered Cathy's hand with his and glanced at Todd. "Tiger and I wouldn't have a now or a future if it weren't for friends like you two and the rest of our basement family. Besides"—he smiled and glanced at Todd—"we're also nosy. If we don't have to, we don't want to have to chase all over town to see how everyone is doing. We've gotten spoiled being able to see and visit with everyone almost every day."

"Please think about it," Billie said. "And let me know. If you're interested, I'm supposed to work with the decorators to personalize each apartment."

"Thank you, Tiger, Keeper. We'll definitely think about it. But now, I need to get Abby changed." Smiling hugely, Cathy got up. "She's being so very patient with me."

"Go and have fun," Billie said, and gestured for them to go ahead. "We adults will party later and we'll do some shopping and planning when we get back in the city."

Almost everyone there stopped to say hello and to offer their congratulations while the two of them ate, and they were almost finished when Maggie and Sandy, with Chase in tow, sat down beside them.

"Sandy has some news," Maggie said as they settled at the picnic table.

"Your internship?" Billie asked, and held Sandy's wide smile.

"Yup. I start Monday."

"That's wonderful," Billie said, and caught Sandy's hand. She winked at Sandy when Chase squeezed Sandy's shoulders.

"And I want you to see what your dad found the other day," Maggie added, and handed Billie an old photograph in a thick frame, captured between two pieces of glass with clear space around the picture.

Billie smiled and held it so Billy could see the two kids standing on a wooden pier with fishing poles in their hands. She looked at her mom. "Us?"

Maggie nodded. "That was the day you two met for the first time. Billy's dad took it. I had it framed so you can put it out and always remember."

"Look at the back," Sandy said with a wide, knowing smile.

Billie turned the picture over and saw the aged, penciled date, *June 18*, and the year was twenty-two years earlier.

"How can that be?" Billie asked, and looked at Billy.

"There was a reason you had to renew your vows today," Maggie said.

Billie turned and looked at her mom and then at Sandy's smile. "Renew? You knew?"

"I knew. Just not when, exactly," Maggie said. "I noticed a change in you two that could only mean one thing: you'd gotten married and your lives had changed."

"Cathy said she noticed too," Billie admitted.

"Tuesday, May the twenty-fourth," he said. "That first walk we took after she was released from the hospital. We went and saw Justice Parker and then I took her to the bank to inventory my safe deposit box and to give her a key. I wanted her as my heir, beneficiary, if anything happened to me, but the reality was that I couldn't wait any longer. Especially after she had been shot and I realized I could have lost her again—really lost her. She had to know I was serious and I had to show her that she was the most important thing in my life."

"Are you upset?" Billie asked, and took her mom's hand.

"No dear," Maggie said. "I knew you had a reason to elope and that you had a reason that it needed to remain a secret. You two have done very well at keeping secrets, but this one you couldn't hide so easily."

Billie smiled. "I'm glad that one was hard to keep. I want everyone to know how I feel about Billy and how he feels about me."

"As often as I can," he said, and leaned over and kissed her again, "I promise to do my best to remind everyone how much Keeper loves his Tiger."

The End

Keeper and His Tiger: The Trap

Glossary

Characters:

-A-

Abby — Daughter of Cathy (Lynx). Seven years old.

-B-

Bennett, Dave — Owner of a well-known and respected paving company located in a Chesterfield suburb, Briar's Green.

Bennett, Tom — Son of Dave Bennett. Stacy's latest boyfriend.

Betty — Mike Hammersmith's secretary at Boster, Lange and Hammersmith Designs.

Billie Mattis — See, Mattis, Billie.

Billy Carson — See Carson, Billy.

Boster, Carl — Partner in Boster, Lange and Hammersmith Renovation and Design Consulting Company.

Butch — An undercover cop helping in the City Center.

Butler, Sid — Owner of The Streetcar Diner.

Butler, Mary — Sid Butler's mother. Sister of Dorothy Hawke.

-C-

Carson, Billy — 31 year old homeless man. Has worked as a dishwasher and scullery man at The Streetcar Diner for seventeen years.

Copper — Streetwise drug dealer. Competitor of Pink's. Tries to sell drugs in the city center after Pink died.

-D-

Davis, Lori	26 year old, blonde woman, Accountant for Swaggard's Drugstore at Main and Branch Water Street. Long-time friend of Billie Mattis.
Diner Staff, Streetcar	Sid Butler – Owner and Head Cook
	Billy – General Scullery duties – Sid's background assistant
	Angie – Dining Room Manager and Head Waitress
	Julie – Waitress and Counter Attendant
	Carole – Waitress
	Melony – Order Organizer
	Niles – Assistant Cook
	Kevin – Assistant Cook
	Ned – Assistant Dishwasher
Donna	Frederick Westman's secretary at Westman Associates.

-F-

Filton, Grier	An Executive officer at the First State Bank and Trust. Billy's financial advisor.
Fowler, Gilbert	Sandy's college boyfriend. Medical Grad School student studying Neurological Medicine.

-G-

George, Rebecca	25 year old, brunette woman, the Assistant Curator at the City's Arts and Culture Museum. Friend of Billie Mattis. Aka, Becky or Beck.
Gibson, Walter	Attorney specializing in Business Law. Billy's personal Legal Council.

GC — General Contractor. The lead contractor on a construction job. Often referred to as the General.

-H-

Hammersmith, Mike — Principal partner and founder of Boster, Lange and Hammersmith Renovation and Design Consulting Company.

Hawke, William Carson III — Son of W. C. Hawke II and Dorothy (Dottie) Hawke (both mudered).

Herb — One of Mike Hammersmith's henchmen. A mean sort.

Homeless People — Department Store 'Street People' & their '(Street name)'

Billy (Keeper)

Max (Stretch) and Mindy (Cat)

Todd (Hammer)

Cathy** (Lynx), daughter Abby

Russell (Mace) and Barbara (Pigeon), son Ernest

Paul (Ferret*) and Donna (Mouse*), son Richard

Buddy (Falcon) and Jane (Sparrow*), son Rusty

Curt (Cutter) and Judy (Owl)

Josh (Red)

Randal (Spear)

Junior (Ditto)

* have a talent for hearing what's happening on the streets.

** Cathy's maiden name was Nikleson, married to and abandoned by Clark Jefferson.

-J-

Joey	One of Mike Hammersmith's henchmen.
June	Contracts Administrator at Westman Associates.

-K-

Keeper	The street name of a homeless man that has protected a number of blocks and properties in the City Center. Tiger's squeeze.
Kelly, Chase	32 year old owner of a Medical Supply business. Volunteers at the Crescent Street soup kitchen.

-L-

Lange, Robert	Partner in Boster, Lange and Hammersmith Renovation and Design Consulting Company.
Lawrence, Blake	Billie's recent ex-boyfriend. A con artist with a bad temper.
Leonard, The Knife	Street-wise, self-proclaimed 'exterminator' known for removing two-legged problems for a price.
Lori Davis	See Davis, Lori

-M-

Majors, Stacy	26 year old brunette woman. Works as a sales clerk and stocker at Pages Bookstore. Friend of Billie Mattis. Dating Tom Bennett.
Markins, Jack	Son of Billie's parent's long-time friends. Fiancé of Katie Biggens

Mattis, Billie	Wilhelmina Georgiana Mattis, a red haired woman, 27 year old daughter of Bob and Maggie Mattis. Works for Boster, Lange and Hammersmith Real Estate Developers and Renovations Consultants. Graduate with Master's degree in Business and Business Law (non-Barred). One older sister, Sandra, living away.
Mattis, Sandy	aka Sandra Mattis. The 30 year old daughter of Bob and Maggie Mattis; Billie's sister. Studying to become a Doctor in Pediatrics.
Mattis, Bob and Maggie	Robert (Bob) and Margaret (Maggs, Maggie), parents of Sandy and Billie. Owners and operators of a viable horse ranching business.
Maxie	Street vendor selling flowers on the north side of St. Charles Street, across from the park nick-named "The Forest."
Mitchell	Frederick Westman's 'go for' person.
-N-	
Nolan, Detective	A Chesterfield city police detective. A friend of Billy Carson.
-P-	
Pink	Street-wise drug dealer with his eye on the Chesterfield's City Center to expand his area of business.
-Q-	
Quinn, Hannah	A local socialite woman, once engaged to Mike Hammersmith in his younger days.

-R-

Rebecca (Becky), George   See George, Rebecca

-S-

Simmy   Street vendor that has a newsstand business near the west side of City Center.

Stacy Majors   See Majors, Stacy

-T-

Tiger   Keeper's squeeze.

-W-

Westman, Collin   Daughter of Nancy and Frederick Westman. No siblings. Student at Michigan State University, East Lansing, Michigan, studying to become a veterinarian.

Westman, Frederick   Real Estate Developer. Daughter Collin. Ex-wife Nancy, divorced sixteen years.

Westman, Nancy   Frederick Westman's ex-wife.

Places and Things:

-B-

Baily   A small farm town NE of Chesterfield. Mike Hammersmith's sister lives there.

-C-

Chesterfield   A middle sized, sprawling mid-west city in the United States. The city had an eighteen block City Center core with high rise buildings, the tallest being fourteen stories. The city is serviced by a regional airport and local and interstate bus services.

CR Associates   Circular Reference, Subsidiary of Pastoric Group – General Manager: John Collier.

Custer's   An eating and drinking establishment located in a strip-mall on the NE corner of Lakota and Fourth Street East.

-D-

Daisy's   A Wine Bar, NW of City Center located at Emmit and Fifth Street West.

Danny's Steakhouse   Distinguished Steak and Beverage Restaurant on Calvin and Duberry. Owned by Danny Willis and his three daughters, Lydia the youngest, Monica in the middle and Nikki (Nicole) the oldest.

Duckard's Department Store   Deserted department store building in a shared block in City Center. Situated at the corner of Second and Baker St

-F-

Forest, The   A city park in west Chesterfield bordered by St. Charles Street on the north, St. Anne on the south, and by Fifth and Sixth Street West on the east and west sides.

-K-

Kelly and Lloyd Architects   Chicago based Architectural Firm specializing in large commercial renovation projects. Owner: Jim Donaldson

Site review architects: Bob Dawson, Joseph, Jane, Lucy

-M-

Marquee Cocktail Lounge   A modern downtown cocktail lounge on the NW corner of Main Street and St. Anne.

-O-

Olive and Onion   A Martini Bar at David and Twelfth Street West.

-P-

Pages Book Store   Book store on Main between St. Anne and Arapaho. Stacy works here.

Pastoric Group   Investment group holding and protecting W. C. Hawke's assets. Controlled by W. C. Hawke III and daily operations managed by Gregory (Greg) Madison.

-S-

Streetcar Diner, The   A shiny, metal-look diner on the west side of City Center. Owner: Sid Butler.

Swaggard's Drug Store   Drug store on Kiowa and 7th Street West. Lori works as an accountant and general clerk / stocker here.

-T-

Tri-Funds   Subsidiary of Pastoric Group.

-W-

Westman Associates   A land development and construction company owned by Frederick Westman.

Whiskey's Bar and Grille A rustic casual dining bar and grille on the NE corner of Blackfoot and Sixth Street, two blocks south of "The Forest."

Books by Aidan Red:

Keeper and His Tiger
(After living homeless to find his parents murderer...)
Book 1: An Unexpected Complication
Book 2: Deadly Undercurrents
Book 3: The Trap

Paladin Shadows Series
Terran Assignment
Book 1: Things Are Not As They Seem
Book 2: When Luck Is Not Enough
Book 3: Fate Has A Different Idea
Terran Recruits
Book 4: In the Wake of Chaos
Book 5: Terran Talents Join Forces
Book 6: New Rules of Engagement
Operation Retribution
Book 7: The Training Phase
Book 8: Taking the Fight Off-World
Book 9: Luring the Prince Into the Open
Garda Nua
Book 10: The Proliferation of Talent
Book 11: When A Planet Is Stolen
Book 12: Right Does Not Ask Permission
Assignment: Casha-Six
Book 13: No Warning
Book 14: The Best Laid Plans
Book 15: A Change of Heart?

Fearin' the Banshee

More Books by Aidan Red

Eight's Warning
A West's Ghost Ranch Trilogy
(A tale in the world of high octane aviation fuel and restored warbirds)

Book 1: The Past Hunts
Book 2: The Past Attacks
Book 3: The Price of Escape

About the Author

Aidan Red's passion for aviation and aircraft design, engineering, and a deep interest in space and space travel go back many years. An avid reader from an early age, Aidan, with great trepidation, ventured into the world of writing during college. With real world experience in business aviation, Aidan's creative side led him to create an alternate world where the beautiful Riggs Valley was born and Shara's life became chronicled in his epic science fiction series, Paladin Shadows.

Paladin Shadows consists of the five triptychs (three-part works), *Terran Assignment, Terran Recruits, Operation Retribution, Garda Nua* and *Assignment: Casha-Six*. In between the Paladin triptychs, Aidan has penned two, three book series, *Keeper and his Tiger,* and *Eight's Warning,* a West's Ghost Ranch Trilogy, and a novel, *Fearin' the Banshee.*

The unpublished books in his various series are scheduled for release on a regular basis in the coming months.

You can visit

www.RedsInkandQuill.com or www.AidanRedBooks.com

for more information on books published by Aidan Red books and where to purchase them.